LUNA STATION
QUARTERLY

Issue 054 | June 2023

Editor-in-Chief

Jennifer Lyn Parsons

Editors

Katrina Carruth • Sara Doan • Cathrin Hagey
Sarah Pauling • Carly Racklin • Shana Ross
Cait Ryan • Katrina Schroeder • Gô Shoemake
Bridget Siniakov • Izzy Varju

LUNA STATION PRESS
NEW JERSEY

Cover illustration:
A Kind Face copyright © 2023 Indicreates

First Paperback Edition June 2023
ISBN: 978-1-949077-42-1

Luna Station Quarterly publishes short fiction on March 1st, June 1st,
September 1st, and December 1st. For more information and submission
guidelines, please visit our website at lunastationquarterly.com

For Luna Station Press

Creative Director - Tara Quinn Lindsey
Editor-in-Chief & Founder - Jennifer Lyn Parsons

LUNA STATION PRESS
www.lunastationpress.com

CONTENTS

Editorial

Jennifer Lyn Parsons

Jennifer Lyn Parsons is a writer and senior software engineer. Currently, she enjoys writing fantasy stories about middle-aged people who aren't into the whole "going on a quest" thing but do it anyway. When not writing code or prose, she is also the editor-in-chief of the venerable Luna Station Quarterly. She finds joy in baseball, tea, discovering music new and old, and making analog things.

This editorial was not written by an AI. I probably shouldn't need to make such a declarative statement and yet, this year seems to be the time when that kind of clarity is required.

As you might imagine, as the editor and publisher of a long-running short fiction magazine, I have been thinking about AI a lot lately. Throw in the fact that I'm also an experienced software engineer and you can double whatever amount of time you thought I was thinking about AI.

So much of what I'm feeling boils down to "if something is free, then you're the product" and the fact that we're now watching the repercussions of that play out in real time. These AIs have been trained on data that was scraped from the internet. You know, that place where so many people are often their worst selves? Yeah. If that doesn't make you uncomfortable, perhaps it should.

When Clarkesworld had to pause submissions earlier this year due to the influx of AI-generated content they were getting, the staff of LSQ had a chat about the situation. I'm pleased to say we're all in agreement that we will not knowingly publish anything generated by an AI.

We felt pretty confident that we can recognize the difference between a human-written story and an AI-generated one for now after one of our editors experimented with ChatGPT and asked it to write "a Luna Station Quarterly" story. While the result was readable and hit on a lot of themes you'll regularly see in a story we would run, the writing style was very immature and the story was very unpolished. Even without knowing this was AI-generated, it would have been rejected.

Yet, these tools are getting more and more refined every day. How long is it until the stories, essays, and articles they produce are indistinguishable from human-written works, but with far more hidden biases than we can account for? More importantly, what can we do about it? That's the big question of the moment, from where I'm sitting. Is there anything we can do to get these companies to slow down and consider the impact of what they're doing?

Artists and writers in particular are currently bearing the brunt of the impact of these rapidly deployed tools. It's astonishing how quickly this technology is being adopted and with no option to turn them off, no protections in place for the creative humans that have worked so hard to hone their craft, who put their heart and souls into their work.

Interestingly enough, in our submissions this round there were a handful of stories about various AIs, their inner lives or how the technology could be manipulated in the not-to-distant future. The latter of these stories is within these pages. It's a cautionary tale and I encourage you all to read it, along with our usual wonderful collection of new tales written by humans about humans, and other dark and complex creatures, making their way through the world.

I'll leave you with two quotes from a few other creative folks who have thoughts in line with my own on this topic. The first speaks to the limitations of what this technology actually is at the moment and the second speaks to why, at the end of the day, the idea of accepting a story generated by an AI will continue to be anathema to us here at LSQ.

"Two things about 'artificial intelligence.' It's not artificial - it's built on as much human activity as can be shoved into a database. And it's not intelligent - it is very fast manipulation of spreadsheets." - Warren Ellis

"ChatGPT has no inner being, it has been nowhere, it has endured nothing, it has not had the audacity to reach beyond its limitations, and hence it doesn't have the capacity for a shared transcendent experience, as it has no limitations from which to transcend." - Nick Cave

L S Q | 054

The Broken Princess

K.R. Segriff

K.R. Segriff is a Canadian writer and filmmaker. Her work has appeared in Atlanta Review, Greensboro Review, and Prism International magazines, among others. She won the Space and Time Magazine Iron Writer Prize, The Bumblebee Prize for Flash Fiction, and the London Independent Story Prize. Her debut short story collection "Trash Pandas" will be published in 2024.

Somewhere between the melting mountaintops and simmering seas was a magical land called Polk County, Iowa. The people there worked tirelessly for almost no money, and what little they could save, they wagered on horses at the Altoona Raceway.

On the outskirts of Altoona sat a pittance of a farm, ironically named "Queen's Acres." Its owner was Juno, an ornery woman who had inherited the property "fair and fucking square" from her thankfully departed mother, Sybil.

The farm had passed over Juno's sister Pinky who had once been the apple of Sybil's eye but had failed so spectacularly at life that even her own mother could not, in good conscience, bequeath her any more resources with which to finance her ruin.

Some years before going AWOL from rehab and presumably ending up dead in some forlorn alley, Pinky became pregnant by Ace Jenkins, a local gambler and hard-living man. She birthed a girl-child named Vicky-V, who, despite her luckless life, grew up to be as self-possessed as a wild-living mule.

After Pinky's departure, Ace and Vicky-V lived in a rusted-out trailer parked in a vacant field adjacent to Queen's Acres. Ace had come to realize that, although outwardly unyielding and rotten, Juno was sometimes surprisingly soft-hearted and was likely the only person in town who would not call the sheriff when he spliced her power line to steal hydro.

This uneasy arrangement might have persisted indefinitely were it not for a horse named Princess. Around the time of Pinky's escape from rehab, Juno returned home with the hardest-muscled mare Polk County had ever seen. Juno told everyone in town that she intended to succeed where both her mother and sister had failed, tame the fearsome animal, and bring home the Altoona Tri-State cup.

Unfortunately, the horse proved wild and unmanageable. No fence could contain it, no saddle would stick, and two broken arms and a missing tooth later, Juno was forced to concede that Princess could not be broken and set the horse loose in the pasture.

The sight of the magnificent beast galloping through the nearby fields presented too great a temptation to Vicky-V, who, being a motherless child, was in search of a more worthy vessel for her adoration.

After several clandestine journeys over the electric fence, Juno pulled Ace aside and told him to keep his creep kid away from her horse unless he wanted to find himself with a throat full of teeth. Ace was not entirely drawn in by this bravado but did sit Vicky-V down to explain the possible downsides of messing with her Auntie Juno.

"Juno's a witch just like her mother Sybil was," he said.

"Horseballs, and you know it," Vicky-V replied.

"Nope. Your grandma was fiercer than Satan's left nut. It was her curse that killed our Pinky."

"Curse?"

"Didn't like that Pinky was a partier. Thought she should be on horseback 24/7 so she could sweep Tri-State."

"Sounds like a better option than the one she took."

"Trouble with our Pinky was, the only sure way to get her to do something was to tell her she had to do the opposite. Also, she hated to be in the saddle. Tri-State was Sybil's dream, not hers."

"So Mama's dream was to get herself addicted to Percs, pull a runner from rehab, and leave you to raise her charming child?"

"One thing I know is your mother loved you. Just some things are bigger than all of us. She wasn't strong enough to break Sybil's curse."

"Which was?"

"Sybil told your mother if she didn't quit the drugs and win Tri-State, she'd curse her to a life of shit."

"Parents are always saying stuff like that."

"But Sybil's curses were legend. Back in eighty-nine, when your Aunty Juno's only pal Darla said Juno was ugly as a cow's udder and called off the friendship, Sybil told her she'd see soon enough what ugly looked like. The very next day, she got that face-fungus that never really cleared up even after they sent her to that hotshot clinic in Boise. Not gonna tell me that's a coincidence. Polk folks say the reason I've got such rotten luck is that I was fool enough to hitch myself to Old Witch Sybil's prize horse."

"Probably got more to do with you always betting too much on the long shots."

"Smartass like your mother. God, I miss her."

"Tell you what, Dad. You can take that whole curse nonsense and shove it. I love that horse. Don't ask me why, but something glues me to Princess. I almost feel like I can read her thoughts. As far as Princess is concerned, Juno can eat shit. It's me Princess trusts, and if Juno would just let me ride her, I bet I could make Tri-State, and then Mama and Sybil both would have to rise from their filthy graves and congratulate me."

Ace and Vicky-V were so deep into their conversation that they didn't notice Juno approaching.

"A fifteen-year-old punk will never make Tri-State," Juno growled. "Especially one who's spent more time in the ditch than the saddle."

Vicky-V planted her hands on her hips and took a stance so aggressive it almost made Ace's heart break from the memory of her mother.

"Just you two jerk-offs try and stop me," Vicky-V declared.

***

Despite appearances, Juno was not entirely immune to the plight of her wayward niece. She started turning a blind eye to Vicky-V's visits to the barn and eavesdropped on her one-sided conversations with Princess. At first, Vicky-V's words were tentative, but eventually, her association with the horse became a sort of confessional.

One evening while Juno was out chain-smoking Virginia Slims beside corn stalks, she heard Vicky-V say, "Why didn't she quit like Daddy did, Princess? He said I deserve better than two parents underground, and that's what keeps him clean. But he's not the sharpest knife. So probably he's wrong." Juno leaned closer as Vicky-V dropped her voice to a whisper. "Sometimes, I think I deserve all that comes to me because I'm so rotten."

Princess only whinnied in response to Vicky-V's musings, but the girl seemed to take some comfort from the horse's listening ear.

Soon after that conversation, Juno confronted Vicky-V.

"This farm is mine, girl, and you've got no claim to it. You want to ride the horse? You work for me, as an employee, mind, not as family. You haven't got a chance in hell of succeeding, but maybe it's about time someone taught you your limitations. And if by some miracle, you do break Princess and make her a champ, maybe you'll reverse the curse your mother brought to this family."

"If I ride Princess," Vicky-V said, "It'll only be because I feel like it. I've got nothing to prove to you or my witchy old Granny. Got no curse on me, have I? Mama wasn't much, but she never wished me ill."

Suddenly, Princess squealed from inside the barn.

"Oh, have at her, you old nag!" Juno yelled. "Show her what it feels like to be a failure."

Vicky-V balled her fists into her armpits and got right up in Juno's face. "This time next year, it'll be Princess and me in the winner's circle at Altoona. Just you friggin' watch."

Juno waited as her niece marched toward the barn and, when she was sure Vicky-V was not going to turn around, she allowed herself to smile.

***

The first time Vicky-V attempted to climb into Princess's saddle, the horse seemed skittish, and Juno had second thoughts.

"Maybe you should leave it," Juno said. "This family's had enough tragedy."

But Vicky-V had determined eyes. "Nah. Princess is just excited. Look how her nostrils are quivering."

"Can't tell shit from the twitch of a horse, girl," Juno said. "Old Sybil doesn't need to curse you. You'll have all the trouble you need on account of your bull head."

"I'll have no trouble from my Princess. We have an agreement. She'll never hurt me because she knows I love her."

"Can't see how you'd make an agreement with a damn horse," Juno said.

"Princess is my best friend. I know what she needs."

"What a horse needs is lots of hay and an occasional kick in the ass."

"Attitude like that; it's no wonder the only folks that like you are livestock."

Juno dropped her eyes, and Vicky-V was startled to realize she had hit bone.

Vicky-V softened her tone and slipped into Princess's saddle. "All any animal needs is someone to be in their corner."

Vicky-V urged Princess forward, and without so much as a snort, the horse complied.

"I'll be damned," Juno said.

Princess trotted haughtily past, and as she did, she pursed black lips and spat atop Juno's boot.

***

It wasn't many months before Vicky-V and Princess stood at the gate at the Altoona Raceway.

"How old are you anyway? Twelve?" sneered the jockey beside them.

"Sixteen," replied Vicky-V, "and old enough to kick your pickled butt."

Princess stomped the dirt beneath her powerful legs.

"Can it, will ya? Vicky-V hissed as she smoothed her hand across Princess's jaw with more tenderness than her words seemed to justify. "Save it for the track and stop being such a dumbass." Princess snorted with her typical rudeness but proceeded past the bars.

"Come on, girls!" Ace cried from where he sat in the stands beside the cross-armed Juno. The bookies had said that Vicky-V and Princess were the longest shot in Tri-State history, so, true to form, Ace had bet everything he had on the race. Despite his long list of past failures, both father and daughter were sure today was the day they would finally spit in bad fortune's eye.

"Do it for Pinky!" Ace yelled.

Princess threw her head back, and Vicky-V snapped the reins. "Settle," she said. "He ain't talkin' to you. He's talkin' about my Ma."

The pistol fired, and as soon as Princess's feet hit the dirt, the air seemed to grow thin around them. It felt like something seismic was shifting just below the track's surface as Vicky-V and Princess sliced through the atmosphere as one continuous being. Before long, the conclusion was foregone, and the crowd erupted into mystified cheering.

Vicky-V raised a victorious fist as they burst through the ribbon, but Princess skittered to an abrupt halt, let out an unholy howl, and fell to her knees. Vicky-V tumbled from the horse, and as soon as she had rolled clear, Princess righted herself and took off running. The crowd scattered in the stands as Princess burst through the confines of the racing circle and tore off across the parking lot.

Ace and Juno clamored their way onto the track as Vicky-V rose unsteadily to her feet. Juno turned and bolted after the disappearing Princess, howling like a wounded animal. "Come back, you asshole!" she cried. "You won't get away from me again! Come back!"

Vicky-V came to stand beside her aunt and rested her open palm on Juno's shoulder. "Don't worry, Auntie," she said. "Princess always finds her way home."

When they returned to Queen's Acres, there was a rustling in the barn, but when they reached the stable, Princess was missing. In her place stood a woman covered, from her hairsprayed bangs to her acid-washed jean-cuffs, in translucent slime.

"Goddamn you, Juno! What'd you douse me with here?"

Juno's gentle laughter filtered through the barn.

"Can't expect a transformation without making a bit of a mess, Sister."

The woman stomped her foot against the barn-boards and

hollered, "Get your ass over here and make me presentable for my daughter."

Juno smiled and raised her hands before her. Then, a bright light appeared, and the slime vanished.

Ace's voice was thick with disbelief. "Pinky?"

"No, asswipe, it's Mr. Blond come to cut your goddamn ear off. 'Course it's me. Now get over here and kiss me."

"But Juno said...."

"I goddamn know what Juno said. Went up to that rehab, but by the time she got there, I was already gone? Lost me to the streets once and for all, and the best thing for everyone was if they told themselves I was dead?

"But..."

"Don't try to catch up, Ace. You'll only confuse yourself." Pinky turned to Juno. "Why don't you tell him what you did, you old cow?"

Juno snorted. "Turned you into a horse right there in the rehab parking lot, didn't I? Stuffed your sorry ass into the trailer and brought you on home."

"All this bellyaching about me being mom's favorite, and who'd Sybil give her magic to?"

"Why a horse?" Ace asked.

"Because she hates me," Pinky said.

"No," Juno said, looking beyond Pinky to the empty stable. "I did it because you were my best friend, and it was the only way I could figure out to keep you alive. Needed to keep you from the percs for long enough to dry yourself out. I can't hold onto much in my life, can I? The only thing I know how to keep is horses."

"Oh, buck up, Juno! I hate you when you're mopey like this. Now listen. You didn't even give me a voice! I had to communicate with my own kid through blinking and bloody horse sounds."

"Let you see her, didn't I? Even made her think it was her idea, so she'd be sure to stick with you. Couldn't tell her outright. She'd have gone all hero, discover her own magic, and screw up my plan."

"My own magic?"

"Come off it, Vicky-V. You never wondered how a 16-year-old kid could stick to the back of a racehorse no adult could tame? It's obvious Sybil's line runs to you."

"Three years you kept up this friggin' hoax!" Pinky interjected.

"Problem was," Juno continued, 'It wasn't only my magic we had to contend with. There was also Sybil's."

"She'd live a life of shit unless she won Tri-State," said Ace and Vicky-V in unison.

"And what did she just do, Einsteins?"

"She won Tri-State."

"You see? The old bitch never specified which role Pinky had to play. There's always a back door exit to a curse if you look for it."

"What happens now?" Ace whispered.

"Happily ever after," Pinky said, opening her arms toward her family.

"If you believe that," Juno said, "you're a bigger horse's ass than you were five minutes ago."

Truer words were never spoken.

There were more broken teeth, visits to rehab, and fortunes lost at the Altoona racetrack in the years that followed. The seas simmered, the mountains melted, and by the time the good citizens of Polk County were wiped from the face of the trembling earth, there was barely enough dry land to contain them. But everyone lived longer than they ought to have, and between their plentiful heartaches lived tiny moments of joy.

And maybe that is the happiest ending any of us simple animals can ever hope for.

Left at the Alter

Lindsey Duncan

Lindsey Duncan is a chef / pastry chef (CPC CSW), professional Celtic harp performer and life-long writer, with short fiction and poetry in numerous speculative fiction publications. Her soft science fiction novel, Scylla and Charybdis, is available from Grimbold Books. She feels that music and language are inextricably linked. She lives in Cincinnati, Ohio.

Berran cautioned her ward to silence with a raised hand. Her other hand rested on her sword hilt as she edged towards the window. Viatrese held her breath as if even its slightest motion would set off a tempest. Branches rustled. The night shadows outside swelled in the shape of a man.

Berran pressed her right shoulder against the wall as she drew. The intruder shifted his weight.

"Berran, the door."

Her ears told her what she needed to know. A coordinated attack, not a lone assassin. In a way, it was a compliment. A blood-daughter of Viatrese's lineage would only have the best of bodyguards, and Berran understood her skills well enough to accept that distinction.

She also would have been just fine with being underestimated.

The man in the tree jumped, landing on the windowsill. Berran lunged. He swung aside, dropping to the floor. The door burst open. No crack of wood; the attackers had a key. She wasn't surprised.

She stabbed down. He caught her sword on his blade. The figure in the doorframe–taller, broader, in padded armor–charged towards the bed. Viatrese rolled off, landing behind Berran. Berran didn't want to allow the first man time to recover, but she had no choice. She spun to confront the larger man. Her sword glanced off his arm, forcing him back a step.

The first man tried to dodge past her. She blocked him, knocking his blade aside. She buffeted him with her arm, sent him sprawling. Once again, she couldn't follow through on her advantage: his ally was instantly upon her.

Three rapid exchanges showed her where his weakness was. She drove the blade beneath the padding under his arm. He staggered back. She shoved him into his ally. The smaller man struggled against the weight, but was able to brace himself quickly enough to use the injured man as a shield. Berran broke off, took a half step back. The smaller man let the other slide to the floor. A muffled groan rose up.

Once free, he snarled and lunged. Berran let him come. She faced him unflinching until it was almost too late. A flick of her wrist brought her sword under and around his blade, catching the hilt. A twist, and it flew out of his grasp.

The clatter of its landing echoed absurdly. Voices stirred outside. The assassin turned to flee, then drew up short, as he found himself confronting a brick wall where the window had been. Berran gave him no time to contemplate. She knocked him out from behind.

The illusion dissolved, miniature fibers of light swallowed by the moon. "I'm sorry I couldn't do anything earlier," Viatrese said. "It all happened so fast."

Berran turned to face the princess. Viatrese was currently raven-haired, slender as fashion dictated. Like every member of the blood, she could change her shape. Every face she had worn had one thing in common: Berran wanted to gather her close and shelter her. She felt, as always, like a looming giant, and a homely one. Her skin was rough copper, her hair cropped and dull corn in hue; she had lost most of one ear in a training bout.

"Your only responsibility to me," she said, "is to let me protect you."

"Then I suppose I failed my responsibility to myself, to always be of use." Viatrese flashed a strained smile.

Berran shook her head. Viatrese was already doing more than anyone could have asked, traveling to a hostile kingdom to marry a prince she had never met. The alliance would end the threat of war between the two realms...a war which their home of Taona would lose. That this attack had occurred in Anaras did not bode well. Their hosts had clearly been involved.

It was not a detail Berran intended to mention. "You've given us a chance to get answers," she said. "That's no small thing."

The royal steward barged in, followed by members of the household. Answers would have to wait.

**

The assassins would not reveal who had hired them. Berran left the manor with only the promise of thorough interrogation. She downplayed her concerns to Viatrese, who had enough to worry about.

Viatrese distracted herself by creating folktales and epic poems in miniature. Berran recognized some of the stories. The talent for illusion was rare among the blood. Berran admired Viatrese's gift of details, tiny flecks of imperfection that bound everything together.

Upon their arrival in Anaras' capital, Viatrese was presented to King Feldar, his queen Thiora, high warlord Urnek, coinmaster Sagilin, interminable other advisors, and prince Diyan. Her intended always wore a handsome face and directed every conversation to the subject of hunting hawks.

"He has a passion," Viatrese said to Berran that night. "That's a good thing."

Berran confined her response to a nod. She wondered if Diyan would have his new bride looking like a hawk. To the blood, shapeshifting was vanity, not disguise: they sensed the person beneath the face. Berran had the knack as well, rare among humans. It was partly why she had such an important ward... and she would have known Viatrese anywhere.

The day of the marriage ceremony was dismal and foggy. A thousand candles lit the royal temple, but failed to enliven the stained glass windows. The pressure of bodies made it hot without relieving the damp. This was the first time in weeks Berran had not been within five paces of her ward, and her veins itched. The reassurances of the royal guard only made her study every angle they might have missed.

The bell sounded, echoing deep in her spine. On opposite sides of the hall, doors opened. As tradition dictated, bride and groom were cloaked and gloved, not even a flash of wrist for distinguishing mark. They approached the heartline that speared through the center of the temple. They faced each other. Viatrese's breath carried, short and sharp.

He bowed his head to her. They faced the priest together, an arm's length apart but separated by the heartline.

"We come this day to bind together the souls of Prince Diyan of

Anaras and Princess Viatrese of Taona," the priestess said. "In each other's eyes, let them find their true form."

It was neither poetry nor metaphor. The blood spent a few years in birth form, but as soon as they learned to change, they did, a weaving of flesh that took skill and time. The marriage ceremony gave each person a form they could assume without thought, a soul body matched to their spouse. It seemed too intimate to Berran for people who married for alliance and strategy.

Viatrese removed her hood. The blonde, waifish face widened into a full moon beam, deepened into coppery skin, a conflagration of red hair...one flowed into the next.

He lifted his hands to his hood, then hesitated. Viatrese reached out as if she would reassure him, even as she took on the visage of an old woman.

He pulled off the hood. The face revealed was unkempt and unchanging. "Prince Diyan sent me with the message he has no wish to marry this creature." Under the gasps and murmurs, he added a mumbled, "I'm sorry."

He fled. Berran wanted to rush after, but he was only following orders. She should not have taken her eye off Viatrese for even that instant: the princess had made a dozen transformations, spanning age and gender, sometimes slight, sometimes towering.

"Where is that boy?" the king said, springing off his dais in military ire. "He forgets–" The coinmaster silenced him before he could paint a full picture of Diyan's failings.

The gathered courtiers seemed to prize the spectacle more than anything else. Viatrese was their theatre of choice, along with the royal family–the queen as flat as the back of a mirror, other relatives marble white. The high warlord said something that contained the word "war," and the single syllable exploded around the temple.

Viatrese's changes grew ever more rapid, as if the interruption of the ceremony had left her soul spinning. No storm could have pulled Berran's eyes away. Why did no one interfere? Someone must have the ability to end the ceremony.

Viatrese wobbled, her body blurred. The changes were almost too fast to perceive, a current where each drop was invisible. She mouthed at the priestess. The woman stared at her...stared through her. Anger piled up in Berran. Her training kept her rooted. She was an observer to all aspects of Viatrese's life, except for ensuring the princess had one. Her duties did not extend to the quality of that life.

Yet if they did...

The queen strode up to the priestess. Berran tensed herself against the weakness of relief.

"...do it again?" The end of Thiora's words carried.

"If we halt the ceremony, your highness," came the reply–Berran had to strain to hear, "she will remain unmarried the rest of her life and never assume a soul body."

Was that really such a terrible fate, when such pain wracked her? Berran edged closer. She could catch Viatrese if the princess fell...and she needed the proximity to hear over the furor.

The queen shook her head. "Unacceptable. Continue. The guards will find my son."

The priestess hesitated. "She could die."

"Let her. Her only use to me is this marriage."

"Your highness…"

"Do not move."

The priestess rocked back a step, lowering her hands. Berran didn't wait for her to finish her retreat. She surged across the temple, crossing the heartline they all considered so momentous. No god struck her down. She reached Viatrese in two breaths. She clasped Viatrese's hands in a moment between copper and cinnamon, childhood and calluses. The princess lifted her head, rising out of the haze of herself.

Their eyes met. Viatrese's eyes blossomed into impossible blue and held. Her body became slender, a cloud of saffron curls, a few inches shorter than Berran with arch cheekbones…and remained that way, so beautiful it reverberated in Berran's bones. Viatrese was in every way perfect. She always had been.

Viatrese clutched her hands. "Berran."

"Princess." The two syllables took all the air she had.

"It's Viatrese," she said, "considering we belong to each other now."

At those words, Berran realized what she had done. She tried to figure out the next step, but before she could move, even speak, the crowd went mute. The wave surge of silence surrounded her, then shattered on the rocks.

"Someone stole the bride!"

"The princess belongs to us."

"A common bodyguard?"

"This is a calculated insult from the kingdom of Taona."

Berran wrapped her arms around Viatrese. Viatrese retreated into her shelter. Despite the chaos, Berran knew she was in exactly the right place.

"Enough!"

The king's command cut through the noise. The crowd subsided as he advanced, advisors Urnek and Sagilin a step behind. "What is going on here?"

"The ceremony is complete, your highness," the priestess said.

"She's married? To that?" The king cast a desultory down Berran's frame. She had height on him, but his regard squashed her beneath his notice.

Viatrese stiffened, taking Berran's hands. She took one step out of the embrace, not enough to separate. "Be respectful as you address my wife."

The color drained from Thiora's face. The king squeezed his wife's hand in comfort. "You were promised to my son," he said.

"Your son," Viatrese replied, "ran away."

"Watch your tongue."

"And this," Thiora added, "is no fit substitute."

"The insult is grave," Urnek said. "Wars have been started over less."

"Yes," Viatrese said, "they have. I'm fortunate Berran chose to step in."

The crowd's whispers buzzed, increasing in pitch. Berran tried to ignore the eyes assaulting her, a thousand pinprick blades. A commoner–worse, a servant, a foreigner–had stolen their prince's bride. Never mind Diyan had abdicated.

King Feldar frowned. "Nothing in this situation is fortunate. You should depart the temple before the fire explodes. Guards! Escort them out."

Berran could have fought through the crowd if it had been necessary, but she was grateful for the human wall. She kept a hand on Viatrese's shoulder, the other on her sword hilt.

***

The guards left them in Viatrese's temporary quarters. Everything but the essentials had disappeared, whisked away in anticipation of the wedding.

Viatrese rotated to take in the bare room. She exhaled, dropping the marriage cloak to the floor. "This is what we are worth to them now."

"I acted without thought," Berran said. "I should have considered how a strange woman claiming your hand would anger them."

"Strange, perhaps—" gentle affection surfaced in Viatrese's voice "—but not because you're a woman. Shapeshifting means the blood can be what they need to be, even bear children. It is rare, but families have wished to form alliances and had only daughters between them...or even less common, a love match. There's no point in marriage without heredity." Her words were as removed as a scholarly tome discussing the formation of mountains.

"Besides," she continued, "clearly it doesn't bother you, or I would be a young man now."

Berran tried to wrap her head around the statement. "I wouldn't want you to change."

"And I'm comfortable just the way we are," Viatrese said.

There were whispers here, hope Berran didn't know how to hold. She had admired Viatrese from afar, and now they were too close. "We have a lot to talk about, but I'm not sure it is safe here." It was easier to rely on the obligations of a bodyguard.

"You will keep me safe. I think we should—"

A servant cracked the door open. "Coinmaster Sagilin wishes to speak to you, your highness."

Berran turned away from the arguments on Viatrese's lips. "We should see what he wants."

Viatrese huffed, as much a child as Berran had ever seen her. "Send him in."

Sagilin entered, forcing a smile. "I should offer my congratulations, but I fear they would be lonely."

"I'm sure I have Diyan's," Viatrese said, "under the circumstances."

Sagilin barked laughter, then looked guilty. "The prince can be flighty, but he's a good boy at heart."

"Boy" was the problem, not the word for a future monarch. "What can we do for you?" Berran asked.

"Not for me, but for yourselves, if you will permit some advice." Sagilin cleared his throat. "Marriage to a common human—and a foreigner—could be insult enough to declare war."

"Urnek?" Berran said.

"Not as much as you might think. He knows a successful war needs the support of the people–and I'm not sure they would understand the finer points of this insult."

"I'm not sure I do," Viatrese murmured. The anger in those words took Berran aback.

"With respect, your highness," Sagilin said, "you do." He cast an apologetic look to Berran. "There is a service she might do that would change minds. There is a waterbeast in the mountains near the capital. It has flooded towns and destroyed bridges. Our warriors have withdrawn from hunting it because of a seer's claims it can only be slain by an outsider."

"I'll do it," Berran said.

"We need to talk about this," Viatrese said.

"We can talk, but this is what needs to be done to protect our homeland and you."

"You no longer get to make unilateral decisions about my safety. We have entered into partnership."

Berran hesitated. She would have pointed out that partnership meant no more obedience to orders, but her training ran deep– and they were arguing in front of a foreign dignitary, possibly an enemy. "You are right. We have much to discuss...but we need all the information." She turned to Sagilin. "Tell me where we can find this beast."

"It is a two-day journey." He spoke to her for the first time, responding to a shift in authority she hadn't intended. She had no place in the court structure...did she?

Sagilin's directions were straightforward. "Whatever you decide to do, I suggest you act soon."

"Thank you, coinmaster," Viatrese said.

He bowed and showed himself out. Viatrese sighed, sprawling in a chair.

"If slaying this beast is necessary to make amends," Berran said, "I'm prepared to do it." Putting her sword into action was familiar territory.

"There's nothing to make amends for." The words punched out of Viatrese in exasperation. "Their prince abandoned me. You saved me. If anyone deserves an apology..."

"You. For being put in this situation."

"Not exactly what I meant." Viatrese smiled wryly. "It needs to be done. And I'm going with you."

"You should," Berran said.

That halted her like collision with a wall. "What?"

"Someone tried to kill you before we even arrived," Berran said. "Now would be the ideal time to try again. We have a lot of enemies here. You're safest with me."

"Because no other guard could protect me as well?" It was teasing, sly.

Berran arched a brow. "If I pondered that and said you had a point, you're perfectly safe here?"

"I wouldn't let you do yourself such insult."

Something eased in Berran's chest. The banter felt so easy, so right, pulling Viatrese into the circle of her thoughts. Maybe there was a chance for this strange marriage.

"We make the journey together," she said, "but when it comes to the waterbeast, I have to face it alone."

"We can discuss that on the way." The levity in Viatrese's tone didn't fool Berran into thinking the princess would easily give in.

"Agreed. We should leave as soon as possible, and with discretion."

"You mean we need to sneak out." Viatrese sobered. "I can make us invisible. We can reach the stables that way."

"I'll pack."

A royal entourage wasn't set up for traveling light, but Berran made the best choices she could. She offered Viatrese a maid's cloak. "You'll need this for warmth."

"Let's go." As they stepped into the hall, Viatrese placed a hand on Berran's arm. "We'll have to move slowly to maintain the illusion."

Berran inhaled sharply as her arm seemed to turn to mist, a faint outline. She could see them both, but only as a haze. She shortened her stride to match Viatrese's definition of slow. They passed a maid, then a messenger hustling past. Neither noticed them.

A phalanx of guards stood at the entrance to the dignitary wing. While they weren't there to keep Viatrese prisoner–yet–they would insist on escorting her. Berran tensed, instinctively quickening her step.

Viatrese tugged her arm. "You'll break it."

Berran checked her stride, despite her instincts. She waited for the guards to challenge them. They slouched and joked amongst themselves. Off-duty behavior.

Five steps past. Ten. Viatrese tightened her grip. Berran forced herself to halt.

Boisterous laughter behind them. It faded out.

"Don't look so surprised," Viatrese said. "Of course it worked."

"I didn't..."

"Your face did."

Berran flushed, chastened...and then she saw the little smirk at the corner of Viatrese's lips.

Five non-encounters later, they reached the stables. Berran saddled up two horses, picking a mild mare for Viatrese.

Viatrese stared intently at the horse, body braced. Berran was about to assist when she grabbed the saddle and scrabbled up. She clung to it, panting. "I'm fine."

Berran decided to take her at her word. They rode out through the back gate. Berran threaded a hand through the reins of Viatrese's mare.

"Hold on," she said. "We're going to make some time."

She urged the horses faster.

* * *

Shortly before sunset, Berran eased the horses into a slower pace. Viatrese's cheeks were pale and wind-wracked, but she smiled fiercely.

"I've never ridden like that," she said. "Without a parade, that is."

Berran chuckled. "Are you well?"

"I will be, once I catch my breath." She reached up to rustle the leaves. The forest path wound on a slow incline, heading into the foothills. "Is this marriage taking you away from someone? From family, friends, a loved one?"

The question cut deeper than Viatrese could have known. Berran's whole life had been in training, then in service. She had never been allowed anything else. "No. My work is all I have."

"And I'm still your work, hmm?" It was a delicate balance between humor and irony.

"You are my ward. Anything else...we can figure out." She cleared her throat. "Perhaps the answer is there is nothing to figure out. This can be in name only."

Viatrese flitted her a startled, anxious look. "Is that what you want?"

No; Berran had been fascinated with Viatrese since their first meeting. She could have remained perfectly content in her shadow. It was no longer so simple, and too fraught to lay those expectations on Viatrese's shoulders. There was a safe answer. "I want what you want."

"Don't do that. Tell me the truth." Viatrese lowered her eyes to the reins, fingers tangled infinitely. "I'm sure you never pictured yourself with someone so fragile, so sheltered–someone who can't even lift a sword, much less wield it."

"Swords aren't as heavy as you'd think," Berran said by reflex. "You may be sheltered, but you're far from fragile. I don't want to make your life more complicated, or the answer would be easy."

"My life already is more complicated." Viatrese lifted her gaze. "When this is done, we have a lot to talk about."

"When this is done."

When the shadows became too deep, Berran chose a campsite. The air was damp and chill. She set up a fire.

Dinner was candied almonds and crackle buns. Viatrese laughed. "Strangest meal I've had since I was a child."

"I'll forage in the morning, scare up a rabbit or fowl," Berran said.

"I don't mind," Viatrese assured her. She peered into the fire. She stretched out a hand, wiggling her fingers. Sparks seemed to spin out in threads to greet her, forming ephemeral figures, faces, a fleeting festival. Berran couldn't help her smile.

"We should get some sleep," she said at last.

Viatrese dismissed the illusion with a wave. She climbed into the mound of blankets made up for a bedroll. "Berran? Thank you stepping in."

Berran paused before answering. The pat reply–that it was her duty–seemed to bother Viatrese and could start an argument she didn't want to have. "I would do it again," she said, only to find she spoke to herself. The princess was already asleep.

Rueful, Berran settled into watchful slumber.

***

The next morning, Berran found bird eggs and wild greens. She used a gold platter to make an omelette. It was a less than effective cooking vessel, but she persevered.

Viatrese stirred, rolling out of the blankets with bleary eyes. Even disheveled, she was poetry made flesh.

"I'm sorry it's such a plain meal," Berran said. "I couldn't find any herbs."

"It's lovely. I've never had anything like it."

"That's because your chefs have skill, unlike myself."

Viatrese shook her head. "Maybe they make things too complicated."

After breakfast, they mounted up. The princess suppressed a little groan. "Everything is stiff."

"That's normal for a novice."

"I expected as much." Viatrese made a face. "It's only three more days."

There...and back. Berran admired her confidence. "Why don't you spin an illusory tale for us?"

Her face glowed. "With pleasure."

Viatrese created an illusion of four birds turned into humans, trying to find their way in the world. It distracted them as they rode. They passed the last village before noon. Berran detoured to the tavern and traded for food.

Soon after, Berran dismounted to lead the horses up the steep path. The rest of the day passed swiftly, until she judged she was close enough to reach the waterbeast's cave within an hour. She called a halt.

Viatrese nodded off in front of the fire once, twice, catching herself each time as she slumped over. "I could sleep like the dead."

"Do that," Berran said. "The waterbeast is the only large predator here. I'll come back to get you."

Viatrese nodded. "Strength and fortune to you."

Berran frowned; something about the response bothered her, but she couldn't pin down why. "Wait until mid-day. If I'm not back by then…"

"You will be."

"Go to the village and tell them who you are. It's the best move."

"It won't be necessary."

Berran surrendered. "Sleep now."

Her own sleep was restless, streaked with nightmares. She awakened at dawn. Viatrese did not move, buried under the blankets, only a streak of blonde escaping like sea mist.

Berran regarded the bag that held breakfast. She left it there.

She climbed over rocks, heading for the cave. She heard the growl of the waterfall first, masking other sound. The waterbeast should be in its lair; it did its hunting in the rain. She crested the ridge.

The landscape dipped to a pool, the waterfall feeding it. The cavern lay behind. She stared at its shadows until she felt herself imagining movement. No. Too much thinking.

She eased over the rock, picking her way through the ruts made by claws. A narrow space between waterfall and cliff allowed entry. She drew her weapon, following the line of stone.

Sticky mist clung to her skin. As she passed behind the waterfall, a raspy thrum filled the air and pressed against her bones. Even before her eyes adjusted, she realized it was the waterbeast snoring. The swell of its body arced like waves, ebbing and flowing with its breath. The motion seemed boundless, skin warping beyond the possibility of bone.

The waterbeast curled away from the entrance. Berran edged deeper into the cavern. Scattered bones glinted white in the shadows. Previous kills—she hoped animal, but they could as well be human.

The creature's head was shaped like a conch shell with a ruffled rose beard. With its eyes closed, it was impossible to see the lids. Berran hesitated. Could she estimate where the eyes should be?

The thrum stuttered. Berran forced herself to stillness, waiting for some flicker of lids. The snoring resumed.

If not the eyes, then the gills. She angled closer to the water-beast's neck. She had trouble making out the gills until they fluttered, reacting to its breath. She readied her blade, feeling across the slick stone with her feet.

As she lunged, the waterbeast awakened. Roiling coils surged towards her. She pivoted out of her strike, narrowly avoiding their swell. Her feet skidded. Its head whipped around, the conch parting into a sea of teeth. She dove, rolling under its jaw. It followed, teeth clashing. She swung her blade up. An aching, scraping connection of metal on bone.

The waterbeast reared back. She had a precious instant to spring past it. Her footing almost betrayed her. She couldn't see clearly, couldn't map the littered stones and bones that were no hindrance to the creature, but could send her tumbling.

Fixate on that, and the beast would have her. She tracked its claws as it climbed upright, its tail dim thunder in the depths of the cavern. It snapped out. She ducked aside, running down its flank. For a beat, she was out of its reach. She thrust at its side, expecting nothing. She was not disappointed: the blade cut only as deep as a hand.

Black blood sprayed her arm. The waterbeast snarled, more in annoyance than pain. It whirled faster than she would have thought possible. Its neck buffeted her. She slammed into the stone. Blind, instinctive, she shoved to the ground, body throbbing. Jaws snapped above her. She rolled to her back and drove upwards.

This time, the blow struck true. Blood poured as the waterbeast screamed. Its head jerked up with such force it nearly ripped the sword out of Berran's hands.

She gathered herself, sprinting towards the waterfall. The waterbeast sucked in air and blew out a torrent of water. It knocked her backwards. She pivoted out of the stream. Now she got a good look at the eyes, all five. Even as she watched, the eyes shifted, flowing in a spiral across its face.

Plan in place. She let the waterbeast home in on her. The bulk of a boulder behind her. The waterbeast's chest swelled in readiness, the conch beard arcing upwards.

At the last instant, Berran spun to the right, thrusting at one of the eyes. The waterbeast twisted instinctively; her sword skidded along the lid. The contact squished, peeling away flesh.

The waterbeast jerked away, its shriek reverberating off the walls. In its gyrations, its claw connected with her shoulder. Scarlet pain rushed over her. She landed hard.

Her fingers went to the injury. Deep, bloody, but she could bear it; it was not on her dominant side. She still hadn't allowed herself to consider failure. If she lost, so be it...but the consequences for her homeland were not acceptable.

Humor flickered. If she could think of a way to kill the water-beast by expending her own life, she might take it. Certainly easier for Viatrese than dealing with a commoner wife.

She ducked behind the boulder, kicking aside a bone. The water-beast tried to recover. The eyes rotated again, one drooping. She had no idea of the mechanisms that made such eyes possible, but it made sense it would be vulnerable, softer than bone.

The waterbeast scanned the cavern. The conch unfurled, three tongues rolling out. Each was tipped with a pale pad. The ten-drils tasted the air. Berran suspected they could scent blood. She had also chosen her next target.

The waterbeast's head swayed over the boulder, tongues feeling out like fingers. One curved about, probing in her direction. As the appendage neared, she swung. The blow severed the end of the tongue.

The waterbeast's head plunged down. Berran flattened herself to the stone. Teeth scraped her back, but could not connect. She lifted her head to sight her escape route. It was not going to be a pleasant crawl.

Horns sounded from outside. The creature's head lifted as it tracked the sound, ocean coils undulating. Berran freed herself from behind the boulder. She wondered at the intrusion. Knights hunting the beast? Sagilin had told her no one was willing to pursue it.

Later. It was distracted; she had an opening. She darted along its flank. Its neck started to swivel. She drove the sword between its gills.

The waterbeast hacked air and blood. Its body shuddered,

convulsing in on itself. The coils bended, knotted, guarding its body and neck. Berran backed off, searching for another opening.

Light flashed behind her. She flinched into her shoulders, startled but refusing to turn. The waterbeast cringed away, its eyes closing in sequence. She took the opportunity without thought. She leapt near, held back for a beat...

Its eyes opened, attempting a squint.

She thrust her sword home. The flesh gave way. Her arm sunk in to the elbow, like into marshland deeps.

The waterbeast thrashed. She could not pull free. Its wild momentum flung her to the right, then the left. She was trapped in its second flail, the third...her arm slid free. She dropped.

The waterbeast slowed in its writhing. Berran inched forward until her hand encountered a discarded bone. She pushed into a crouch, wary. The waterbeast might be waning, but it was still dangerous.

She knew where the flash of light had come from, as well as the horns. "I thought we agreed you were to stay at the camp," she called.

"I don't recall agreeing," Viatrese said from within the waterfall.

The waterbeast gathered itself, snarling. Berran spun to place herself between it and the entrance. She held the bone low; it would not serve to deflect bite or claw. The eyes had stopped spinning, fixed in place. The one she had stabbed was lowest, her blade still embedded.

The waterbeast huffed out a breath. She braced against the torrent, letting it surge over her. As soon as the spray slackened, she plunged the bone into the softness of its palate, putting the full weight of her body behind it.

She jumped free as the waterbeast's jaws snapped shut. It jerked one final time, claws skittering across stone, then collapsed. It did not move again.

Viatrese rushed to her side. "Are you all right?"

"I think you made my heart stop," Berran said. The throbbing in her body made her legs wobble.

"I think you mean 'thank you.'"

She coughed laughter. "Thank you." That moment of levity was too much; it dissolved the last of her adrenaline. She slid to the ground, landing on her tailbone.

"How do I help?" Viatrese asked.

"I can't ask anything more of you. I just need time to gather myself." She probed the injury, winced.

"You're not asking. I'm offering." Viatrese knelt beside Berran. Her eyes reflected sapphire in the shadows. She took hold of her sleeve. "You could bind it with..."

Berran jerked away. "Please stop."

"You first." Anger frosted Viatrese's voice. "Is it pride? Do you still think of yourself as my servant?"

"That's what I am." Berran peeled the cloth away from her shoulder, wincing. "Do you know where my name comes from?"

"I assumed it was a name from Old Kerrish," Viatrese said. "It has the sound."

"It is Old Kerrish, but it's not a name." Focusing on the wound gave her an excuse to keep her eyes averted. "Berran is a word, meaning 'six.' I was the sixth child in my training unit. I was never a person, Viatrese. I am a number."

"A number would have remained in its rank. It would never have stepped forward to rescue me." Viatrese laid a hand over hers. "You may have started as a number, but you have become boundless. Besides," she continued, "do you think I would have come to the rescue of a number?"

The laughter rumbled up from Berran without her willing. "You didn't come for a number. You came for your kingdom."

"That, too—but not only." Viatrese pulled the hand to her heart. "Let me help you."

Berran told herself it was exhaustion that made her give in. It felt good—too good. "Please. If you have dry cloth, that would be best."

Berran directed Viatrese in bandaging the wound. Once the binding was secure, Berran rose and made her way over to the fallen beast. She bent down to withdraw her sword.

Viatrese crinkled her nose at the squelch. "Eww."

"We'll need one eye," Berran said. "For proof."

Cleaning her sword was a messier business than her wound. Once her sword was sheathed and the eye wrapped, they left the cavern and started down the slope to the campsite.

She halted Viatrese within sight of the smoke. "Someone is there."

"Locals?"

Berran shook her head. It was unlikely to be bandits, her first fear: the sole path led to the waterbeast's lair, with nothing else to recommend it. "Stay behind me."

Viatrese nodded. Berran advanced, hand on her sword. Six men in the white and red livery of Anaras. Unlikely they had been followed, but if someone knew their destination, it was not hard to meet them on the way down. She stepped out of the trees.

The captain, a rangy man with a hawk nose, turned her way. "Greetings. Have you slain the waterbeast?"

"Have you come to escort us to the capital?" Berran asked. The soldiers had tied their horses to the same tree as her mares.

"Come to the fire and tell us the story. Are you well, princess?"

Berran lifted a hand to hold Viatrese back, but she had already halted, body tense. "Why are you here?"

The captain sighed, irritated. "Suspicious, aren't you? Well, it's warranted." He gestured to the soldiers. They spread out. "You won't be returning to blemish Anaras further."

Berran wished she could be surprised. "By whose command? If we are to die—" which she had no intention of doing "—I would like to know who wields the blade."

He hesitated, but arrogance won out. "We act with the will of the queen. You could slay a hundred waterbeasts, and you would still not be welcome in our home."

Berran glanced back at her ward. "You assume," she said, locking eyes with Viatrese, "that we killed this waterbeast. We only escaped from it."

Viatrese's lips twitched in a moment's delight. She understood perfectly.

The waterbeast's tsunami cry echoed overhead as trees shuddered and rustled. The horses bolted. So did two of the soldiers. The others fell back, scanning the sky. Berran surged forward, blade flashing out at the captain. He jerked instinctively, shoulder twisting into her blow–enough to turn it from fatal into debilitating. He collapsed. She whirled to his right, disarmed the man next to him, then faced the other two.

Uncertain, still with half an eye skyward, the first man lunged. She parried him even as she dodged the other. The disarmed blond searched for his sword, but could not find it. Berran didn't have to guess why.

"Idiots," the captain gasped, "there is no waterbeast."

It took them a moment to believe it. In that space, Berran wounded the taller of her attackers, coaxed the other away from Viatrese. Her shoulder screamed, but she refused to heed it.

The shorter man's sword lashed out at her flank. She twisted away, grimaced. She still had to keep an eye on the blond, even though he was unarmed, and that divided her attention. She saw the blow aimed at her hip, but could not avoid it. She thrust out an elbow to disrupt the angle of the blade, succeeded in turning it into a shallow cut.

That gave her an idea. She drew back, moving towards Viatrese as she did. She flitted a glance behind her, then to the captain, without really looking–enough to suggest she was distracted. The taller man took the bait, jumping to the attack. She threaded her blade inside his guard, laying open his arm. He gasped, dropping his sword before it could connect.

"Call your men off," Viatrese said, voice shaking as much as the sword she gripped in both hands. She levered it at the captain's throat. The soldiers halted, uncertain.

He glared. "You have no power over me."

She leaned closer. It threatened to tip her over. "Are you sure?"

Berran moved to her side, supporting her elbow with her free hand. "You had better do as she says."

He spat curses under his breath. "Stand down." The men backed off, lowering their swords.

"Take your horses and go," Berran said. "You can return to the capital, but I'd consider how your failure will be met."

The soldiers scrambled backwards and grabbed reins. They retreated out of the clearing.

Viatrese sagged against Berran. The captain shifted, propping himself up. One look at Berran convinced him not to move further.

Berran hesitated. She had killed men before, but only in the heat of combat. "Viatrese?"

Viatrese let the blade fall. "We take him with us, of course."

***

The ride back to the capital was swifter than their arrival, even with their captive bound to his horse. Just shy of the gates, Viatrese insisted on hooding the captain. As they rode up, she announced herself in a ringing voice. The gates swung wide. Royal men scurried to clear their path. Berran followed in Viatrese's wake, dragging their captive.

The royal audience hall was not empty; the queen and a handful of advisors were present, engrossed in debate, which ended when the guards opened the doors. Viatrese strode in, Berran a half pace behind. Sagilin stared, astonished and visibly relieved. When Berran caught his eye, he flushed ruddy and ducked his head.

"My wife has slain the waterbeast you all fear, and with ease," Viatrese said. "But despite that service, someone did not want us returning alive."

The queen turned slate pale. King Feldar thrust himself from his throne. "Is that the man?"

"It is," Berran said, removing the hood.

Feldar raised his brows. "This is one of your men, is it not, wife?"

Before she could speak the denial poised upon her lips, Sagilin interjected. "I told the princess where to find the waterbeast. Queen Thiora insisted upon knowing where they had gone. To my knowledge, she is the only other person who does."

"This is ridiculous," Thiora said.

The captain roused, struggling to his feet. "I was only following orders."

Calculation flashed across the queen's face, followed by concession. "We should never have let Taona across our borders," she said. "Even worse, to have sacrificed my perfect son to this flighty frill. Someone had to put things right."

Had she encouraged Diyan to flee the marriage ceremony? If it was so, she had put Viatrese at risk of a painful and public death.

And otherwise, Berran would never have married her.

Feldar's face hardly changed, but his voice came as iron. "We have much to discuss, my wife. Great ladies," he continued, his tone expanding as he addressed them, "you have done this kingdom exemplary service. Let no one ever doubt your right to stand in the highest halls."

Berran recognized a dismissal when she heard one. She laid a hand on Viatrese's shoulder. "We should go."

Berran and Viatrese soon found themselves in the same chamber that had begun their adventures. So much had changed, Berran couldn't wrap her hands around it. She slumped against the wall, relying on the strength of stone.

Viatrese collapsed on the couch with an excess of dramatic posture. She remained for only a moment before she pierced Berran with her gaze. "You can no longer say you are not worthy to stand with me," she said. "A high authority has proclaimed it."

Berran had no argument. She retreated with, "I will always have the habits of a lifetime. I was born to guard and serve you."

"Which is what a spouse should do, and I will guard and serve you." Despite her serious tone, Viatrese's eyes glinted. "Can you deny I did a good job?"

"I can't," Berran said. "I might not have survived without you. That isn't an invitation to make battling beasts a regular pastime."

"If you wanted to abandon the court, travel out into the world, and hunt monsters, I would do it gladly," Viatrese said. She was wholly sincere, and for two beats, Berran agreed with as much heart. Then she came to her senses.

"Let us not," she said.

Viatrese laughed. "Oh, very well. I suppose we must return home now. Things will be very different when we arrive."

That was an understatement. It swirled past Berran, inexorable as the waterbeast's coils. Still..."They don't have to be. It can still be in name only."

"I'm going to ask you again." She rose, chin notched, eyes gone to a blaze. "Do you truly want that? If a man as distinguished as King Feldar can acknowledge you, then I defy anyone else to do otherwise. Perhaps when we come to know each other, we will find nothing to hold us together, but that is the future."

Exhaustion or not, moving away from the wall was as easy as a feather floating. Berran went to her, taking her hands. Pale, delicate, capable of great things...and nearly dwarfed within her own powerful palms, callused and tough.

"I want to try," she said. "I know I will always find you fascinating..."

"If you are going to say that I might get bored of you," Viatrese replied tartly, "I may just scream."

Berran surprised herself with her own laughter, deep and full. "Your bodyguard wouldn't come running."

"Oh, she had better."

It was the second time Berran had held Viatrese's hands in this fashion. They had fought together, almost revealed secrets, and for the first time, Berran thought they might be able to exist in the same world.

Viatrese was braver than she had imagined. It was time for a different kind of bravery.

"In all this time," she said, "we've never kissed. We should fix that."

"It does need righting." Viatrese leaned up as Berran tilted her head down, closing the distance between them. Their lips met, breath joined. It was not a perfect kiss, awkward and searching and bright as fire. It was a kiss of beginnings, and it hoped for a thousand more.

We're Sorry, This Number Has Been Disconnected

E.A. Brenner

E.A. Brenner writes short and long fiction, loves hardware stores, making jam, and stories about magic spilling everywhere. She lives in Salem, Massachusetts with a spouse, a book hoard, a yarn stash, and rumors of a vagrant ghost in the basement.

Indira Chant never did anyone a favor. Her elder sister Jorie, graduated last year, had arranged and provided all favors, selecting the lucky few graced with a spell from the Chant family, whose magical talents were believed and doubted and shrouded in mystery. Jorie had been friends with everyone and no one, moving effortlessly through social circles because she did not care about the boundaries other people lived by. But Jorie had graduated, and those in need of a little magic had suffered a drought in her absence.

Indira Chant was friends with no one, and she offered no favors. That didn't stop hopefuls from asking. All school year long, she found notes in her locker, received messages on her phone although she had not given out her number, was cornered in the bathroom with a request or a demand. She declined them all. The lucky few were referred to other members of the Chant family but thereafter forbidden to share any details of their transactions. The unlucky were met with stony, silent refusal.

This week brought a strange reversal. Instead of a girl pining after a boy, Indira was suffering through a monologue from the soon-to-be-crowned-prom-king Chris about how soon-to-be-prom-queen Ella wouldn't talk to him anymore, but they just had to go to prom together or it would all be ruined, and Indira was going to help him. Not "just had to help" or "I need your help" or some variation of a plea. Chris declared Indira was going to help him. Three of his friends stood guard at the bathroom door, preventing anyone from interrupting them. He should have only brought two, Indira thought idly. Three was a powerful number. Four not as much. He had already unbalanced things. She had already declined to help.

Chris waited impatiently for her capitulation. Indira tried to hide how uncomfortable she was by mimicking her sister's nonchalance. Jorie had never been impressed by or scared of anyone.

"What do you imagine I can do about this?" She was pleased by how cool and unconcerned she sounded. She already knew all the things he'd imagined, the spoken and the unspoken. But she wanted him to believe she wasn't intimidated, that being backed into the corner of the bathroom wasn't a novel experience or a fast track to securing her services.

"You work your," he twiddled his fingers in her face instead of saying the word, "on Ella and get her to go to the prom with me. I pay you." He said it like he thought her in need of money, ready to be grateful.

Indira sighed, and then stalled. "What did Ella say when you asked her?" She already knew. Everyone knew. He'd done one of those dumb prom-posals in the lunchroom. But Indira needed him to say it, so she could form Jorie's bored drawl and say, "You can't afford me," and decline again to solve his self-created problem. Indira wasn't in the game of making people amenable to rejected romantic overtures. Or secret ones. The women of the Chant family didn't subvert consent or facilitate rape. Of course, none of their hopeful clients ever thought that's what they'd asked for. They imagined they were creating consent and romance, with some assistance. They thought themselves a gift to the ones they pursued, overcome by the power of love, deserving reciprocity. None of them saw what they truly were: Apollo poisoned by Eros's punishment arrow. Indira refused to be the bow that shot the other arrow at an unsuspecting Daphne.

"She said no, why do you think we're here, you dumb bitch!" his fist came toward her. She flinched away. His punch stopped just beside her head. Arm raised, resting on the wall, he boxed her in. His face spilt with an unkind smile. "You're going to convince her to say yes. I pay on delivery. No one says no to me."

She was momentarily baffled by this turn of events. In all her years as Jorie's silent shadow in these meetings, this had never happened. Jorie had never been threatened. Indira's role as the muscle (her magical strengths didn't run to the gentle and subtle) had never been needed. But Jorie, as far as she knew, had never been ambushed.

Now that she thought about it, Indira was not so surprised by this violence. Chris was a hole people poured yesses into. She was surprised Ella had said no. Indira could also say no, right now, but not without causing a great deal of damage and harm. A moderate but firm no required supplies she didn't have with her.

Two of Chris's goons drew closer. Three faces pressed her into the corner. Three, a powerful number. She swallowed and wished she had a reputation as one to stay away from. She thought: Jorie will have an idea of how I can get out of this.

She swallowed again and lied her assent: "The fee is a thousand. Twenty-five percent now, the rest on delivery."

Jorie didn't answer Indira's call. She hadn't answered for over two weeks, and Indira was worried.

Jorie, older by sixteen months, was on her labyrinth year,

traveling the world, visiting the vast network of the Chant family witches, absorbing new magical knowledge, earning her second set of tattoos, and deciding who she would apprentice under. She was "emerging from the labyrinth of herself and finding her path through life." Indira was still at home, a novice with only initiate tattoos. It was the first time in her life she'd felt the gap between them; even when slightly out of step as Jorie transitioned to middle school, then high school, ahead of her, she'd never felt the distance. They had the same father, a rarity for sisters in the Chant family, where the women never married and seldom kept lovers for long. They looked so alike they were often mistaken for twins.

Jorie always answered Indira's calls. Until recently.

To distract herself, she considered her predicament. She could make Chris forget he'd asked her. That was a simple spell, already learned though not practiced enough. But she'd also need to make his friends forget, lest they remind him. A simple forgetting would not stand up to questions or recountings from his friends of their bathroom deal. She needed a better plan. She needed a Jorie plan. She heaved herself off her bed and went to consult the family books.

At the bottom of the stairs, the door to the house's library stood ajar, and she heard her mother's voice within. "She hasn't arrived at Maisie's. No one's heard from her in three weeks." Indira knew she spoke of Jorie.

"She's never listened or followed the rules, what made you think she'd start now? I'm impressed she made it this long before running off." Her aunt's voice this time.

Indira pushed into the room. Two stony faces greeted her.

"This is why you should've let me get my GED and go with her," she said. "Jorie wouldn't be missing if we'd gone together." This was an old argument. Indira and Jorie had crafted the plan, eager to take their labyrinth year like they did all other things: together. But the family refused.

"The thing you most need," Indira's mother spoke the same words now that she'd spoken a year ago, "is to stand on your own. And to stop eavesdropping."

"The door was open," Indira said, instead of saying, "I need help." She turned and left. They'd only tell her she needed to solve the Chris situation on her own, too.

As she climbed the stairs to her bedroom, Indira felt a prickle in her left arm, in the stamen of the flower inked near the fold of her elbow. Someone, somewhere, was attempting a magical work against her. The mole in the very center of the stamen pinched liked when she took tweezers to a hair growing out of it and caught the skin by mistake. She rubbed it with her thumb. Now the back of her neck prickled, all the hair on her body rising. She knew this feeling. She was being watched.

Perhaps it was Jorie. She wanted it to be, even though it didn't feel like it. Indira knew the feeling of her sister's magic. When Jorie scried on her, it felt like a companion in the room, like sitting with a cat but not touching each other. If this were Jorie, her tattoo would not be alerting her to outside intrusion and threat. Indira kicked the door of her bedroom closed and stalked over to her dresser. It was low and long, backed by a large mirror, suitable for many kinds of work and perfect for this. She shoved aside the detritus of school papers, notebooks, pens, costume jewelry, and empty soda cans. She pulled a silver tray and a purple pillar candle from a drawer and struck a match. When the candle was lit, she placed it before the mirror, put her index finger against the burning mole in the center of the flower on her arm, and asked, "Who is watching me?"

The watcher was either too lazy to ward themselves or their wards so poor Indira's scrying blew them away like smoke. An image formed in the mirror, haloed by the light of the candle's flame, small but very clear, the scrying made powerful by the reflection.

It was Ella. This was as surprising as her refusal of Chris. She sat cross-legged on a floor somewhere, staring down into a glass bowl of water set beside a lit candle. It was a decorative taper candle, bright orange with bats and pumpkins. Indira snickered. Ella was an amateur for certain, using a leftover Halloween candle and a clear bowl. Had she thought the association with the spooky season would help, or was it the only candle she could find? Orange was for ambition, opportunity, success, justice. Unsuitable for scrying, spying, and seeking hidden knowledge.

As she watched Ella, Indira saw a bloom of purple appear in the bowl's water. Another surprise. Despite everything, Ella was getting results. She had some latent magical ability then. That, or something was boosting her. It was possible she'd purchased a magically powerful object, knowing or unknowing how it would aid her. Indira couldn't imagine whom Ella could have bought it from, as the Chants were the only practitioners of any real skill in town. Perhaps Ella had gotten lucky online. With her finger, Indira drew a circle in the air around her purple candle and the image in the mirror, said, "So may it be," and blew out the flame.

She put aside the purple candle and took a black votive from the drawer. Lighting the black votive, she whispered a basic invocation for protection, and left the candle to burn itself out.

This time it was Ella who cornered Indira in the bathroom.

Different bathroom, at least, Indira thought, and she finished washing her hands. A girl needs a little variety in her life.

Ella turned the lock with a definitive *snick* and stood in the doorway, staring at Indira. Indira dried her hands on paper towels and stared back. Neither said anything for a long time. Indira tossed the paper towels into the trash and waited.

Ella drew something from her pocket and manipulated it in her cupped hands. She was whispering down at it. Indira's mind flicked through the possibilities and landed on the most likely: sympathetic magic with a doll or other representative object. Ella was brave to try something like that when she could barely manage a decent scry and clearly knew nothing about wards. Brave and foolish. Without wards, sympathetic magic could easily get away from you.

At the same time that Ella's voice grew bold enough for Indira to make out the words, she also saw the white string trailing from Ella's pocket into her hands. "I bind you, Indira Chant. I bind you, Indira Chant. I bind you Indira Chant, from doing harm against me." Ella wrapped the white string around a small doll in her hands. Indira recognized a scrap of fabric from her favorite scarf that had gone missing from her locker last week. If she was smart, Ella would have taken hair from the brush in her locker, too. But Ella wasn't smart. No, she corrected herself, Ella wasn't knowledgeable. She was clearly smart, had talent and moxie. The attempted binding prickled over Indira's skin, settled on the curling leaf of the vine tattooed on her right arm as a warning. It wasn't purchased magic, and it wasn't going to take.

Indira lunged forward and smacked the doll from Ella's grasp. Ella's eyes went round in her face, and she stumbled backwards into the door. "This isn't *The Craft*," Indira hissed into Ella's face, crowding her against the heavy, scarred wood. "For fuck's sake. What is wrong with you?"

Ella twisted around, shouldering Indira away from her, and scrabbled at the door lock. "Leave me alone!" she cried. "I won't go to prom with him. You can't make me."

Indira sighed and stepped back. Of course Chris had shot off his mouth about hiring her to make Ella go to the prom with him. What an idiot. Magic was best worked in secret, didn't he understand that?

No, of course he didn't. He was an ignorant, entitled boy.

"Calm down," she snapped. "I'm not gonna make you do anything. But you need to stop fucking around with shit you don't understand before you hurt yourself."

Ella stilled, hand on the lock, and glared over her shoulder. "Don't lie, I know Chris hired you to spell me into going to prom with him."

Indira rolled her eyes. "He 'hired me' in the sense that he literally backed me into a corner and forced me to say yes. I don't do that kind of work. Seems to be his M.O., though. He didn't think you'd have the guts to say no to him in front of everyone, did he?"

Ella released all the air from her lungs in a long, slow sigh and slumped against the door. "He asked me in private, first. Twice. The first time he called me, and the second time he came around my house. Luckily, my mom was home, so he didn't come inside. I keep saying no, and he keeps asking. I'm afraid to go anywhere alone, or be home by myself. My friends don't understand why I won't just say yes. If he asked any of them, they'd say yes. I tried a spell to make him stay away, but it didn't work." She eyed Indira with suspicion. "You're not protecting him, somehow, are you?"

"Fuck, no. You're just not very good at magic."

Ella opened her mouth to protest, but then closed it, looking grumpy. Indira was the opposite of grumpy. She was finally landing on a good idea. The Chant family had a code, and that code demanded that when you found a new witch and they were solitary, no mentor or family to show them the way, you had to do it. What better way to wiggle out of her deal with Chris and prove she could stand on her own than to teach Ella? Ella could put Chris off herself. Indira could claim she wasn't able to get past Ella's defenses. All problems solved.

"How long have you been trying magic?"

They sat cross-legged and facing each other over the braided rag rug in Indira's room. Over Ella's shoulder, Jorie smiled from a framed photo, and Indira pretended for a moment she was facing her sister. Now that she knew Jorie wasn't answering anyone's calls, that the family didn't know where she was, she worried every moment she was awake. Was Jorie safe? Alive? Would Indira feel if something terrible happened, the way real twins said they felt their other half's pain or fear? She clung to those stories. Feeling something terrible happen was better than knowing nothing.

"Not long."

Indira turned her attention back to Ella. Ella's voice carried the faintest traces of a southern accent. "I've been interested since I was a little girl, but never had the guts to try before now. I guess I just didn't want to be disappointed if it didn't work. If I was bad at it, or it wasn't real after all."

That sounded like what little she knew of Ella. Overachiever didn't begin to describe. Top of the class, graciously declined captaincy of the cheer squad so she'd have time to be president of the honor society, run all the senior class fundraising, and be the seniors' representative to the local rotary club. Kind to everyone, never got in trouble, about to be prom queen. Preppy clothes, dazzlingly white sneakers, perfection walking. Never took risks.

She was Jorie's opposite. Indira had never seen Ella wear black, boots, or a bored expression.

"What did you see when you scried for me the other day?"

"You know about that?"

Indira made a noncommittal sound. Ella was an open, earnest book. It was obvious she thought Indira was impossibly cool and mysterious, and Indira was not about to do something so mundane as explain herself. Teaching always started, her mother said, by showing the other person how much they do not and cannot know. Ella could never be told the tattoo's secrets. Only the Chants held knowledge of their strange, impossible flowers.

"What did you see?"

After a moment, Ella said, "I saw you. But not the way I expected. I saw your face, like you were peering over my shoulder into the water."

"I *was* peering over your shoulder."

Ella shivered the way Indira knew she would. Indira smiled.

"But everything was purple," Ella said. "Does that mean I did it wrong?"

Color was a good place to start. She walked Ella through the basics of spell work, what each color was for, how to set wards and select proper tools. She explained everything she'd done wrong, and everything she'd done right, about her attempt to scry.

Ella absorbed it all. She was quick, asked good questions, and wasn't afraid to say she didn't understand because she wanted to understand—nay, she wanted to gain mastery—as quickly as possible. Indira liked this about her. Jorie might have rolled her eyes and dismissed Ella as a goody-goody teacher's pet, but Indira recognized what Ella's enthusiasm and drive for perfection had been masking all this time: ambition.

It was time to see if Ella had the talent to back it up. Indira clambered to her feet and clapped her hands once. "Ok," she said. "You're going to do a spell. Properly, this time."

"Really?" Ella sat up on her knees, all excitement, no trepidation.

Indira nodded with authority. "You're going to spy on Chris."

Under Indira's direction, Ella set a ward with a circle of salt around the rag rug. Ella filled a black plastic bowl with water and set it in the center. Ella set the silver tray beside it and took a fresh purple candle from the drawer. She hesitated when Indira advised her to hold the candle for several minutes, thinking about all the things purple was good for, thinking about how she wanted to see Chris. "This feels silly."

"Where's your intention?" Indira pushed. "Do it."

And Ella did it. She lit the candle and commanded, "Show me that stalker," into the dark surface of the water. Indira heard steel in Ella's voice.

Immediately a picture formed on the surface of the water. Chris, kissing a girl. Ella recognized her. "Scarlett. Why doesn't he just ask *her* to the prom, then?"

"Isn't she dating one of the sportsball players?" Indira surprised herself by knowing even that much about this girl's social life. Usually she was happy to pay no attention at all.

Ella nodded and murmured, "Lacross. Aaron. Bitch."

When Chris pulled off his shirt and started on Scarlett's, Ella leaned forward and blew out the candle. "She's been telling me how lucky I am he asked me, that I should go with him and 'get your V-card taken care of, El'." She mimicked a syrupy-sweet voice. "She calls herself my friend but calls me a frigid bitch with a stick up my ass. To my face." Her hand lashed out and knocked the bowl of water askew, sending a wave of water over the rag rug. The bowl tipped, then settled, remaining water sloshing furiously inside.

Ella leaped to her feet. 'Oh my god, I'm so sorry!" She scanned the room for something to mop up the water.

"It's okay," Indira grabbed a towel from beneath the bed and pressed it into the rug. "Not the first time someone has spilled a bowl of water in here. Why do you think we sat on the rug?" She and Jorie had tipped many a bowl, causing water damage to the plaster ceiling of the dining room beneath, before the rag rug and emergency towel made an appearance.

"It sounds like your friends aren't really your friends." Indira let it hang in the air. She didn't know why she was asking. She never cared about friends, so why did she care about how Ella's treated her?

Ella sighed and pulled at a loose thread in the hem of her t-shirt. "You know how every group has a punching bag?"

"Not really. I've never been part of a group." At school, Jorie had been her group. Outside of school, she had the family. She'd never needed anyone else.

Ella sighed again, this time in frustration. "Well, most groups have one," she snapped. "And I'm it. Last year it was Megan, but she left. They decided this year was my turn. I've just been waiting it out, but now they've all decided to support Chris's graduation goal of banging an Asian girl. God, I hate this whole stupid school, and this whole stupid town, and I can't wait to leave." She threw up her arms but had nothing and nowhere to direct her anger, so she drew them back in and crossed them. "I'm going to UCLA, you know," she huffed.

Indira made a suitably impressed noise. "I'm going to Europe," she said. "I have family there." She wasn't permitted to say more, and was relieved when Ella didn't ask. "So, what do you want to do about Chris?"

Ella turned to face her. Her face had gone from closed and pensive to open and blazing. "I want to go full Carrie on his ass. Show up at prom on his arm, then dump buckets of blood on him and his stupid prom king crown. I want to magic his ass into next year. Can you help me?"

"Indira." her mother confronted her in the family library after Ella went home. She was flipping through books looking for the right spells to create a true send-up to Carrie, sans the out-of-control fire, as fun as that sounded. "What are you doing with that girl?"

"Helping her out with a guy problem. He's made a nuisance of himself. And she's a natural, Mom. She scried on me first, so I have to teach her." A lot of these spells needed blood but didn't produce it. Guess they'd have to buy that. She'd enjoy the irony of using Chris's money.

Indira moved to flip the page and find other spells to fulfill Ella's vision, but her mother stopped her with a hand on the book. "You're supposed to consult with the family first," she said. "Since you failed to do so, we held counsel without you. The auguries say nothing good will come of whatever it is you're planning. You need to stop."

"What, you held counsel while Ella was still here?" Indira realized she'd never been in this position before. Jorie had always been told no, stop that. Indira was always lurking behind her, ready to follow when Jorie did it anyway, but Indira was never the one under scrutiny, never the one denied.

"You brought an outsider into the house without notice or permission and did a working with them. So, yes, we held counsel immediately. And we saw attention on you, on the family. Lots of attention. That kind of attention is how witch hunts and wars start, and we will send you to your father's people before we let you do that."

Indira tried to capture her sister's insouciance, the way she'd used a few words to duck and dismiss their mother. But Indira had always been intimidated by their mother, and now she was stunned. Sent to her father, whose name she didn't even know, meant exile from the family. No labyrinth year around the world, no higher magical training, no catching up to her sister. "So Jorie breaks the rules, sells spells and favors all through high school, and gets to go on her labyrinth year. But I do my duty to help one person and you threaten to exile me? That's not fair!"

Her mother sighed and rubbed her forehead. "Jorie dealt in small things. She never brought anyone to the house, drew attention, or gave away family secrets!" She gestured at the spell book.

"I'm better at the big stuff!" Indira shouted. "And this guy deserves it. He tried to buy a rape spell."

"Your sister should have taught you her subtlety, but all she taught you was rebellion." Indira's mother lifted both their hands from the book and flipped to another page. A forgetting spell, using a knotted web, that could be worked small or big. The pattern sprawled over the page like a spider's web, a dreamcatcher, a mandala. She tapped the page with her long fingers. "This is the spell you need. Make the girl and the boy forget about all of this. Extricate yourself from the situation. You need to protect the family, not waste your time on a girl that will drop her magical hobby before the first semester of college is over."

"But, Mom," Indira protested. Her mother was already turned away. Beyond her, in the doorway, stood one of Indira's aunts and two of her cousins. Three impassive faces holding her in place until she capitulated.

"Whatever you're planning," her mother repeated, "is how witch hunts and wars start. End it now."

Before Indira could tell Ella the Carrie plan was off, Ella agreed to go to prom with Chris, publicly. Not as public as his lunchroom prom-posal, but she marched up to him in the hallway in front of their friends and said, as they planned, "Ask me again."

Indira dropped a note in his locker to meet her in the bathroom at the end of the day for payment. He and two of his friends were already there when she arrived. She felt flustered. She'd arrived early so she'd be lounging mysteriously against the back wall when they entered. Instead, she hesitated on the threshold, surprise hanging out of her like a piece of toilet paper stuck to a shoe. And one of the goons was missing. Damn. She needed them all together for this.

Indira squared her shoulders and entered the bathroom with false confidence, locking the door behind her. She marched up to Chris, held out her hand, and demanded, "Payment upon delivery, as agreed." The memory charm web was tucked in her pocket. She itched to pull it out now. This moment when they were all looking at her was perfect, and it was slipping away.

He looked down at her palm, and his mouth curled at one corner into a sharp grin that made Indira's stomach sink. "I'm paying for the whole prom experience. You'll get your money after Ella gives it up. If that frigid bitch doesn't deliver, you don't get paid."

Rage bloomed in her belly and swallowed all the plans. Indira lowered her hand and spun away. "Guess I don't get paid, then," she said as she walked toward the door. "I don't deliver girls to coward rapists who pretend the word no doesn't exist."

Instantly, she regretted everything. She could have deployed the memory web, she could have found a spell to make Chris impotent forever and then made him forget he ever talked to her. Hell, she could have worked the Carrie plan with Ella. She didn't have to blow everything up like this.

Except she did. Surely the family would understand. She couldn't do nothing. Forgettings and stay-aways meant Chris would turn his attention to some other girl. Maybe the next girl would say yes, but maybe she'd say no and he wouldn't listen. She'd made herself complicit when she tried to play him, and now she had to pay the price.

She hoped the price wasn't exile. She grabbed at her tumbling thoughts. She needed a new plan, a better plan. She needed Jorie, but Jorie wasn't here.

Someone shoved her from behind, hard enough to propel her into the door. Her face hit the heavy wood and pain bloomed along her cheekbone. "Bitch!" Chris hissed in her ear. He crowded her against the door, tall and heavy behind her, pinning her in place. "You owe me my money back, then." He wrenched her bag from her shoulder and tossed it behind them, then grabbed her free hand and yanked her whole arm into a painful hold behind her back. "Look in there," he barked at his friends.

"Get off me!" she yelled. "Stop it!" She struggled against him, tried to leverage her weight to throw him off, but she couldn't. Every move was agony on her arm.

Her other arm was trapped between her and the door. On the fingers of that hand were three rings. One had three garnets embedded in real silver. One was a circle of flowers, blackened and smooth with age. The third was a spiky pyramid ring, with a skull in the pyramid instead of the eye of Providence. She eyed the skull ring. That would do it. She tried twisting her hand into a better position.

Chris used his full weight to push her into the door. "Freak," he said directly into her ear, breath hot and sour. "Stuck up bitch. Is this the most action you've ever gotten? You should be paying me." He pulled her arm even higher. She couldn't stop the whimper of pain that escaped. He chuckled in her ear, and the sound made her cringe. His free hand dipped in and out of her pockets. It felt like being groped.

Behind them, his goons dumped her bag out onto the floor, went through her things. "Her wallet's empty," one of them reported.

"What the hell is this?" Chris found the memory spell. She'd spent hours laboring over the complex pattern. Don't pull the thread, she silently pleaded. If he pulled the trailing thread, it would collapse the web. Without the words, the intent of the spell, it would render it useless and unrecoverable.

Chris threw it to the floor. "Where's. My. Money."

"I told you. I had to buy supplies to work on Ella." She grunted and pushed back against him. It felt useless, a gust of wind against a mountain, but she was able to raise her hand. He grabbed her by the hair and smashed her face against the door. She ignored the pain. She was eye-to-eye with the grinning skull in the ring.

You're the muscle if anything gets out of hand, Jorie always said before they met with clients. *I got this small stuff. But you, you can really fuck up someone's day.*

No one ever got out of hand. They wanted test answers, clear skin, confidence, a win. Jorie gave it to them. They didn't care why Indira was there.

With the sharp tip of the pyramid, she scratched a sigil into the door. The wood was old and soft, layers of varnish and dirt surrendered beneath the spike. The sigil came out wobbly, but solid. She felt it take hold, all that potential waiting, an earthquake building, a storm about to break. "Where's my money!" Chris screamed in her ear. Indira placed her fingertips against the sigil and didn't even need to speak aloud. She had only to think her invitation, and the storm moved through her.

Chris was blown backwards. From the yells they let out, so were his friends. Indira heard three thuds as they all hit the walls, the stall doors...

A sink.

When she turned, ears ringing from the summoning, she saw Chris falling away from one of the heavy porcelain sinks, limp body slumping to the floor. His head came to rest at an angle it shouldn't, and blood leaked from his left ear.

She looked away. On the floor at her feet lay the forgetting spell, a crumpled pile of string. Fingers numb, she picked it up. She looked again. She stepped toward him. Chris's eyes were open, and they seemed to both stare directly at her and at nothing at all.

"Oh my god, he's dead!" one of his friends revived enough to speak. "You killed him. You fucking freak, you killed him!" He scrambled for the door, fear in his eyes. He dragged his buddy to his feet, woozy and shaking his head.

She couldn't let them walk out. They'd tell anyone who would listen. *This is how witch hunts and war start.* This was what her family saw. This was why they avoided outsiders and were careful when taking clients. This was why her mother was adamant she make the situation disappear, not help Ella take public revenge.

The boys fumbled with the door. Indira untangled the web.

"Look at me," she demanded. Even she was impressed by how authoritative her voice sounded. Accustomed to following the leader, the boys froze and turned their gazes.

She pulled the dangling end of the thread and said, "You were never here. This never happened. You've been out looking for Chris, because he was supposed to meet you but didn't show up. You can't find him anywhere, and you don't know where he is."

Their gazes were caught on the thread as it tightened and closed, capturing and binding their memories of the past few hours. While they stood dazed and unmoving, Indira reached past them, unlocked the door, and maneuvered them into the empty hallway. She closed the door behind them and locked it again. Then she took out her phone and dialed Jorie.

Jorie didn't answer. She tried again. The phone rang and rang, but didn't connect.

Indira sank to the floor and stared at Chris's dead body, unsure what to try next. She couldn't call her family. They'd already chosen her path, and she hadn't followed it. She'd created a mess, and she had to get herself out of it, or instead of a labyrinth year, she'd be exiled to her father's people, strangers. Fathers of Chant women were a secret guarded by the mothers, only revealed when necessary. She was, she knew, creating a necessity right now.

She didn't want to meet her father. She wanted to catch up with Jorie.

Indira selected another contact and called.

"Hello?" Ella's voice was quiet. "Indira?" she asked, uncertain when Indira didn't speak.

To her everlasting embarrassment, Indira started crying.

Ella arrived twenty minutes later. She knocked on the bathroom door, and when Indira opened it, Ella handed her a packet of tissues. "Thanks," Indira muttered.

Ella stopped on the threshold and stared at the dead body. She was very quiet, face unreadable. Finally, she said only, "Huh," and stepped the rest of the way inside. She closed the door behind them and flipped the lock.

The two girls looked away from Chris and stared at each other. Indira said nothing. She had nothing to say. She had no idea how to get herself out of this.

"So, we need a tarp or something, and a place to hide a body." Ella squared her shoulders and set aside her bag. Her top was sleeveless, but her motions carried all the sentiment of someone rolling up their sleeves. "What else? Is there anything we can do to keep people from seeing us, or finding the body? Can we make them forget, if they do?"

Something about the way Ella said "make them forget" snapped Indira out of her paralysis. An idea, a Jorie-level idea, was forming in her mind. Or maybe, an Indira-level idea.

"We need string, lots of string."

"You mean rope?" Ella had approached the body and was nudging it with her sneakered toes. "I can run to the hardware store down the street. Tarp and rope," she spoke her list out loud. For a moment, Indira wondered who the hell Ella really was. What kind of person showed up for a crying acquaintance and was immediately prepared to hide a dead body? She added ruthless to her appraisal of Ella's ambition. What a thrillingly dangerous combination.

"No," Indira shook her head. "Not rope, string." She held up the forgetting spell she'd used on Chris's friends, as though it would mean something to Ella. "We need to make the world forget about Chris."

Ella gawked at her. "You can do that? Just, make everyone forget a whole person existed?"

Indira shrugged, trying to look nonchalant instead of uncertain. "We can try."

"Will yarn work?" Ella reached into her bag and pulled out a skein of pale blue yarn. "It's cotton and linen. Does the fiber content matter? Is this enough?"

"You work with fiber?" Now Indira was gawking. Then, shaking her head, she confirmed, "That looks like enough, sure."

"I crochet." Ella produced a small pair of scissors and clipped the skein from a half-finished project somewhere in the depth of her bag. "It's relaxing."

"So, you have a strong affinity for thread magic, probably. That's good. That helps, because I don't." Indira collected her things from where they'd been scattered across the floor. In her notebook was a sketched copy of the spell's design. She showed it to Ella. "But I do have an affinity for big and powerful. And we have to make this big and powerful. Big enough to cover the body. But it has to be exact and perfect, or it won't work."

Ella picked out the construction of the design and its many nuances within minutes. Indira couldn't help but be jealous; it had taken her hours to understand the spell well enough to build it properly. She couldn't help but recall her mother's words: *She'll drop her magical hobby before the first semester of college is over.* Watching Ella work, Indira knew her mother was wrong. She was seized with a fierce feeling that Ella could become a once-in-a-generation thread witch. And if this spell worked the way it should, Ella would forget she built it. She'd forget finally trying the magic she'd always wanted to. She'd forget she had a reason to be friends with Indira. Without Chris—awful, unrepentant Chris—they'd never have spoken to each other.

If she stopped now, Indira thought, and found another way, a place to hide the body until she and Ella both were gone from town, she didn't need to do this. She didn't need to make everyone forget. But, if she messed that up, if she didn't make this and her connection to Ella go away, she could lose everything. Her labyrinth year. Her whole family. Her sister.

Indira comforted herself with the notion that Ella would discover this again. With so much power and talent, it would find her, if she didn't find it first. She had UCLA waiting for her. Indira had Jorie waiting for her, on the other end of their labyrinth years and apprenticeships. A whole lifetime she could not throw away for a temporary, convenient friend.

Ella constructed the web within an hour, perfectly knotted, every line in place, and draped over Chris's cold body. "Now what?" she asked.

"Now," Indira took a deep breath. "You wait in the hall."

"But don't you need me to cast it?"

"It's a single caster spell."

Only one person could hold all the intention of what needed to be forgotten. Otherwise, it would go awry, or not work at all because no two minds could be so synchronized.

"Won't it be more powerful if we do it together?" Ella argued. She didn't understand the interior subtlety as well as she'd understood the mechanical. She thought she could escape the forgetting.

Indira could not go home and face her mother until Ella forgot. All the ends tied up neatly.

She was at war with herself. She wanted this to be over. She wanted to take her labyrinth year, catch up with her sister, find out if some other Chants did big magic and could show Indira her place in the world. She wanted Jorie to come and take charge while she stood silently behind her, at the ready for violence that wasn't coming. She wanted to be friends with ambitious, ruthless Ella. She wanted this to never have happened.

When Indira didn't answer, Ella charged ahead. She wrapped Indira's hand around the pull thread of the spell, and then wrapped her own hand around just behind. "Tell me when to pull."

Indira looked down at the body on the floor; Chris's usual smug expression slackened to a vacancy that rendered him near-unrecognizable. "You stupid piece of shit," she whispered. "Why couldn't you let it go?"

This was not the quick pull and done of the spell she'd worked on Chris's friends earlier. That was limited to a single event, a few hours of their lives. She needed to erase nearly eighteen years of Chris's existence. It wasn't possible. Even if successful in removing knowledge and memory of him, he'd leave behind a presence. Photographs of a boy whose name no one could recall. A room full of things in his parents' house become a sad and frustrating mystery. A college acceptance letter for a ghost.

Ella, unbothered and unmolested at senior prom, free to have a good time and then leave this town running toward a happy future instead of away from a terrible past. Other girls, women, in the future who would not be raped by a boy grown into more of a predator as he became a man.

Indira thought about all these things, about how positive a world Chris's absence would leave behind. She held all of the intention of the spell inside herself and spoke it into existence through one word: "Now." Her voice echoed in the empty bathroom. They pulled the string together and collapsed the web.

Knowing if the spell had worked or not was impossible in the moments following. She was not going to forget about Chris. But then Ella looked at her, eyes gliding over the dead body on the floor and immediately dismissing it as unimportant, and asked in a vague, confused voice, "Indira? What's going on?"

She thought she would feel worse, but the guilt and loss were not as strong as the desire to move on to the next thing. She maneuvered Ella into the hallway. "Wait here for me."

Ella nodded, murmured a vague *okay*. She stared vacantly at the floor, a puppet with strings cut, all her ambitious, ruthless energy, gone. Indira felt sick, felt like she'd stolen something vital. But Ella's energy would come back when the spell was done reworking her memory. Indira hadn't stolen anything; she'd found her own determination and ruthlessness inside herself, as huge and destructive as her magical talents. She finally knew herself. She had no one to share this revelation with.

She burned the spell webs in a sink. The thread and yarn stank as they charred. She felt sorry for whoever discovered the dead body tomorrow when they came in to use the bathroom. She took Chris's wallet from his pocket to slow the police down. Eventually, they'd link Chris to his school file through a photo, make their way to his parents' house, and be utterly baffled by everyone's claims to have no memory of him. But none of that was her problem.

Indira imagined Ella waiting in the hallway. Maybe she'd woken up a little, shaken off the confusion and disorientation, told herself she was here to use the bathroom but found the door locked and had gone away.

Maybe she'd kept her memory after all. She'd said Indira's name. Maybe she remembered they were friends now, even if she couldn't quite recall why or how. Maybe she was waiting for Indira to finish up and join her.

Indira unlocked and opened the bathroom door.

The hallway was empty.

She dialed Jorie's number. The phone rang and rang, but never connected. She tried again. Again.

Again.

No connection.

All Our Whiskered Idols

Kahlo Smith

Kahlo Smith was born in the redwoods of Santa Cruz, CA and is pursuing her MFA at the University of Nevada, Reno. When not hunting Bigfoot or navigating catacombs, she can be found on Instagram at @vellumgarden.

Grandma Dinah died just after my tenth birthday. At the grief camp my family schlepped the cousins to, kids huddled together in the craft tent, sketching mothers and grandmothers smiling down from heaven in yellow crayon.

I grew up without a god, caught between a lapsing Jewish mother and a bold agnostic father, and by the time I turned ten it was too late to take comfort in a storybook.

"That's not true," I said, smashing my finger into cousin Lisa's crayon portrait's face. "Grandma's in the ground. She was in the box we buried at the funeral. Mom told me!"

For the third time that day, Lisa burst into tears. I started crying too. Great Aunt Ruth bundled us up in her arms and lugged us across camp to the cafeteria. Lisa and I held hands while she nagged the staff into giving us ice cream, and we both ate it salty as tears and snot dripped onto our spoons.

Even then, I knew I was going to die someday. When it happened, every thought and memory would be snuffed out like a yahrtzeit candle. The kind my mom never managed to light. I wouldn't be an angel shining on high; I'd be a pile of metal fillings and decay.

"Vey is mir!" I imagined my mother would gasp when I was gone, one hand flying up to cover her mouth and the other to smack the side of her head. "I forgot to light a candle for Tehilah! Next year; next year for sure."

In the next twelve years, Mom only remembered to light Dinah's yahrzeit candle twice.

By then, I lived in a university-owned apartment in Lower Pacific Heights, nestled between Temple Sherith Israel and the First Church of Christ, Scientist. I tried not to stare at worshippers. They sort of scared me.

When Great Aunt Ruth died, I turned my back on those temples and schlepped to Chevra Kadisha Mortuary in LA. Aunt Ruth loved synagogues. She liked the stained-glass windows, and would stand in beams of colored light, twisting her arms to shape new patterns of shadow. Sometimes she'd take my hand and we'd dance through shades of blue and yellow.

People stood in line to bury their grief with Aunt Ruth. After each sniffling relative scooped their clods of dirt onto the casket, they impaled earth with the shovel and stepped aside. I stood in the back of the crowd fingering the edge of my black ribbon. When I got tired of hating the Rabbi, who hovered behind the grave marker and recited the Tziduk Hadin, I took turns resenting my extended family. They floated around the cemetery with matching placid smiles, comforted by faith and duty.

On the way out, someone set up a basin for us to wash our hands of impure spirits. Uncles and grandchildren hovered around it whispering praises to god. Watching them, I felt ghosts gnawing through my stomach. I pushed past and let my hands stay dirty.

We all ate at Canter's Deli the next day, because Aunt Ruth loved their pickles, and cousin Lisa spent lunch crying into her soup.

"She's in a better place now," Aunt Lieba whispered, rubbing Lisa's back with a fat-fingered hand. "She was suffering."

I left the deli clutching a take-out container. Halfway home, my clenched fingers tore through the cardboard, and I slammed it into the garbage, dripping pickle juice.

Aunt Ruth loved Earth, suffering included. She wore heavy jasmine perfume and ate chocolates straight out of the box. She taught me to sing loudest in my row on Shabbat so everyone in front would compliment my voice. Every time her high school class sent an announcement of another classmate's funeral, she'd crow, "That's another one I've beaten!" Even as her memory failed, she'd ask me to "push this chair a little faster, motek!"

My parents raised a girl who couldn't explain loss as a transformation of the soul, so I missed Aunt Ruth like someone had bitten my left ear off.

A week after the funeral, I was back at school, waiting for the bus with my earbuds jammed in deep.

I only spotted the rat because she moved. She was big. Bigger than any rodent I'd ever seen, her fur slick and glossy, her stomach fat. She snuffled around the iron legs of the bus stop. Crumbs of discarded Twinkie clung to her whiskers.

When the bus dropped down to meet us, she skittered along with the crowd.

I hung near the back of the line and watched her pause at the curb cut. No one else, not even the driver, saw her spring up onto the bottom stair. With a quick hop she was inside. I followed, holding my breath, sneaking glances at the other passengers. No one screamed "Rat!"

I crept through the aisles. The rat and I were in on the same delicious secret.

She nestled under a row in the back of the bus, clutching a chunk of granola bar between her trembling paws. I took the aisle seat. The fabric under my thighs came alive, rippling like fur.

I was breathing hard enough to hear it through my earbuds. I popped them out, straining for the quiet sound of crunching, but all I caught was her toes tapping the floor. I kept thinking I felt her tail brush my ankle. Each time, I looked down and found her crammed into the corner, holding her chunk of oats like an old woman with a purse on her lap.

My stop came too early. I dragged myself off the bus, stealing glances over my shoulder to see if the rat would follow.

She didn't. Still, she ruled my mind all day. During class, while the professor lectured about Art Spiegelman like we hadn't read the book, my head reeled with visions of her.

In my mind, she perched on the bus seat beside me holding a whole granola bar. Every time my lecturer clicked over to a new slide, I imagined it was my rodentine seatmate snapping a cluster of oats.

I spent a week in agony. Every leaf twitching on the wind was a rat's tail, every shoe tapping under a desk was a furry body huddled in shadow. I kept a candy bar squirreled away in my pocket. I'd scared her off before, but maybe I could earn her trust with food.

Straining to be close to her, I went back to the bus stop. I waited two hours for something that never came.

It was dark by the time I walked home. Usually, out late at night, I called Aunt Ruth to chatter me along. Instead, I scanned miles of gutter, hoping for a flash of fur.

The next day, a pink tail peeked out from under an empty bus seat. I wasn't sure if it was real. I wandered to the back of the bus in a daze. Crouched under the padded seat was my chubby brown rat. She stretched a piece of iridescent blue fabric between her paws.

A scarf? I wondered as I curled into the seat above her. *A belt?* Grinning, I raised my eyes to the ceiling, picturing a little brown rat with a head scarf tied under her chin. I fingered the candy bar in my pocket.

She brushed my shoe as she scuttled out of hiding, and I jumped up to follow.

We shot down the steps and followed the sidewalk. I dodged shit-stains and chewed clumps of gum. She did too, fabric clutched between her teeth, and I wondered if all rats avoided filth on the streets. Until I met my rat, they'd been their own kind of city dirt to me.

We rounded a corner onto a deserted residential block. She ran to a manhole cover in the center of the street. Nose twitching, she circled it three times, then scuttled into the gutter. She disappeared down the storm drain.

"Oh, come on," I whispered after her.

I turned my attention to the manhole cover. It was ajar, which was a safety hazard, and yet another sign that I was meant to follow my rat. Still, it was over a hundred pounds of iron. Eventually I heaved it aside, exposing the first few rungs of a maintenance ladder. "Hello?" I whimpered into the black hole.

A squeak rose up out of the dark. That was all the encouragement I needed.

The air inside the manhole was thick. I breathed in through my mouth, tasting something foul. Warm underground moisture hung around me like fog. The ladder rungs were damp. Scrubbing my hands clean would loosen my grip, so I swallowed bile and kept climbing.

When I slid off the ladder into a slick of stagnant water, I was alone. I craned my head from side to side, listening for her skittering. In the distance I heard squeaks. With one reluctant hand trailing the concrete wall, I followed the noise. Mildew collected on the pads of my fingers.

There was a dim light in the distance, growing with each step. At the end of the tunnel, I was bathed in weak sun streaming through another manhole grate.

The rays illuminated a throng of rats.

City rats coated the floor, some fiddling with their whiskers, others scratching their nails against stone. Hunks of discarded food trembled in their paws.

A pile of junk loomed over them. Atop it sat a single rat.

She was more beautiful than any pampered pet rat. Her patchy fur made a perfect mantle of black on her head, leaving a soft white underbelly. Heavy whiskers twitched in time with her nose. Her tail was lithe and flexible, light pink.

Sharp black eyes watched me from her throne, a tangle of pizza boxes and clothing scraps. A pair of hot pink panties hung like a war banner.

The Rat Queen, I knew without thinking. Rats clustered,

chirping, all around me. Fur brushed my ankles. I didn't flinch, too consumed by the tapping of her clawed toes.

She looked right at me. With a twitch of her nose, she acknowledged my presence. She gave a demure squeak.

The rats that packed the room surged towards her, carrying their offerings of crumbs and meat casings and chocolate-slicked wrappers. My fingers clenched around the candy bar in my pocket. I inched closer to her throne, shaking with anticipation. For once, I could be a believer.

I'd never been so close to something holy.

Her worshippers dodged my ruinous feet. Easing to my knees at the edge of the pile, I split the candy's wrapping. A chorus of approving shrieks heralded the first glimpse of chocolate. I peeled plastic from my sacrament and raised my gaze to hers, searching for approval.

Surging up from her seat like a splash of rancid water, she skated down the hill of boxes. I bent my head and stretched the candy out for her to take.

She grasped it with her paws. After a long sniff, she dug her teeth into the corner. Gnawing through the chocolate, crushing caramel and nougat and peanuts between her jaws, I thought I'd never seen anyone eat more gracefully. Not even Aunt Ruth at Canter's.

There was a restrained satisfaction in the way she ate. Her eyes shone like methane fires and her tail jittered, but she chewed slowly. With only a quarter of the bar gone, she dropped it. It slapped the cold cement.

She clicked her claws. High-pitched mewls poured from a

thousand open mouths and bounced off the cement walls. If every drop of rain pouring from the clouds made a sound like a baby bird being crushed to death, a typhoon would sound like that.

They converged on the candy with reckless glee. Crumbs of chocolate flew through the air as sisters and brothers scrabbled for a taste.

I opened my mouth and joined their wailing chorus. My voice broke over and over again, rubbing my throat raw with exultation. I was swept up in a haze of warm air, echoing shrieks, and a sense of total unreality. Thrashed by waves of noise, I decided there was no reason for a rat to fear death. We were a collective. We would eat our dead, and they would never disappear.

Regally detached, the Rat Queen paced back up the pile to her seat. Ruckus quieted under her gaze. My candy bar was gone, every crumb licked up by starving mouths.

I watched her, rapt and adoring.

She nudged a pizza box out of place. It slid down the stack and stopped at my feet. It was an empty box from Luigi's Pizzeria, labeled on the top in sharpie: XL pep, 2x cheese.

An empty box. I'd been overstuffed at a dozen family tables—I knew the way you fed people was always a kind of test. I picked the cardboard up and pressed it to my chest.

She streaked down the back of the trash pile and was gone. The congregation of rodents exploded around me, scampering down the tunnel or disappearing into cracks in the stone.

I sat alone in a dark sewer.

The smell of waste crept into my nostrils again, and I wrinkled my nose shut. Hard cement pushed into my knees. I staggered to my feet, ignoring the wet patches on my jeans, and wandered back down the tunnel.

The manhole cover was still ajar, and I was gripped by the fear that someone might walk by and see it open. A water management authority would rip through the Rat Queen's tunnels like a blaze of sterilizing fire.

I heaved myself up the ladder and onto the street. Midafternoon sunlight seared my eyes and skin. I cowered back against the manhole, head reeling with red and white flashes. The distant echoes of voices and thrumming engines assailed my ears. Far from her musty throne chamber, the air brimmed with loud scents of gasoline and hamburger and hot asphalt.

The pizza box covered my face. I breathed through damp cardboard and waited for my eyes to adjust.

That walk to Luigi's Pizzeria was the most fulfilling pilgrimage I've ever taken. I was buoyed forward, city sidewalk turned to airport moving walkway. The Rat Queen gave me a mission. I would buy an extra-large pepperoni pizza with extra cheese for her followers' feast.

Every pedestrian I pushed past looked miserable. Their faces were buried in phones or glued to concrete sucking them down like it was still wet. My feet were light pink-clawed paws.

The city was made new. Every stinking alley was a site for worship, cradling its overflowing dumpster bounty. My chest was bursting with brilliance that threatened to blow through my teeth and blind passing cars. I lived in a beam of sunlight streaming through an open manhole.

At Luigi's, the boy behind the counter saw my brilliant grin and stuttered.

"Extra large pepperoni, please," I declared. "Extra cheese."

"Got big plans?" he squeaked, pawing at the register.

"Yes!" I replied. It was the most I'd said to a stranger in the past two weeks.

While I waited, a pigeon outside destroyed a hot dog bun. I admired the way its feathers glinted iridescent in the sunlight. Flashy and crass, I thought, but beautiful in its own way.

Endorphins overflowing, I navigated the maintenance ladder one-handed. I found the chamber empty. Awkward, I waited in the center, holding the steaming pizza box.

A squeak came from the throne of trash. Skittering claws sounded behind me, and a quartet of rats appeared in the mouth of the tunnel. I set the box on the floor and backed away.

They leapt on it, rending cardboard like flesh. The four rats worked as a team, sinking their teeth into the crust and dragging slices away. Some to a pit draining wastewater, some down the maintenance tunnel, some into holes left by shut-off pipes.

I watched them with respect. Trusted, valiant workers of the Rat Queen.

When I was alone in the room again, a single slice sat untouched in the torn box. Something rustled in the Rat Queen's throne. I set the box on top of the pile, dispersing stray cardboard shreds at its base, and opened what was left of the lid to display the final slice. I backed away and got to my knees.

Hesitant, the Queen emerged from her nest. She was just as

regal without a rodentine army at her feet. Ignoring the slice of pizza, she clutched something from the pile in her paws. I kept perfectly still as she padded in my direction.

At my feet, she laid a single square of dirty silk. I took the scrap.

I stood, and she turned and retreated to her nest. My next mission was clear: clothing fit for her royal regalia. I left the sewer stinking of waste and grinning so hard my teeth hurt.

I wracked my brain over where to find clothes. There was always the thrift store, the donation bin, but I needed something nicer— something I couldn't get on a student's budget.

The answer came that night, when for the first time in days I checked my calendar.

On Saturday, the cousins were meeting at Lisa's house to paw through boxes of Aunt Ruth's keepsakes, which she'd driven home from LA. Without visits to the sewer to mark my days, the week floated by in a haze of missed due dates and microwaved meals.

I was late to Lisa's house because I spent all morning in bed, smelling my own sweat and wondering what the Rat Queen's favorite color was.

Cousin Lisa's apartment was in a nice neighborhood. On the walk over, I passed Wise Sons Deli. Lisa liked to take me there after class when I first moved to the city. It reminded us of after-school trips to Aunt Ruth's.

She would heave open the loaded refrigerator door. "You want eggs?" she'd call over one shoulder. "I've got potato salad, some lox; we could make toast. How about some juice?"

"We already ate lunch," Lisa would moan.

"Just a little snack! I made cake. You want some coleslaw?"

We always ate everything.

A wave of disembodied family greetings rang out from Lisa's crowded apartment. Aunt Ruth kept all her things sparkling; cleaners came by every Tuesday and left the house spotless. Cousin Lisa liked her place just as tidy.

I tried not to flinch from the bright white walls. A tangy, acrid scent hung in the air.

Perched on the couch, Lisa's friend Osnat breathed deep. "God, it smells like your aunt's lemon cleaning spray in here. Liz, is that from you or did it come with the boxes?"

Most of the artifacts and heirlooms had already been divvied up and shipped off to their keepers. In my own apartment sat an untouched box of pictures, two dancing musical teddy bears, and some books Aunt Ruth set aside for me. I wasn't interested in that kind of finery.

I pushed past people clustered around jewelry boxes and scrapbooks. My destination was the box Lisa packed from the infamous walk-in closet.

Aunt Ruth kept her clothes more pristine than her home. Each dress or coat was freshly dry-cleaned and wrapped in a plastic bag—not that it mattered, with everything stuffed into a cardboard box. The nicest pieces were gone, but at the bottom sat a pile of scarves.

It was just what I needed. Handfuls of silk and cashmere glossed over my grubby fingers. Nearby was an empty shoebox, and I stuffed it with my hoard of scarves.

Someone tapped me on the shoulder and I flinched like I'd been bitten.

"Tehilah?" Cousin Lisa asked. "Are you going to take all those scarves?"

"Do you want any?" My voice must have been edged with desperation, because Lisa pulled her hand away and twisted her fingers together.

"No, they're all yours if you want them. But you never really liked wearing them. I thought maybe you'd rather take some gloves."

"Okay, well, it's not about what you think. I want these." I held my box of scarves close to my chest, certain she was trying to steal them from me. They were exactly what the Queen needed, and I wouldn't let her touch them.

Lisa took a small step back. Blood rushed to my face as her eyes filled with a sticky emotion halfway between pity and fear. "That's fine! Everything in the boxes is up for grabs."

"Fine," I snapped.

She dropped her voice. "Are you feeling okay? I know you took Aunt Ruth's death hard—we all did—and I know that you weren't interested in grief counseling with the Rabbi, but maybe..."

"I don't need to talk to any Rabbis!" I didn't give a damn about our family's stares. "I've got my own community, okay? Stop trying to force yours on me!"

"I'm sorry, Tehilah, I didn't mean that you should go! I was thinking instead we could—"

Her hand drifted towards mine. I yanked the box away. My eyes burned. Cousin Lisa was right—I'd never liked scarves for dress-up. But I needed them for something more important.

"Leave me the hell alone," I choked, and hustled out the open door.

Tears trickled slowly down my cheeks on my way back to the bus stop. I got on with aching eyes and salt-crusted cheeks, but the bus driver didn't comment as I fished three floating dollar bills from my pocket.

She wore a high-collared blue shirt in soft jersey knit. I wondered if the Queen would like it. I realized when the driver made eye contact that I'd spent too long in front of the machine.

"That's a pretty shirt," I blurted.

She gave me an indulgent smile. "Thanks, sweetheart."

I kept my head down until my stop, avoiding eye contact with strangers. I held the box of scarves against my side and hurried through a familiar tangle of side streets.

I put my burden down to shift the manhole cover aside. I wasn't sure how to navigate the ladder, so instead I closed the lid and dropped the box into the sewer. I scrambled down after it and found it right-side up in a quarter-inch of standing water.

My merciful Queen wouldn't mind.

The sound must have echoed, because when I entered the grand hall, dozens of skittering feet paced the edge of the room. I waited by the door until their leader graced the top of her nest. Every step full of ceremony, I made my way to the center of the chamber.

I turned the box upside down and let Aunt Ruth's scarves

cascade onto cement. Dregs of sewer water seeped into silk. The rats held back, awaiting their Queen's will.

She tiptoed off the stack of pizza boxes. One of her claws caught the edge of a fine lace scarf. She considered it. With her usual elegant pride, she dug her teeth into the fabric. A strip of off-white finery came off in her mouth, and she turned to me, allowing me to tie it.

My fingers trembled against the soft fur on her throat. I jittered through the movement of a bow. Lace sat tight against her fur, and she looked more regal than ever.

The holiest of holies lay before me. All I had to do was open my heart and be part of it.

The moment that thought washed over me, I realized it made no sense. Wasn't I already part of it? I'd carried offerings to her altar, I'd squealed my praises along with the horde. In front of me lay the proof of my dedication. A bundle of fabric, silk and lace stained with rank water.

In that moment of doubt, something fragile and irides-cent snapped.

I missed my Aunt Ruth. She wouldn't like the sewer.

I started crying. Wailing, tears spraying from my eyes like bus wheels in a gutter. I was hunched over in the rotten dark, breathing in shit-laden fumes, surrounded by skittering rats.

They were tearing apart Aunt Ruth's beautiful clean clothes.

I grabbed one of her favorite scarves, a pink one with embroidered roses in one corner. I clutched it to my chest, feeling sobs flutter through the fabric. Rats scattered from my jerky movements.

The whole sewer was crawling with them, and I panicked, every breath scraping my throat as I stumbled to my feet.

My eyes rested for a second on the one with a bow around her throat. Her tail was slick with grease. Flat black eyes didn't meet mine as she fled into the trash pile, scared off by a loud human.

Sniffling and gagging on the air those sniffles pulled in, I sprinted out of the room. Behind me, fabric tore, whiskers twitched above squeaking mouths, and I did not belong.

I crawled up the ladder. One of my feet slipped on a damp rung, and I dropped, screaming as my shoulder wrenched. I hung there, crying too hard to open my eyes, until my floundering feet touched metal. When I finally emerged, snot-streaked and panting, I was covered in mildew. Streaks of rust defaced the scarf. My shirt was torn and damp.

Still whimpering, wringing Aunt Ruth's scarf between my hands, I trudged down the street. My aching legs carried me to the bus stop.

I scanned the gutter. It was all wrong. I should never have followed that rat into the darkness. "Please," I wheezed to the empty street, begging for someone to protect me from a threat I couldn't name. Nothing had followed me out of the sewer, but I felt chased.

The bus pulled up. The people who filed off didn't linger on me. To them, I was scenery. A ragged young woman crying at a bus stop. I could feel the dirt streaking my cheeks.

And the smell—for the first time, I noticed the smell that followed me from the manhole. I stank. Not just like the sewer, feces and mold and metal. I stank like sweat and wet fur and salt.

"Hey kid," called the bus driver, "you getting on?"

I stood without thinking and wobbled to the steps. Dimly, I realized I had no money. I'd left my purse at Cousin Lisa's house. Still, I made a show of patting my empty pockets. I wanted to prove I had a reason for stepping up.

It was the same bus driver, still wearing her blue shirt. She waved a dismissive hand towards the seats. "You look like hell, honey. Go sit down."

"Thank you," I said. "Thank you."

I chose an empty row in the back of the bus. There was nothing under the seat.

Really, I decided, I wasn't riding alone. A man in a baseball cap slept against his window. At the very back sat a high school student with their face buried in a comic book. Two girls shared earbuds, listening to the same music and giggling out the same window.

The robotic announcement scared me at my stop. "Thank you for letting me on," I rasped as I passed the driver. "It's a really nice shirt."

She chuckled at that, and her laughter followed me off the bus and down the street.

I kept my gaze at eye-level. A man walked towards me on his way out of the First Church of Christ, Scientist. I knew what I looked like, but I stiffened anyway as his eyes darted over my damp jeans and tear-streaked face.

He smiled at me. It was warm and welcoming, probably engineered by pity, but I smiled back as hard as I could. "Have a lovely day," he called over his shoulder as he passed.

"You too," I cried back, remembering how to be human.

I made it home, shoulders aching, my eyes wrung out. With every step up to my third-floor apartment I could feel water soaking through my socks.

A beat-up shoebox sat in front of my door. I opened it to find my brown leather purse and a pristine yellow sticky note. *Tehilah,* it read, *You forgot this at my place. I grabbed you those earrings you used to wear for dress-up (front pocket). I miss her too. I saved some gloves and I thought maybe we could look through them together. Let's get lunch soon.—xo Lisa*

I wrapped my purse in the pink scarf, pressed them both to my chest, and went inside. My shades were down. Mold speckled my unwashed dishes, and clothes were scattered on the floor.

Thank you, I texted Lisa. It was all I knew how to say.

I threw the windows open, plugged in the fan, and switched on the radio. With bland pop music blaring from the speaker, I shambled to the bathroom to rinse myself clean.

Tracks

Elizabeth Guilt

Elizabeth Guilt lives in London, UK, where history lurks alongside plate glass office buildings and stories spring out of the street names.

I never told you that I had a scar like a train track around my waist. I never told you about my dreams. I never told you how I stuffed belongings into a bag, slipped away from my parents' house, and ran down the road in the early hours of the morning. How I leaped joyfully into a rusting Ford Mondeo, and squeezed in among the bags and boxes. How it had a huge black cabinet strapped to the roof rack. I never told you how I, and the driver, flitted from city to city, zigzagging slowly south until we reached a tiny village somewhere outside Seville.

I told you that I preferred to live my life on my own. I told you I was not looking for a partner. I told you that you could be a friend, but nothing more.

I told you– when you found that old playbill– that yes, that really was me in the picture. The Great Biondini's glamorous assistant, climbing night after night into the huge black cabinet. I told you how he looked directly into my eyes the first time he brought down his gleaming saw. How I stared, amazed, at my own toes wiggling from the other side of the stage. I told you how the audience screamed and applauded when he took me by the hand and I stepped bravely out of the cabinet again. I did not tell you about the faint mark on my skin afterwards, tracing the path of the saw.

Yes, I told you, night after night he concluded his act by saw-ing me in half and putting me back together again. The people cheered, and clapped, and called for more, but he would whisk me away as the curtains came down. We piled everything back into the Mondeo, and raced to the next town, laughing into the darkness.

Yes, I told you, I loved him. And every night I trusted him, and never worried about the band around my stomach that grew a little darker, a little redder, every day.

I told you the adventure came to an end. We stayed a while in Southern Spain, then I came home to England. I did not tell you why, although you asked. Everything comes to an end, I told you.

I never told you about the night someone in the audience caught his eye. A beautiful redhead, a few rows back, and he smiled brilliantly up at her as he began to slice me in two. He looked away from me, just for a moment, and I felt the saw. I cried out. His head jerked back, his eyes guilty, and together we finished our show. The crowd—the redhead—stamped and whistled and begged for an encore. He swept me up, carried me tenderly to the Mondeo, kissed me and told me he loved me.

I never told you his hand on my neck could make me tremble, how his lips felt like magic in the night. I told myself there could never be another.

I never told him how often I felt the saw after that. A little nick here, a slice of agony there. I smiled, and stared into his eyes, and wiggled my toes, and bowed to the standing ovations. I never told him as the pain got worse.

I never told you about the final night. The night where I felt the saw's teeth bite into me, and chew through the whipcord-tense muscles in my stomach. The night I began to scream and could not stop. The night when he pulled the halves of the cabinet apart and there was nothing but blood, and the audience stared in open-mouthed silence. I staggered to my feet because he told me I had to get up, had to get up, had to show these people I was fine, come on, come on. Look, she's fine! We slunk from the stage to a cold and terrified stutter of applause.

I told him that I couldn't do it again. He told me I'd be fine: we'd take a villa outside Seville, some rest, some sunshine, some time off. I told him no, I could not do it again. He told me we'd see.

I never told you about our sun-drenched weeks in that villa, because I didn't think you would want to hear. An easy, lazy, lovers' life of late mornings and gentle strolls and carafes of wine. He wrapped himself around me, and his hands stroked a glow from my skin. The bloody gashes healed. I gloried in his love, bathed in it, and wished it would go on for ever.

He told me it was time to go back on the road, and I told him I could not do it. Not again. Not after that last night. He told me he would take that memory away, and I ran. Stuffed belongings into a bag, slipped away, and ran down the road in the early hours of the morning. I told myself I had to, that it was the only way to be safe.

I told you I had not heard from him since.

I never told you how my heart stops with every knock, every call, every clatter of the letterbox. How my stomach clenches under the scar, wondering if he has found me.

Silk

Alyssa C. Greene

Alyssa C. Greene (she/they) is a writer
and amateur weaver currently living
in New York City. Her fiction has
appeared in Fence, Pleiades, North
American Review, and elsewhere. She
also co-hosts Say Podcast and Die!, a
podcast about the Goosebumps books,
queerness, and horror. A graduate of
the Clarion Science Fiction and Fantasy
Writers' Workshop, she has an MFA
from the University of Utah and a PhD
in German literature from Columbia
University. Find them on Twitter (@
acgreenest) and check out pictures of
their (probably not haunted) weaving on
Instagram (@caffeinemotivated).

I don't know how long I've been at the spinning wheel. I'm in my body less and less these days; it feels like a place I visit rather than live. She only lets me back when major physical needs hinder her work. The equivalent of *check engine light* for a human body.

Last I remember, I had just finished dinner. Now morning light peeks in under the shed door. How many days have passed since that dinner, I can't yet guess.

I stop treadling and flex my hands. Raw, red lines have etched themselves between the fingers. Even silk threads will wear down skin, given enough time.

As I rub salve into my hands, I realize something's different this time. Normally my hands and my body would already be shaking from exhaustion and low blood sugar. A glance at the spinning wheel only makes my suspicion stronger. Silk filaments have been spun and plied into yarn—perfect yarn. Marie-Louise would only let go of me if the shakes were spoiling her handiwork.

I'm not sure if the thought comes from my gut or from Marie-Louise or if there's even a difference anymore, but suddenly I'm certain: someone's coming.

***

Gran built the shed on the furthest corner of the property. It's a long walk back to the house. You can't see the shed from the house, and some mornings when I wake up, there's a brief, blissful moment where I forget about its existence entirely.

Most of the shed is taken up by the menagerie. Before I go, I look in on the few remaining silk moths. They're laying eggs, beginning the cycle anew. Their part in this has always haunted me; I'm grateful not to remember the harvesting stage. The first time I watched Gran toss handfuls of cocoons into boiling water, I ran screaming from the shed. When Gran came to, she found me at the foot of a mulberry tree hugging my knees to my chest and sobbing.

Outside, it's morning. The fog hasn't completely burned off, and even though I've walked this footpath a thousand times since I was a girl, for a moment it feels magical.

The hill crests and I can see the house. There's a strange car parked in front of it. My instincts were right: the cycle's begun again. It's already in motion.

The car is well-maintained but not a newer model, nothing fancy. A figure sits in the front seat, backlit by morning sun. When I'm fifty feet away the driver emerges from the car and slams the door hard. Something in their stance feels aggressive—not something I'm used to seeing from visitors. They're usually supplicants, come to throw themselves at my feet as a last resort.

I shield my eyes as I approach. And then I recognize the face: Gina.

Last I saw Gina, she was forcing the doors of her overstuffed hatchback shut, refusing to look at me so I wouldn't see the tears running down her face. "I'll be back for the rest of it later," she said. She drove off and never came back. Her winter clothes and knickknacks are still boxed up in my attic; I've never been able to bring myself to throw them away.

"I thought to myself, 'It couldn't be,'" Gina says. No *hello* or *nice to see you*. She's the kind of person who always says those things, even to someone she hates; her anger doubles the shock of seeing her again. "They told me I was going to see someone named Marie-Louise. So imagine my surprise when I got *this* address."

There's so much I want to say to her. *It's good to see you. I've missed you. I wish I hadn't pushed you away.* But that's not how this works. There are rules. Or maybe 'rules' isn't quite right—there are rituals. There's a way these things are done, and it's the same for a pauper as for a president. There's no exception for when the person you wanted to spend the rest of your life with shows up on your doorstep.

"Sorry," I say quietly. "I can't help you."

("I can't keep living like this if you won't even admit something's wrong," she'd said as she crammed toiletries and books into her bags. I'd emerged from a frenzied haze to find her packing, and was still too weak to do anything but watch, shakily eating sliced bread straight from the bag, only half-comprehending her words. "And I can't help you if you won't let me in.")

I turn away and start up the porch steps. The same steps she used to climb as she called out half-jokingly, half-sincerely, *Honey, I'm home!*

"Are you fucking kidding me?" she shouts. "Natalie, are you seriously walking away from me right now?"

She tells me to come back, to talk about this like adults—don't I owe her at least that much? But I'm already turning away, reaching for the door, trying to keep my face from crumpling.

***

I was eight when I found out I had a grandmother.

"Does she live far away?" I asked, figuring this must be the reason I was just now hearing about her.

"About a day's drive," Mom said. She told me we'd be visiting her that weekend.

On the drive up, I bombarded Mom with questions. Why hadn't I met my grandmother before? (I had, once, as a baby.) Why didn't we visit her sooner? (We were busy.) Did she bake cookies? (Could bake, but only begrudgingly.)

"Do you talk to her a lot?" I asked.

"Not really."

"Why?"

"We don't have much to say to each other." Her tone told me to stop asking.

I couldn't fathom Mom's disinterest in the joyful woman who threw her arms around me the moment I emerged from the car. Her home had everything the movies taught me a grandmother should have: freshly-baked cookies, needlepoint samplers mounted on the walls. A refrigerator covered in pictures, including of me, the only daughter of her only child. Gran, as she told me to call her, dug out old picture albums and told me stories about anyone I pointed to.

Mom never said a word more than she needed to. She watched every interaction with appraising eyes.

The next morning, before my mother awoke, Gran showed me around her small farm. She had a few sheep and goats, a modest flock of chickens. And then she led me to the barn.

The interior had been turned into a workshop. Walls were mounted with spools of yarn and thread; the place was full of gizmos whose purpose I couldn't even begin to guess. At the center of the barn stood a contraption that looked like it had weathered centuries. A wooden frame that extended up, taller than me. Atop it, a boxy machine, down from which emanated thousands of fine threads. The threads fed down into the wooden frame, through harnesses fitted with strings, and somehow, what emerged from the machine was lustrous red cloth.

I could feel my grandmother's eyes on me.

"What is it?" I asked.

She patted a low wooden bench in front of the machine. I sat down, transfixed. I ran a hand over the smooth cloth before realizing I should ask first. I jerked my hand back and started to apologize, but she only smiled, eyes alive with light.

"Go ahead," she said, and I touched the cloth again, traced my fingers over its stylized pattern.

"This is a Jacquard loom," she said. "For many generations, my ancestors—*your* ancestors—were master weavers. They made silk cloth like this. Here,"—she gestured to an object hanging near my face—"pull this."

I had to stand on my toes to reach it. When I pulled it, something shot from the left side of the machine to the right. I moved back instinctively, nearly tumbling over the bench.

Gran chuckled. "That was the shuttle. It delivers the yarn." She put my hand on a bar attached to the machine. "The beater," she said, and swung my hand forward. When she swung the beater back, the thread from the shuttle had become a part of the cloth. I gasped in delight.

She pointed to a chain of punched cards sewn together and showed me how the pedal at my feet made the Jacquard machine advance to a new card. The cards looked like someone had gone wild with a hole punch, but in fact, there was more order than first met the eye. She showed me how they engaged a series of hooks that lifted certain threads and not others, allowing the pattern to bloom. I found the rhythm of it quickly—pull, beat, step, pull, beat, step—and before long I'd woven an inch of silk cloth.

Gran examined my work. "A natural," she whispered. Then she glanced at her watch. "We should get back to the house."

The quickness of her movements, the way she looked around as she locked the barn door—all of it told a story. When we got to the house and found Mom reading the paper, she looked from Gran to me.

"What have you two been up to?" The question kept so casual, as if it were nothing.

"Gran introduced me to the animals," I said. "Did you know that goats have four stomachs?"

The tension dissipated. There had been some test, some tinder that hadn't sparked.

We passed the rest of the weekend pleasantly; we didn't return to the barn. But for weeks I dreamed of the *clack* of the shuttle as it found home, the sound of thread on thread, the gradual emergence of a pattern, the whole of which I couldn't see.

***

Normally I'd crawl into bed to recover from the things my body did without me, but Gina's visit leaves me too wired.

I head to the barn to get some work done. Not only have I taken over my grandmother's workshop, I've added a computer-controlled loom, a big Swedish rug loom, and a table loom for sampling. The Jacquard loom is there, too, but I don't consider it mine; it belongs only to Marie-Louise. Normally it's hidden under sheets, but they've been pulled off, the whole thing dusted and oiled and readied for use.

In my everyday work I don't use punch cards. A production weaver doesn't have time for that. I plug designs into my laptop, and the laptop tells the machine which threads to raise. I weave yards and yards of fabric for designers and retailers. If you've seen my work, you've probably seen it as upholstery on loveseats and chairs in boutique furniture shops, or perhaps as the dishtowels on your more persnickety friends' wedding registries. Occasionally more glamorous assignments come in: historical fabrics for expensive Hollywood period pieces. But hardly anyone stops to think about the chaise lounge an Oscar-winning actress sits on when she says, *Let them eat cake.* My work is part of the background of something grander. You wouldn't know my name.

That used to bother me, the anonymity of the work. I made a good enough living calibrating my weaving to seasonal trends, anticipating what colors and structures would be in demand.

But I hungered to be seen, to have my technical and design skills recognized.

It was a hunger Marie-Louise shared.

I could give you that, she whispered each night as I drifted off to sleep.

Never, I thought.

But over time, *never* eroded into *maybe*, became *what if*.

These days I try to focus on the work itself. The flow state of movement that bonds body and machine. The everydayness of cloth. Watching threads become something substantial, something durable, something that might become part of a stranger's daily life. I've loved these things since Gran first showed them to me, and I wish I'd never felt the need for more.

***

Gina returns the next day, and I refuse to leave the house. She hurls invectives at me, calls me vindictive and cold and mendacious.

"I always knew you were hiding something from me," she shouts.

She bangs on doors and windows, stands on the porch screaming. Not even words: just primal sound.

The person who gave her my address must have coached her to keep coming back. They tell each other things, I've learned, though not always accurately. And often enough, they withhold the most important information. The cost of these services.

After an hour or two of this, I hear her at the front door. But she doesn't knock, doesn't ask to be let in. She walks to her car and sits cross-legged on the hood for another two hours, waiting, daring me to come out, to face what she might have to say to me.

I can't.

When she finally leaves, it's somehow worse. Even when she screamed, I realize, there was comfort in the fact her presence. Without her, I feel how empty this house is, how alone I am out here, just as Gran must have felt before I came to live with her.

I open the front door, ready to sprint after her car, and something flutters to the ground. An old brochure, stuck in the door handle.

Silkwork, it reads, *Textile Art from Ancient Times to Now.* It's been opened and closed so many times that the paper's creases threaten to become tears. We were young and in love when we went to that show.

The night it opened, I practically sprinted through the museum, looking for the object I'd come to see. I found it, spotlit in a glass case. A silk-woven prayer book.

Gina caught up to me a few minutes later. "There you are!"

"I can't believe it." The words came out half-whispered.

She slipped a hand into mine. "Tell me."

"That's Joseph Marie Jacquard on the cover," I said. "Jacquard, like my grandmother's loom. He invented the machine with the punch cards. And it took maybe half a million of those same punch cards to weave this book. And do you even *know* how many warp ends this took?"

"Um," she said. A caterer came by with a tray of wineglasses, and she took one. "Obviously, yeah. But let's say for argument's sake, maybe I forgot."

"Four hundred—per *inch*!" I was nearly shouting now.

"That sounds like...many threads."

"*So* many," I said.

She smiled and bumped a hip against mine. "I like it when you talk nerdy to me."

"And it was woven in Lyon," I said. "Where my people are from."

I had told Gina the story my grandmother had handed down, about being descended from a master-weaver who took part in a silk-weavers' uprising. The Canut Revolt. He and his family—a family which doubled as his workshop staff—were killed when French soldiers retook the city.

What I hadn't told Gina: the dreams I had about that bloody week in April 1843. The chaos, the black flags, the dreams of a new republic. Over and over, Marie-Louise bending over the corpse of her father, shot dead in the street. His blood staining her hands.

Gina squeezed my hand. "Would you ever make something like this?"

Marie-Louise's words burst from my mouth: "I could do it better."

***

Mom died within a year of our visit to the little farm. I packed a bag and went north to live with Gran. We cried together over lost mother and child. I began a new school; we began the work of becoming a family.

She was a kind, doting guardian, until one day she wasn't. She woke up early and went to the shed; I didn't see her until hours after school, my stomach rumbling with hunger.

"Here," she muttered, pulling a can from the larder. She thudded it down in front of me without looking at the label. "Can opener's in the drawer."

"Coconut milk?"

But she had already wandered out the door.

Days passed. I tried my best not to bother her, cobbling together meals from shelf-stable goods after finishing the perishables. I laid awake at night listening for her boots trudging up the stairs, the box spring creaking as she collapsed into bed.

Just as abruptly as she'd become a stranger, the grandmother I knew returned to me. She straightened the house and filled the kitchen with groceries. She made breakfast and dinner and packed my lunch. She spoke to me.

I had no explanation for any of it. I was probably being too sensitive, I told myself. She came from a different generation; she must have simply expected a child of ten to be more self-sufficient. Practically a grown-up.

Things went back to the way they had been, and I tried not to question my good fortune.

And then a man turned up asking for Gran. He was nearly her age. He wore a hat and doffed it when she emerged from the house. "Ma'am?"

Gran's mouth hardened.

"Ma'am, I have a problem, and I hope you'll do me the kindness of hearing me out."

Gran turned on a heel and slammed the door in his face. When he didn't leave, she called him names that shocked me. He returned the next day and she charged at him with a broom, screaming "aiyeeeeeeeee!" as she ran. On his third visit, she invited him in.

From my room I could hear only the muffled cadences of the conversation. After a few minutes, he was gone.

Gran disappeared again, replaced with a furious automaton, scribbling impenetrable code, graphing shapes I couldn't understand. Then she moved into the barn. I listened at the door, hearing the *thwump* of the beater and the *click* of the machine rotating its cards. If she slept at all, she must have slept in the barn.

After many feverish days, she emerged. Crawled into bed and slept. Her exhaustion was so total that when the stranger returned, she couldn't get out of bed to greet him. She sent me to the barn to fetch a package wrapped in brown butcher paper. I handed it off and never saw him again. I didn't see what was inside, but it felt like cloth.

***

My heart doesn't know whether to sink or soar when I hear the car coming up the road. Her third visit. I'm supposed to help her.

This time, when she gets out of her car, I open the front door. She seems to know this is the procedure—she must have been coached. By someone who loves her or hates her or a little of both.

Usually I'd guide a visitor to the living room, offer a cup of tea. It seems like a witchy thing to do. But Gina walks straight into the kitchen and sits in a chair by the window, the same spot where she used to eat breakfast every morning.

"How does it work?" she says.

"Nice to see you, too." I immediately regret my words.

"Did I forget the pleasantries? Oh, excuse me, I was busy driving three fucking hours to get here when I should be with my wife in the hospital."

"Sorry," I mutter. It feels like the last months of our relationship. Me shutting down, her exploding. I clear my throat and try to channel Marie-Louise and her indifference to everything but her loom. "Here's how it works. You tell me what you want. You bring me something valuable. And a, uh, donation. Whatever amount is significant for you." My face flushes; that last part is always uncomfortable, but the fact that it's Gina makes this worse.

"Anything else?" Her voice is hard.

"Yeah." I swallow hard and then look into her eyes. I've never needed anyone to understand as badly as I need her to understand this now. I open my mouth to tell her to leave, but Marie-Louise takes over: "There is another cost. One that will be dear to you. Maybe not today; maybe not soon. But there will be another price to pay."

"What does that mean?" she asks, but Marie-Louise holds my mouth shut.

She sighs, reaches into her bag. She's come prepared. There's cash, lots of cash—she's done well for herself, evidently, or maybe her wife has. On top of the cash, she places a ring. A family heirloom. She put it on my finger once, and I wore it proudly until the day she left, and I handed it back to her.

She gets up to leave, and I grab her arm to stop her. There's so much to say. *I wanted to protect you. I thought I was making the right choice. I've never stopped missing you.*

What comes out: "You need to tell me what you want."

She looks at me for a long time before saying, "Keep my family safe."

***

Strangers came to my grandmother a few times a year. They never announced themselves, but somehow Marie-Louise knew. My grandmother frenzied; I did my best to stay out of her way, to keep the groceries stocked and the house clean. And I tended the silkworms.

In dreams I've seen the small menagerie where Marie-Louise's father kept silkworms. He hoped to create raw silk right there in Lyons, and so not have to rely on farmers in Cévennes or Ardèche, or on foreign imports. But he died before he could realize that he'd underestimated the time and resources farming on that scale would take.

Our silkworms spin red cocoons. Under my grandmother's care, and mine, they've never made the white or yellow encasings they're supposed to. Their red silk won't take any dye. I once tried to ply their silk with wool. The brake band on my spinning wheel snapped; the fibers pushed apart like two magnets of the same polarity.

Gran's mother smuggled the moth eggs from the family menagerie when she immigrated to America. She called it divine intervention that they were not discovered.

They must be magical, she believed, to spin only red silk.

She was wrong.

Bombyx mori—that's what an enterprising young biology grad student determined they are. He delivered the news to Gran with disappointment, having hoped that her moths might be a major discovery. In his lab, generation after generation of caterpillars spun only white cocoons. DNA sequencing confirmed that they were nothing but ordinary silk moths.

"The red must be a trick of the light," he said glumly.

My grandmother nodded with sympathy. He was not the first enterprising young man to study her moths, she told me later.

Over and over I dream of Marie-Louise's hands reaching into the menagerie. The same dream my grandmother had: a moth landing on the back of Marie-Louise's palm, her skin still sticky with her father's blood.

***

After we'd seen the silk prayer book, an itch emerged. To create something wondrous. More than that: the gnawing desire for people to truly know my work. And my name.

There was a national competition for textile artists. I spent fruitless hours at the loom or hunched over graph paper, trying to design something that would dazzle the judges. I hated every single attempt I made.

Let me help you, Marie-Louise whispered. *Together, we'll be unstoppable.*

The deadline crept ever-closer. No matter how much Gina tried to calm me down, the competition felt like a point of no return. Success would mean I was an artist; failure would confirm I was a nobody. And I was tired of being nobody.

Alright, I told her. *Just this once.*

Almost immediately, I felt myself unblock. I sat at my desk for hours, sketching, calculating, planning. I spent weeks in the most beautiful flow of creativity and creation. Everything came easily; there were no bad ideas or failed samples or existential crises.

At the end of it, I had a cloth nine feet long, something approximating a classical frieze. As soon as I sent it in, I collapsed and couldn't get out of bed for a week. Life slowly returned to normal; it was easy to feel like none of it had ever happened, until the email appeared. My piece had won.

The first time I really looked at it was to collect my award. It was a historical scene, depicting the whole weaving process, from spinning to warping to weaving. The same woman worked every step of the process. There are no extant representations of her but I knew immediately who she was.

The title: *La canuse.*

The judges praised my attention to detail and the structure of my cloth. But what they really loved was how I highlighted a forgotten figure from history.

The cost was this: there'd be no more shirking my duties. I'd have to continue her work.

***

Even though she's paid, even though I told her there'd be a cost, I know Gina can't possibly understand that Marie-Louise doesn't strike fair bargains. And so I try to fight her.

Years ago, I did anything I could think of to keep her at bay: spritzing my house with holy water, chanting, meditation, caffeine pills by the handful. The only thing that worked was keeping myself in a constant state of privation. If I was exhausted and hungry, I was of no use to her.

As a solution it was unsustainable. I needed to sleep, eat, work. And so it meant I had to cede my body to her sometimes. We seemed to have a truce in those early days. She respected that I could take away her power. But after Gina left, it was just me, alone, on a farm miles from anything. What did I need those lonely, empty hours for, anyway? I opened the door for her and she walked in.

But this is different: this is Gina.

I bury all the food in the kitchen in the backyard. I walk for hours around the property until my entire body aches. I keep myself awake.

I walk through the night, through the next day. If I keep myself awake, if I drop dead from exhaustion, it'll be worth it to protect her.

Gina calls from somewhere noisy. I can barely make out the words. "Nothing's happened yet. How long does this take?"

"You need to reconsider," I say. "You could die. Everyone you love could die." At least I think that's what I'm saying—I'm so tired it's hard to keep anything straight.

There's a long enough pause that I start to wonder if she even called, or if I'm just dumbly holding a book to my ear and hallucinating. But then she speaks.

"If I lose her, I might as well be dead."

"Gina—"

"I understand the cost better than you think I do, Nat."

I slump to the floor, let sleep take over. There's a lot of work ahead.

***

By evening I'm working feverishly, or rather, my body is, and I'm watching it happen. Punching holes in cards as fast as my hands will allow, sewing them together into a chain. Individually I might be able to decipher which threads she plans to raise in a given row, but I can never conceptualize the whole.

The red silks are always a blur. Designs half-remembered, figures fuzzy in memory, even though I know they must have been sharp and crisp coming off the loom. That's how Marie-Louise weaves.

Ada Lovelace once looked at the Jacquard loom and saw the future. "We may say most aptly that the Analytical Engine weaves algebraic patterns," she wrote to Charles Babbage, seeing more potential in the proto-computer than the inventor himself, "just as the Jacquard-loom weaves flowers and leaves." A future of encoding information, using hole-punched cards.

Marie-Louise encodes more than figures in her cloth, but I don't have a mind like Lovelace. I can't look at it and see beyond the pattern.

***

One morning, I brought in the paper and saw the old man who'd visited Gran on the front page. *Double homicide in Davis*, the headline read.

I showed Gran. No emotion registered on her face. "They always underestimate the cost," she said.

***

I've dreamed many scenes from Marie-Louise's life. It's hard to know which are memories, and which are merely dreams. In some, she begs her father to let her follow in his footsteps as master weaver; he rebukes her, telling her to be practical. She knows she won't be granted that title.

In other dreams, she wanders the streets of Lyon in the final days of the uprising. The smell of cordite, the sounds of screams. She sees the Emperor's soldiers, searching for the last of the rebels. In a moment of impulse, she makes eye contact with one of them, gestures towards a side street. After the gunshots die out and the soldiers move on, she forces herself to walk down that side street and look at her father and his compatriots and the blood congealing in the street. To see what she'd become.

***

I weave Gina's cloth. It's a blur; it always is. But I feel Marie-Louise's energy, her bliss, the way she becomes one with her instruments. I think I see hands, naked female forms. I think I see a loom.

***

Gina comes to collect the parcel. "Should I open it now?" she asks.

"It's yours," I say. "Do with it what you wish."

She tears open a corner of the package, sees the red silk, then thinks better of it. She hugs the package to her chest; the way the paper crinkles in her arms makes me want to cry.

"I haven't seen one of these since your show," she says quietly.

The last moment we were happy. Engaged and looking forward to a life together. Finally feeling like I could be an artist people took seriously. Before I realized that Marie-Louise could take Gina away from me.

Over the years I've gone to the library, sorted through local newspapers. I found some of Gran's visitors there: murderers, arsonists, suicides, accidents. They could have all been coincidences, I suppose, but I wouldn't bet on it.

I couldn't sleep, couldn't eat. When Gina left for work, I had visions of her car totaled in a ditch; I panicked every time she left my sight but refused to tell her why when she begged me to help her understand. I couldn't bear the thought of her knowing that I was the kind of person who put others at risk for her art. For some cloth.

And then I began to lose time.

Gina grew angry with me for the surly, single-minded person I became in those fugue states, but how could I explain that I wasn't myself in those moments, that I was somehow my own ancestor, and no amount of talk therapy could fix it?

She gave me an ultimatum; I gave her back her ring.

I exacted my own price. I pried people out of my life until I was completely alone. At least, I thought, it would end with me. I'd give Marie-Louise no successor.

**

In Gran's last days, I asked her if she had ever woven anything for herself in red silk.

"Only once," she said.

"What did you ask for?"

She doubled over in a coughing fit. I repeated my question when she finished.

"Someone to take this burden," she said.

After she died, I found a paper-wrapped parcel in her closet. I opened it. A long, long roll of red fabric. An image of a body. And all over it, splotches of waffle weave, a textured structure that disrupted the otherwise smooth fabric.

Something about the image looked familiar. It reminded me of the x-rays my mother's oncologist showed her, how he pointed out the tumors and explained her chances.

There was something about the pattern. I couldn't look away. And then I spotted it. There, in the lungs. It was the inch I'd woven when Mom first brought me to visit Gran.

***

Sometimes, when I sink into an armchair with a book of pattern drafts or a textile history, I feel completely at peace. And then that peace is shattered by the question: is this who I would have become without Gran? Without her silk, without the wish she'd asked to be granted?

***

Months pass. I try to focus on everyday life. Tending the garden, feeding goats and chickens. Weaving ordinary cloth.

And then Gina calls. "Thank you," she whispers into the phone. "I can't ever thank you enough."

"I'm just glad you're okay," I say, and I mean it.

"I don't want us to be cut off from each other anymore," she says, and already I'm sobbing. I don't have the strength or the will to push her away. She says she's coming to visit and I let her.

**

All morning I fret, checking for news of car crashes, earthquakes, anything out of the ordinary. But her car comes up the road, safe.

She emerges from the car, eyes ringed with dark circles. She's exhausted, but she's beaming. She waves before opening the back door of her car, rummaging. As I walk toward her it becomes clear she's not rummaging; she's taking something from the car.

And then I freeze. There's a baby in her arms, bundled in red silk. Already I know the child is a girl.

"Natalie," she says, coming toward me. "I want you to meet my daughter. I almost lost her and my wife. I don't know what you did, but they're both alive, and I'm grateful to you."

"Oh," I say. My voice is weak.

"Do you want to hold her?"

I mean to say *no* but Marie-Louise says, "Of course!" and reaches out my arms.

Gina hands me the baby, still cocooned in silk. The baby looks up into my eyes—into Marie-Louise's eyes—and smiles wide.

Marie-Louise nestles the baby against our shoulder and murmurs, "Ma fille."

Mother Mangue

Lis Vilas Boas

Lis is a researcher with a PhD in Oceanography and a writer that likes impossible stories. In oceanography, she investigates the bioacoustics of marine mammals and the underwater soundscapes of Brazilian waters. As a writer, she tries to find in fiction the balance between science and magic that permeates her ideas.

Loneliness rips her apart every time a wave breaks, spreading sea foam and losses over the sand, so she moves further between the trees and away from the beach. Feet sink in the mud, dead leaves caress her skin and branches grab the wet fabric of the old, stained clothes.

Laguna is her name from the life before, she still clings to it. No one remembers it now, or no one ever asked—she often forgets exactly how it happened, how she decayed. When the sun escapes the canopies and hits the water just right, she gets a glimpse at her reflection. Still young on the outside, hollow eyes showing the dark path within, deeper and scarier than the ocean abyss.

The mangrove is not quite home although she has lived in it for many years now. Some days the roots contorting above the water feel like prison, other times the ever-present shade gives as much comfort as a refuge could. That forest, trapped like her between land and sea, offered Laguna the same it gave to every other creature—a place to hide, maybe even a place to grow.

Beneath the sound of waves crashing on the surrounding beach, distant footsteps cross the murky puddles. Muffled voices, laughter here and there. Crab hunters going home, probably, the only ones from the village that ever venture far into the forest—the others are afraid of the mangrove, of Laguna, and the knowledge she carries about those who come to her in dark hours.

They always come.

Sometimes an unwanted child, discovered right after a few moons with no blood. Other times a belly as round as pufferfish, ready to burst open, and yet the baby refuses to leave. Every once in a while, some come for a spell—a womb that won't quicken or eyes that won't meet across the market. The reasons vary and come and go as sure as the tides. The villagers like to pretend they don't want or need her services, but they always come. They cross the mud, jump over branches, pretend they don't see the slimy creatures watching their suffering, and they beg.

And although Laguna despises them, she always heeds.

Night has covered the canopies when she reaches her hut, sitting lonely atop a sandy island. The house has a round shape, built out of fallen trunks so twisted that one might think it had sprouted from the ground. It had been there when she first arrived, waiting like a gift and a curse from the forest, a small place to live safely and to be reminded that there was no one to share it with. An island within a forest, a bubble in the sea, a woman in the world. Later the high tide will bring the waters right to her doorsteps, but it is the moment of the day when the walk is deceptively easy. Silt gives way to firmer sand, leaves scattered around, a seed here and there, and she is home.

The cormorants nesting above the rooftop stare silently at her progress, non-judging and unhelpful and still the only company she has—during the day, Laguna would share her fish with them, and they might share a few secrets in return.

She lights up a fire and stares through the only window. Sleep never comes easy, it is not something she did in her previous existence and still has not taken up the habit. Listening to the slow rise of the water, the sea invading both that unclaimed territory and her memories, Laguna counts her losses. In her wandering, she misses the sounds of sloshed steps, the panting of a tired throat.

Someone hits the door.

It is a woman, barely leaving the girlhood years behind. Her eyes are wide and bulged, she heaves from the recent effort, grabbing the belly of an advanced pregnancy.

"Please...please."

Laguna moves away so she can come inside. This one she has seen before, walking with the crab hunter boys.

"They are going to take her from me." The girl enters, leaning on the walls until she finds the bed. She falls on it and takes a huge breath before going on. "It is not the time yet, is it? But I need to have the child now. You can do it, can't you, Mother Mangue?"

The name always amuses her, she doesn't know where it comes from. When they don't need her, she is just the witch. When they are desperate, she is suddenly a mother ready to help. Mother Mangue.

"Raise your dress," she commands, hearing the dryness of her own voice.

"I'm Nana," the girl says as she obeys. Laguna never asks for names, but they always offer them anyway. It makes them less afraid, as if knowing their names would make her somehow kinder.

"How long has it been?"

"A little more than seven moons, I think. I'm not sure, I...it was my first time, I didn't..." Nana's hand begins to tremble, grabbing the cloth covering the bed. She doesn't cry, even though the tears are threatening to escape. "He loves me, though. We are running always together. I need to have this baby today, so we can run away before they take my child from me."

Laguna listens without comments. They like to talk—to explain—as much as they like to offer names. Telling stories is a way to pretend they are in control of the world.

"Will she live, Mother Mangue?" Nana asks in a whisper, her greatest fear finally slipping through the words. "If it happens tonight...will she live?"

"She?"

Nana nods, a trembling smile reaching her face as she caresses the belly. "I feel it."

Laguna knows better than to question such feelings. Her hand runs through the line marking the stretched skin, sensing the life inside. Not for the first time she wonders what the feeling is like. The title of Mother Mangue sometimes feels like irony—it is an unavoidable fate, it seems, that a woman's life must revolve around motherhood even when she cannot give birth to children of her own.

It is indeed a 'she' inside, although people not always know what that means. The little being is healthy, moving as if feeling the apprehension of the mother. Laguna can do it—has done it enough times before.

"But you cannot travel," she warns.

"What do you mean?"

"She will live, but you cannot travel today. Both of you will need time to recover."

"But..."

"You can't."

There is a hurried knock on the door. Both women jump with surprise, Laguna curses herself for not paying attention a second time in the same night.

It is a crab hunter boy and he barges in. He runs to Nana and for a moment they become a mass of limbs and mouths grabbing each other so tight that it is uncomfortable to watch. The kiss is full of longing and relief and what seems dangerously like true love. He touches the belly and places a gentle kiss there as well, Nana covers her mouth and inhales deep—she still doesn't cry, even though her eyes are as full to the brim as the high tide.

Memories threaten to surface so Laguna drowns them again. It is useless to revisit the past. She once was a girl waiting for a boy that never came, she is now fruit of that waiting and there is nothing to be done about it.

"Will you help us, Mother Mangue?" he asks, still holding them.

"I'd be more willing if you had not invaded my house, boy," she grumbles, turning to the table full of jars with herbs and flowers. "You and your little friends avoid me like the plague during the day, and during the night you come demanding help as if I was a crab ready to be plucked out of the mud."

"You *have* to help us!"

"Ian!" Nana shushes him.

"I don't have to do anything, boy. My obligations are not to you or any person who remembers me only when they need me." Still, she already has a pot in hand to mix the ingredients.

The couple argues through whispers. More than once, she notices how Nana holds him back. Often Laguna wonders if men ever stop seeing women like their mothers, and perhaps she is better off without the boy that abandoned her.

"Mother Mangue...please. I'll do anything," Nana says. She rises slowly and walks to the other side of the table. "Don't mind Ian, he is just desperate. He has already gathered the things we need to run, and we are going to. But it will be easier to hide if I am not pregnant."

"Do you think a child is easy to hide? When you are not much beyond a child yourself?"

"My family will be looking for a pregnant girl, not for a couple with a baby."

"Not for long."

"Not for two moons, this is enough time."

Laguna stares at her from across the table, the dim light casting more maturity than is right for the years the girl has. It could be done, she had before.

"It would be easier to kill."

"No!" Ian rushes to their side, trying to pull the girl aside.

Nana raises a hand to stop him, the other holding her belly. Still, she doesn't cry, and although her jaw trembles like a leave on the wind, her voice comes out unshakable.

"Step back."

Once more the boy obeys, it seems certain who is going to protect who on the days to come.

"She is mine, and I am having her, one way or the other."

It is the glow in the eyes more than the story that gets to her. Countless couples have come desperately to that door—a tea to empty a belly, a blessing for a sick woman, a painful labour, two lives that seemed unable to generate a third one. Always afraid, always something sad to tell. Not that girl. Nana is already a mother, has that fire within that could burn the forest and evaporate the marshlands.

"There will be a cost, at some point. Dabbling with the time of life is risky."

A dry laugh escapes Nana's throat, her eyes without any humor.

"There always is," the girl answers, sounding much older.

So, Laguna nods towards the bed and Nana breathes deeply, nodding back before going to lie down. The spell itself is more about time than life. The potion is less about inducing than about calling. The act is as much about the child as the mother.

The powers gather around mind and heart, guiding Laguna. Being a witch in a hut had not been a choice, it was something that happened like sea currents happened—lonely as it is, the nature within her cannot be denied. She places a hand on Nana's forehead and another on the place where her daughter's head is, beneath the skin both their lives curve towards her call just like the young sharks search the roots of the trees to hide and grow before they can leave.

The mangrove is a nursery, and so is she.

Mother and daughter are children to her years, seeds to the forest, larvae to the fish, ripples to the tide. Laguna closes her eyes, offering herself to the powers that weave creatures together, extending a hand towards the flowing of time. It is not their time, but it never truly is—it had not been her time to fall in love or to leave the sea or to look beyond the surface, and there she was.

Laguna moves to the front, opens Nana's legs, murmurs a chant half an invitation half the wind spreading sea foam. The eyes are still closed, somewhere she hears a scream and a declaration of love but she is now too deep to notice. Beneath the water, beneath the roots, beneath flesh and heartbeats, in the moist darkness the mangrove breathes in and breathes out, heeding to her request. Another child is being brought to the world, another daughter that will leave the drowned lands and perhaps someday return.

***

She dreams of that night many days after Nana and her family have left.

A dream—or nightmare—of walking through the forest at night, patiently moving, feeling mud and air, searching. The girl screams somewhere ahead, somewhere behind. Sounds like Nana when she was in pain, and it also sounds like a baby crying for the first time. Relief and despair swim together among the dead leaves clinging to her clothes. Laguna leaves no trail as she wafts through the water, being called by someone she does not know but wants desperately to.

Seeing Nana leave with a daughter in her arms had been harder than other times. Most villagers went and never looked back, came again if they needed, but never truly saw her. Nana had held her tightly, had smiled, and saw something Laguna barely remembered was there to be seen.

"Thank you, Mother," Nana had whispered before going away. Just Mother, not Mother Mangue. Mother, she said. Mother, the nightmarish dream whispered.

It is a long while before she finally wakes up with a wish. Or maybe a conclusion, an understanding.

There is a way to end the loneliness, after all.

While sleeping, she never finds the person lost in the forest. The dream begins and ends with the search. Laguna is certain that it will happen while awake. So she walks through the mangrove, wandering until the path is right. In a bag there are the things she needs—herbs, dried fish, rainwater, an egg, and a knife. If she doesn't come back, there is no need to carry more than that, and if she does everything else will be in the same place.

The cormorants that nest above the hut's roof follow, watching her progress as if they knew where the journey would lead. Some of the fish go as well, the ones who live their whole lives in the murky waters. She prefers moving through the water, so the crabs are not disturbed. The animals don't offer advice but maintain silent companionship, their gazes glowing under the filtered rays of light as the sun sets and the thin smile of the moon rises.

A crescent moon is the ideal time, she believes, and so she must hurry.

The journey follows the coastline, the same way the mangrove contours the shores of that side of the world. It cannot go inland, the sea is an important part of the ritual—life grows in the water, whatever the form. It cannot be seawards as well, because the ocean is greedy and resentful and she no longer can claim any rights to it. So the coastline it is, between tiny muddy islands and dense aggregation of trees—the trees, she discovers very quickly, are against her, make Laguna's progress more difficult at every turn. With each step, roots weave tightly around each other, branches grow sharper, leaves turn the path darker.

She knows it is close when the forest becomes silent.

There is a clearing and the water is so still it is as if the tides had stopped. The turning of the world is slower, the animals stay behind and the Tree in the middle awaits.

It is so enormous that it is an island on its own, made of thick roots contorted in arches so wide that she could pass beneath them without bowing her back. It is blooming, it is losing leaves, it is growing new branches, it is full of propagules—it has all seasons in a single moment. It contains time and dreams and nightmares and Laguna finally understands how the villagers feel when they knock on her door.

The muddy floor becomes deeper, she must swim—the progress is slow because she has never learned how to swim with arms and legs before, with a tail it used to be so much easier. Slowly, gently, Laguna chants as her movements disturb the surface. Closer and closer, beneath the crescent moon now high in the sky.

"Please, Mother Mangue..." she repeats the words the villagers always say. Suddenly she knows where the name comes from—it is not hers, it belongs to the mangrove, to the Tree. As the words float among the aerial roots when Laguna swims beneath them, a new knowledge surges. When they come to her, they are asking the favor of the forest. Somehow, they knew it. "Please, Mother Mangue, help me."

There is no response. The Tree doesn't want her there anymore than she welcomes the villagers begging for help.

"I need someone."

Further beneath the aerial roots the night is even darker, the silence is heavy, but air and water become warmer. Closer to the core, there is a safe place, she knows—she must beg to that soft spot, the same the villagers appeal to when they come in despair. Laguna begins chanting again.

The song is of her home, so distant and so deep. The words are not perfect because they were not made to be sung above the surface. The story is about the mermaid who fell in love with a sailor, the oldest tale in the world. Sacrifices are not enough for men. The melody thrums with heartbreak and betrayal, beats with the rhythm of pumped blood, reverberates through legs that were once a tail and within organs that are still more fish than human because the transmutation occurred only on the outside and appearances are limited. Mermaids are not enough for men. The truth leaks from her voice as the loneliness of her life fills that body she had to learn how to live with. The memories are vivid even after so many years, colored in shades of blue and green and brown, trapped in the mud ever since he left, preserved in the contours of decayed leaves and rotted feelings. Love is not enough for men. So the song goes and so Laguna sings.

Sings and sinks, telling of her life as she dives beneath the labyrinth of wood, begging to the heart of the Tree because neither of them are men.

"Please, Mother Mangue."

The roots give way, at last.

Maybe it is the sadness that does it, maybe it is that the Tree also had a story of her own. Laguna resurfaces in a knot of roots, branches, leaves, and propagules. A nest ready to be used.

"Help me become a mother as well, help me earn your name."

This time the Tree answers. It speaks in the language of submarine plants that most of creatures don't understand and Laguna had learned through the years. *There is a cost.*

"There always is."

Motherhood is not what you think.

"But it is all there is now."

This is not true.

"It is my truth."

Then do it, child.

Laguna almost laughs. The appearance of her youth is deceiving and she has not been a child for decades, but she knows better than to question the age of the mangrove. The Tree is the mangrove, and the mangrove is a nursery—all creatures are children to it.

She lifts herself to the nest of roots and plucks a large propagule, asking for permission before she does so. The Tree says no more, merely watches and allows. From the bag, she gets the egg—it had been conceded by the cormorants living above her roof, a blessing in its own form.

The spell is new to her, written in the dream and understood in the nightmare. With the knife she cuts the propagule in half and carefully opens the egg—both the seeds and the undeveloped bird inside she offers the sea, feeding the young sharks that have come to watch. She cuts herself, spilling the blood within the empty eggshell until it is full. Chanting, the egg of blood goes into the propagule, and with herbs she closes the gashes and conceals her wish within. Blood and bird and plant and chant, all in layers until she is holding a sphere the size of a coconut fruit—but it is not the Fruit, not yet.

Time is the last component of the magic.

Laguna builds a nest of leaves in the center of the knot of roots and places her future inside it.

"How long, Mother Mangue?"

You will know, as all mothers do.

***

Days, weeks, and months.

It is the first time in her life that Laguna pays attention to the passing of the seasons.

Every day she visits the nest. In the spring the egg is still small and green, pulsing. She takes to sleeping in a saline plain nearby, under the stars. In the summer it has grown, acquired brownish colors. Sometimes she hears the villagers in the distance, calling for her in the forest, and she ignores them. In the autumn the egg is the size of a newborn child and pulses in the rhythm of a heartbeat. She has so many expectations that she barely leaves the Tree's side, it is going to be soon. But when winter comes by, nothing happens.

A year and another season pass and the nest is still gestating.

Laguna chants to the child inside the egg, tells her of the beautiful world they are going to live in, and pretends that everything is fine. She sits in the nest and lays gentle caress, ignoring the thin roots that have started to grow around it.

More springs and summers, more growing and waiting, until she stops counting.

The villagers have found her, now living in a camp near the Tree. They come to her new improvised home, but nothing they say moves Laguna to help. She believes the magic of life contained in her must all go the child—it is her turn this time, she tells them, ignoring their tears joining the saline water of the mangrove.

One day, she meets her reflection in the sea and discovers her hair turned gray. The face is no longer the same of when she walked with two legs for the first time, it has wrinkles and it has been marked by the sun. The sadness of abandonment has been replaced by the despair of uncertainty and at last, after years she has not bothered to count, Laguna wonders if Mother Mangue had removed the blessing.

The Tree is always silent, ever since the day of conception.

The egg is now completely covered in roots. When the tide rises and covers it, a sheen of red light escapes the knot covering the ball the size of a small child—it is the same shade of red her scales used to be and everything is even harder.

In her waiting, Laguna feels lonelier than before.

The forest transforms around her, following the movement of the sea. New mud islands form and disappear, generations of cormorants migrate, the villagers' faces change as they grow and stop coming. Time takes away her power, the strength of her bones, and even the breath of her lungs—Laguna can no longer dive to see the development of the egg.

It comes a night, under the glow of the crescent moon sad smile, when she gives up.

Laguna falls on the mud, and cries looking at the sky, seeing the life before and the life she couldn't have.

***

The rising tide takes her body. With the dead leaves she floats, drifting in the slow pace of the drowned forest.

It is always a competition in the mangrove. Sea and land push their waters against each other, and the path of tides dictates the direction of the streams. Laguna knows this without having to look, lets the world take her wherever it wants because there is nothing left.

She closes her eyes when at last she stops floating, now resting in some muddy beach covered by familiar canopies. Then there is a hand in her shoulder.

"Mother Mangue?" someone asks.

The voice is raspy, old, but filled with wonder.

"It is you, isn't it? Everyone thought you were dead. Consumed by the mangrove," the voice continues and another hand comes to her back and suddenly the person is trying to lift her.

Laguna ignores the attempts, shuts the eyes even tighter.

"I thought you had just gone on to another place, thought you deserved it. So many years you've served, so many live today because of you. My own child and grandchildren..."

With a deep sigh and a push, the person gets Laguna to sit. A gentle touch caresses the mass of muddy hair in her head.

"When I came here, I knew it was my turn. The hut was abandoned, so I did the best I could. My grandson even helped me, bless him, even though they don't like the idea of me living here all alone. But it must be, the mangrove told me so, as it must have told you long ago. So, I am Mother Nana, now...are you Mother Mangue, still?"

Nana.

The memory comes like a sudden downpour of rain bringing fresh water to the salted marsh. Her eyes open and there she is. The girl is now as old as she is, two crones looking at each other. Nana hugs her. Laguna cannot remember the last time she was in an embrace, or when she felt the warmth of a body. For the moment she is a child.

The girl who is no longer a girl takes her inside. The hut is changed, she barely recognizes it as her home—perhaps because it had never been home. Here and there Nana had placed little objects that reeked of affection and human connections, while in Laguna's time there were only useful objects to the craft. The bed is new and the chairs are as soft as pillows as she sits to watch the surroundings. Cormorants above the roof still make the same noise, though, and this brings a little comfort.

"The boys bring good stuff from the new port they are building to the north," Nana says while she pulls a kettle from the fire, the smell of an unknown tea fills the air. "They think I deserve to be pampered...me! Ha!"

Laguna listens as she rattles about her family and her journey coming back to the village after so many decades. Nana is old, but there is spring to her footsteps, a strength that resembles the fast pace of a smart crab feeding around a coconut. Her eyesight is not so good as it used to be, but if she squinted it was there around the other woman—a green and brownish aura, spreading like a tree.

"Well...would you like to tell me your story?"

Nana places the tea in the middle of her hands, the crude pottery warming both their wrinkled skins. Laguna says nothing.

"I...there is a story..." Nana sighs, then smiles. "Forgive my curiosity. It is just that the visions began after the birth of my first daughter, the one you brought to the world, and I have always wondered if you did it on purpose or if it was something else or...You told me there was a cost and I assumed it would mean losing someone later, or illness, maybe even Ian, bless his soul. I understood years ago, in a dream, when I saw a woman coming out of an egg coming out of a seed coming out of a knot of roots. The woman was me, and the woman was you, and the mangrove flourished around. The cost of my daughter's life, I think, was more life. Life for me to deliver into the world, like you used to do."

The cost of life.

Mother Mangue had warned, but even now Laguna does not understand. Her entire earthbound existence had been a cost, she had served and given and lived by the mangrove. Trembling hands threaten to spill the tea, but Nana grips her tighter.

"Mother Mangue..."

"Laguna."

The sound of her own voice is strange. Older and drier than she remembers, with an echo of waves breaking against the rocks like a distant whisper. She cleans her throat.

"My name...is Laguna."

It is the first time she introduces herself ever since arriving in the forest, it is strange and soothing, it brings back the memory of a version of herself that had been buried beneath many layers of salt and mud and decayed leaves. Telling Nana her name is a first step. After a sip of tea, the story of her life goes tumbling out of her, bits and pieces with no coherence or purpose. Being abandoned on the fringes between land and sea, flinging her way amongst the trees, assuming a role she had not asked for.

Nana listens quietly, holds her hand like a mother or perhaps even a friend. There is no judgement, even if there is no comprehension as well. When the story is over the sun had already set and risen, and they share a moment of silence.

"So this is why you have aged." It is the first thing Nana says.

Laguna leans against the back of the chair, she feels tired.

"Mermaids age differently."

"But you didn't used to. For many generations you were the mangrove witch, and time didn't touch your skin or your hair. And now you look as old as me."

"What are you saying, girl?"

"You are aging because of your child. Your years are being given to her."

Although sleep and exhaustion are claiming her mind, a glimpse of understanding sinks through the fog. Laguna nods slowly.

"The cost of life."

"Perhaps...but..."

"Motherhood...is supposed to be a sacrifice, isn't it?"

"No, it isn't."

But Laguna does not hear the response, her head tumbling into a dreamless sleep.

***

Life grows slower and slower, and less lonely as well.

Laguna feels more and more like a tree, movement takes effort and nothing is more comfortable than being still with feet buried in the mud. The water licks her ankles and knees depending on the tide, a caress so soft she thinks she hears the call of home, a touch so gentle she knows there is no going back. She is dying.

Nana takes care of her, tends to her few needs, and asks for advice when a woman from the village comes. Nana is a better forest witch than she ever was, there is no doubt. Helping people had been a duty for Laguna, an exchange with the mangrove, while for the other it comes naturally. One day she tells her that, but the woman just waves her head with a small smile.

When the season ends, Nana leaves the hut to collect herbs and propagules.

Three days pass before she returns, and when she does, Laguna sees in her eyes what she had found. They avoid the conversation, although she is not sure what they are afraid of. It is not as if there is something to change, or that there is more time to her life.

It is night when Nana takes her outside and they sit on the water's edge.

"The Tree is dying."

There is a painful tug at her heart, but she asks anyway.

"And the egg?"

"Still alive, and pulsing. Laguna…"

"Don't."

"I know what to do."

"Has…Has Mother Mangue spoken to you?"

"Not in words, she is sleepy and tired as you are…She has given you a great gift."

A burst of humorless laugh escapes her, bringing out a violent cough in the aftermath. Nana holds her arm, grips it tightly.

"Listen, she has. She is a mother and she has lived your pain, she understands."

"But she has not given me the child I asked for."

"Did you truly want that child, or did you just want to not be alone anymore?"

The truth is in the silence, Laguna has no energy left to pretend so she doesn't answer. By now they know each other well, as intimately as they know the mangrove that surrounds them. Nana takes a propagule that passes floating by, begins to rip its fibers.

"Why…why wasn't the child born?" Asking requires courage, and she feels weaker once the words leave her. "Was it punishment for my selfishness?"

"No, not punishment…" Nana offers her a resigned smile. "For this labour, we are going to need a witch."

"You." A sudden rush of relief runs through her bones, turns her body to mush. Being in the care of a trusted friend is a new sensation in her old life, but she feels lucky and silently thanks

Mother Mangue for calling Nana back. "You are the witch in the mangrove now."

"Yes. But it is not the time yet."

"No...I must go, first."

It is Nana's turn to answer with silence, so they sit quietly for a while. The while becomes long hours, and then days.

Laguna is determined to not rise from there again.

***

Nana's heart is filled with a bittersweet emotion she doesn't know how to name.

Every day she sits by Laguna's side and they talk, she pretends not to see that her friend is half-buried in the mood. Thin roots sprouts from the skin and arch towards the ground, longing for the water, growing with each day. The conversations they share cover memories and stories of their lives, avoiding the subject that one of the is becoming a tree.

It seems unfair that their companionship has been restricted to the end of her friend's life, but it is useless to dwell on it. Life in the mangrove is made of cycles, children become mothers and mothers become witches—not always in that same order. They have both taken care of each other, and she feels lucky to be able to repay the favor.

The day of the birth comes. She places a kiss on Laguna's forehead, now full of new fresh green leaves sprouting, and goes.

The Tree is dried and crumbled, the knot of roots is all that's left.

For a moment, she is not sure if she is strong enough to do it.

Laguna had the power of the sea thrumming inside her, an easy connection with the mangrove. Nana tattles where she once walked, tries while she used to simply do.

"Mother Mangue...it is time," she whispered against the knot, feeling the warmth of a red glow escaping through the gaps. "I am here now, let her go. She is a creature of the sea and to the sea she must return."

The mangrove is part of the sea.

Nana sighs when she hears the whisper.

"I am going to miss her as well."

Delicately, she searches for an indentation, or a breach large enough to insert her hand in the mass of wood, anything she can use to pull. The tide is rising, and somehow, she knows this is a good sign.

The life inside pulses, like a heartbeat increasing its pace. There is movement, a pushing from within joining her attempts to pull.

"Come on, child. You have done this countless times before..." she coaxes, panting with the effort of pulling the roots aside. "You have done this for so many others, do this for yourself."

The forest pulses and breathes around them, power flows through mud and water and salty air. Nana has felt this before, almost a lifetime ago when she was young and begged the lonely witch for help. A familiar presence invades her body, fills her soul and transforms the self—Nana is old, Mother Mangue is even older, together they are ageless. The mangrove is a nursery, and so is she. Mother and daughter are children to her years, seeds to the forest, larvae to the fish, ripples to the tide.

"Push, child, push."

Push, child, push.

She puts a hand inside, breaches a moist surface.

"It is safe out here."

It is safe out here.

She feels the contour of tiny arms moving, trying to rip the membrane apart.

"You are not going to be alone."

You are not going to be alone.

She takes a deep breath, grieving the loss and celebrating the new life to come. Nana pushes the roots aside, making way for her friend.

Somewhere in the forest, near a wooden hut in a muddy island, a woman who was once a mermaid sheds her last breath. Right there amid wood and blood and arms, a newborn mermaid who was once a woman takes her first. Somewhere, the new Tree who was once a woman who was once a mermaid spread its leaves. There, the nest who was once a Tree and who knows what else before falls and sinks in the dark water.

Nana accepts the help of the rising tide, removes the child from the nest and lets her float in the surface. She is beautiful. The same dark hair, the same guarded eyes. It is the first time, and probably the last, she sees a baby mermaid and it feels like a miracle. Something the forest will remember forever, something she will carry inside until her last breath.

"Laguna..." she whispers, and the baby looks at her.

A tiny hand is stretched towards her.

"Do you know who I am?"

The child gurgles something, an attempt of talking, frowns at the bubbles she makes on the surface. Precariously, she swims around inside the protective circle of Nana's arms.

"I don't know if you are going to remember me, in this new life of yours. But I hope you know that I am going to be here, we are going to be here, Mother Mangue and me." At the distance, she feels the concordance of the new Tree. The mangrove flows through Nana, and she begins to understand that Laguna was not the only one to be reborn that day. "The mangrove is part of the sea."

The little mermaid looks up again, as if she had heard. Nana lowers herself in the water until they are eye to eye, wondering and marveling. Laguna had given birth to herself, asked for company when she had been wishing for the freedom to be again who she truly was. Motherhood of others could be a choice or even an undesired fate, but motherhood of themselves is an unavoidable for some women.

Young Laguna swims, gaining confidence in the new tail with red scales, running wider circles each taking her further away from the nest. Now that they are one and the same, Nana knows that it pains Mother Mangue to see her go. The forest had taken in the woman with a broken heart, nursed her as best as it could, and now it is time to part ways.

A pang of loneliness threatens to sip inside, but Nana pushes it aside. It is the fate of mothers seeing their children leave, but it is also true that mothers are always part of their daughters the same way the mangrove is part of the sea.

Birds Are Not the Village

Merri Andrew

Merri Andrew is a writer living on Ngunnawal and Ngambri Country in Canberra, Australia. Her work has been published in Corporeal, Strange Horizons, Daikaijuzine, and Antipodean SF, among other venues. She enjoys baking, naps and watching praying mantises. Merri can be found on Twitter @MerriAndrewHere and Instagram @merri_andrew_here

Baby Thea lay on her stomach, wearing only a singlet and nappy in the warm afternoon. Looking at her big cheeks, her tiny lips, and her lowered eyelashes flooded me with pleasure, as always. The valley between her shoulder blades, her little shoulders, were miniature echoes backwards in time of her strength and size to come. My baby.

I knew that sleeping on the stomach was a risk for a baby, making it easier for their little mouth to get covered by bedding, their tiny windpipe to be constricted, all so quietly, without a sound to warn anyone. I knew that, but it was so peaceful just watching her sleep.

Resting my head on the railing of her cot, my sight blurred until only Thea was in focus, and then...

I jolted awake with fear spiking my blood, alarm shaking the inner muscles of my body. My heart and brain were braced, racing, ready, even as I stayed so still the cot didn't even shake. Thea didn't stir. Only my pulse roared while the quiet in the air remained, a reproach.

Deliberately, carefully, I stood and bent to listen for Thea's breathing. My ear was just a couple of centimetres from her face.

I pulled my hair back so it wouldn't tickle her. I held my breath. Finally, I caught a faint, whispery inhalation but then...nothing.

Had I imagined the breath? Maybe it was enough. At some point I had to decide it was enough. But what if...? I imagined later, knowing I had been so lazy and selfish that I didn't bother to make sure, and all the while my baby was...

I bent a little closer and a stray hair must have tickled Thea's face because she snorted softly and clenched her little hands twice, and made a crying-like face that threatened to turn into full screaming wakefulness, but then relaxed back into sleep.

Resting my head back down, I had a feeling that all of this had already happened. Down the street I could hear another baby crying, then silence, and birds calling. My eyelids dropped again, heavy as honey. Heavy as honey as sweet as sleep.

I jolted awake once more. Dribble wetted my hand where I had been resting my head. Thea was lying on her stomach. How could I have left her in that position? But she was sleeping so beautifully now; if I woke her, she might not go back to sleep. Maybe I could just watch her, make sure she was alright, and then at least it would be quiet and still, and she would be well-rested and happier in the evening, and I would have some peace for a while, even if I could not let myself sleep.

No. I would not delude myself this way. There would be no peace for me without knowing Thea was safe. My sense of duty clunked woodenly into place: graceless, grinding, inevitable.

I reached into the cot and carefully worked my fingers under Thea's arms, gently wriggling my hands down into the mattress foam to avoid pressing on her flesh. Smoothly, quickly, I turned the baby onto her back, hoping against hope that she would stay asleep so I could nap. Instantly, though, she flung her little arms up, rigid, and opened her mouth. It made a pink-black square, in which a cry gathered. The cry gathered, and gathered, and then blasted forth, wailing, outraged, the opposite of sleep.

***

Walking down the hallway, I noticed a bird landing on the skylight above me. Its claws clattered, and it flew off. I caught only a glimpse of its shadow. As I passed the sunroom, I saw a starling pacing on the outside sill, its feathers slick and its breast plump. In the kitchen it waited for me at the open window.

"Having a hard time of it, eh?" the bird said.

I had heard about the birds that gathered at houses where there was a new baby. They bothered people for a while and then left after a few weeks. I hadn't heard about them being talkative.

I tried ignoring the bird. It hopped back and forth irritably, trying to bounce up into my line of sight and get my attention.

"Why is it just you and the baby?"

The starling's voice trilled and scratched, pulling at my last sleepless nerve.

"Where is your mother? And where is the baby's father, hm? His mum? His dad?"

The bird scrawched a chuckle at this last idea. I caught the hint of an oily rainbow in its feathers.

Before I could answer, the bird said:

"I just saw your husband at Domino's Cafe. Business meeting. Lovely big piece of cake."

This was annoying. In the morning when I was making my husband's lunch, I had offered to pack a piece of the birthday cake I made for him yesterday. He said no, he was trying not to eat too many sweets.

"Your mother-in-law is busy-busy too! Work, work! I did see your mother out walking. Do you think she's on her way here?"

I did not.

"Oh well," the bird chirped, "I suppose they all think you're managing admirably."

It left a meaningful pause.

"I have something that might help you, actually. A...method."

The bird fluffed up its feathers and then shook to smooth them down again.

"You get a cup of water, look at your reflection in it, then you close your eyes and say:

Sip away my trouble

Make me split and double

Then you take a sip of the water. If you've done it right, you'll separate, so part of you stays with the baby and the other part can go and rest."

Rest. That sounded good.

The bird seemed to get distracted, pulling at a strand of wool that was caught on a splinter of the windowsill. I thought it had forgotten me, but after a while it dropped the wool and perked up once more with its grating little voice.

"It's genius," the bird gossiped, "I saw Karina from four doors down doing it. But I don't think she invented it."

The other birds hopped a few jumps forward, fossicking out tiny seeds and insects from the flooring of the deck. The spokesbird tilted its head to focus on me, waiting for me to speak.

"Will I...will she, the other part of me, will she take proper care of Thea?" I asked.

"Trust yourself!" the bird chirped. "Just like the midwives said."

"But..."

"Well, got to go. Make of it what you will! Good luck!"

It plucked again at the wool, finally prising it out from the wood, and flew away with it.

***

Obviously I couldn't trust the bird, but I desperately needed to rest, so I decided it was worth a try.

I filled a cup with water and took it to the bedroom. Sitting beside Thea, who continued to grizzle, I looked into the cup. There it was, my haggard reflection.

I was about to start the rhyme when I had a thought. What if I overslept? I didn't want to leave my double in charge for too long. So I pulled an old mechanical alarm clock from a drawer and set the alarm for one hour.

I looked back into the cup and saw my face, wavering. Already I could imagine the relief of resting, truly resting, in the comfort of knowing that Thea was being cared for, by me.

I chanted:

"Sip away my trouble

Make me split and double"

I took the sip of cool water, and looked again into the cup. My reflection blurred and disintegrated. I felt my mind swelling inside my skull, swelling and buzzing as if there was not enough room, and then there was a kind of suction and release and... there I was, standing in the doorway, looking back at the cot, at the woman sitting there: myself.

It was eerie, seeing myself from behind, my tired stoop, the back of my greasy, unwashed head, my hair pressed into odd parts and swirls.

I looked less maternal than I'd expected. My physical appearance did not match the feelings I tried to create for Thea: warm, whole, safe. Instead, I looked frail, lumpen. Above all, tired.

Gradually, though, I began to notice the stoic angle of her neck, the generosity and purpose in her fingers as they stroked the baby's back, so softly, without waking her. I realised it didn't matter that her appearance lacked those qualities of ease and wholeness; they were there in her mind and in the baby's mind. The fact that these qualities were not in my mind, looking at the two of them, only served to confirm that I was released, not needed, free to be elsewhere, to rest, to ignore, to wander.

I stepped quietly out of the room, into the hall, and then into the sunroom. I lay down in a sunny spot and let the warmth cover me. I slept.

***

I woke to silence. Not calm, sunlit silence. Stone silence. Empty silence. Dead silence. The light had moved across the sunroom and the shade was cold, as if the sun had turned its shoulder against me, as if I had disappointed it and was banished.

As I hurried back down the hall, the silence got louder and my knees weakened. How could I have thought it would be safe to leave Thea with her? I had tricked myself. I had allowed myself to believe something I knew wasn't true, just to have a rest. And now, and now...

I approached the cot, the empty chair beside it. From across the room I could see the blanket that I'd left tucked tightly over the lower half of Thea's body, now heaped and crumpled at the other end, over the place where her head should have been.

Heart pounding, I was drawn to the cot. It felt like my blood had drained downward, leaving my head light, empty, shivering, my legs heavy and numb.

The stifling woollen cloth was perfectly still. I looked for the movement that would indicate her breath. Nothing.

I tried to pull back the blanket, but I found that my hands had no force. I could place them near the blanket but I could not touch it, could not move it. The heap of bedding remained motionless, deathly still.

Then I thought, grasping at hope: wouldn't the pile be bigger if Thea's body was under it? Perhaps my double had taken her to another room? My spirit lifted, just the tiniest bit.

Calling Thea's name, I strode down the hallway. Despite the volume of my voice in my own ears, I could tell it was not reaching my surroundings. It was as if I was encased in an invisible bubble. The sound of my voice bounced back to me, grating.

As I passed the doorway to the kitchen, I glanced in. It was infested with birds: starlings, parrots, wrens, noisy miners, wattlebirds. A magpie was tearing open a packet of biscuits; three galahs were scrabbling on the slick metal of the stovetop, pecking at crumbs. As I watched, a currawong pooped on the knitted tea cosy and launched away, tumbling the teapot off the tray.

"Thea!" I yelled.

Entering the living room, I saw my daughter, lying on her back in the middle of the floor. She was pumping her little legs and bringing her arms down and up, smiling.

Thank god, I thought. She's alright. But then I saw the coloured glass marbles we normally kept as decorations in a wooden bowl on the coffee table. They were strewn all over the carpet with some stray feathers.

We hadn't thought we needed to put the marbles away yet. Thea hadn't learnt to crawl, let alone stand. But now I saw her twist her strong little body, rocking, rocking and trying to roll over.

Stupid, stupid. Why hadn't I put the marbles away? And where was, where am, where is...the other?

I moved quickly to Thea and tried to pick her up, but I could not get a grip on her. There was no purchase to be found on her plump limbs, the soft cotton of her singlet. Again and again, I failed, and still she kept flexing, trying to roll.

She finally did it, and I could only watch in horror: she flopped onto her stomach and lifted her head and shoulders, exploring the view from her new vantage point. Her hands reached out, grabbing towards the pretty glass balls, her little pink tongue poking out in anticipation.

Frantic, yelling (though no-one could hear me), I looked around the room, and that's when I saw it, her, me, collapsed on the sofa, one leg protruding, messy hair flung over the armrest, face hidden in the pillows, breathing deeply: asleep.

Blood rushed to my face, stiffening my cheeks into an angry mask, narrowing my eyes into blades, to cut, to hurt, to retaliate. How could she?

I shook the woman's shoulder roughly; I shrieked into her ear. If I could wake her, at least, she could pick Thea up. But I was not really shaking her, and she couldn't hear me. I had no greater effect on her than I had on my daughter.

Desperate, I chanted the words backwards, trying to reverse the spell. Nothing.

I lay down facing Thea, my head just inches away from her. She looked through me and flapped her arms, reaching. In my mind, I conjured all my care for her; I thought about holding her, breastfeeding her, of her looking into my face, our gazes locked adoringly. I tried to channel all of that love towards her, to reach her. It had no effect.

So, I tried the opposite. I gathered all my fear; I thought of all the spiky, poisonous hazards that could injure her, all the cliffs she could tumble off, the power points and flames and blades, the sharp corners that could dent a falling temple, the hinges that could crush tiny fingers. I didn't want her to be scared, but if I could make her feel my fear maybe she would stop. But no. All that fear, it stayed inside my bubble.

And the useless lump on the couch kept sleeping: selfish, negligent. The hated qualities I had to exterminate from myself, day after day, were now embodied, in my own body.

Then it happened, what I dreaded. Thea finally reached a green marble, grabbed it and put it in her mouth.

I had a feeling like standing on a cliff and behind me the land falling away, crumbling, until I stood only on the narrowest, collapsing strip of soil. There was nothing to do but to fall.

But just then the alarm went off, filling the house with noise. Even though I was the one who had set it an hour earlier, it startled me, and for a moment I did not know where the clanging was coming from.

Mixed with the racket of the alarm, I heard a flapping of wings and clatter of pans in the kitchen, and spreading into the hall now, a picture smashing to the floor after wings swept it off the wall.

All the noise scared Thea and she opened her mouth wide. She breathed in to cry, and I feared the marble was going to be sucked back into her windpipe but instead it fell forward, wet, over her toothless gums, onto the carpet. Her scream added to the clamour.

The woman on the couch jolted and sat upright. I hit her and hit her, knowing my blows held no force.

"How could you!" I screamed silently.

Thea was still crying and had rolled again, onto her back and was now facing upwards, wailing.

Gradually my blows began to reach the physical world, but weakly. The other me touched her face as if a cobweb had blown onto it, or dandelion fluff. I slowed. Now she put up her arms to shield herself, not urgently, only as if she was being hit by a foam sword or a plush toy. She was saying something, but her voice sounded far away.

I stopped. If my body was solid now, if I could have an impact on objects, I could...I turned and bent, and picked up Thea. I was still weak, only partially in the world, and it took a force of will to hold onto her and not let her fall through my diluted grasp.

I knew I could not go very far, so I sat down on the couch with Thea. The alarm finally stopped and quiet filled the house. There was only an occasional flap of wings and scrabble of claws in the hallway. I held Thea close, safe, cherishing her weight in my arms.

The other me was fading as I watched. Her head hung wearily, but with an effort she bent to pick up some marbles and placed them back in the wooden bowl. The last few marbles fell, not from her dissolving hand but through it. A downy feather drifted, quiet as sleep, to the floor where she stood. And then she was gone.

Before the Unicorn Hunt

Hesper Leveret

Hesper Leveret writes fantasy and science fiction with an emphasis on the beautiful, lyrical, and strange. She was born and raised in Southampton, educated at Oxford, and is now based in Liverpool. Her previous jobs include selling books at Waterstones and writing questions for The Weakest Link quiz show.

One fine morning, a few weeks before the Prince was due to arrive, Lariselle saw the leaves on the great goldenoak tree start to turn, and she knew it was time to prepare for the hunt. The housekeeper at the royal hunting lodge, she was—officially—the only person who lived there all year round. The rest of her family lived in the village called Forest Gate, which sprawled along the road through the Skydark Forest. The same road took the Crown Prince and his entourage to the lodge for their annual unicorn hunt, his once-a-year chance to show off his skills, impress his friends and enemies alike, drink large quantities of Skydark cider, and not worry about the consequences.

In reality, Lariselle's whole family lived in the lodge with her—there was no way she was living in there all alone, surrounded by stuffed dead glassy-eyed hunting trophies. And there were plenty of small servants' rooms which otherwise hardly ever got used, tucked up under the rafters next to the main chimney so they stayed warm in winter. It only made sense for them all to live in the lodge, and if the Crown Prince never actually thought to check if anyone else was there or not when he wasn't—well, then it wasn't a problem.

Lariselle picked a leaf from the lowest-hanging branch of the goldenoak tree, and took it inside to show her mother.

Masena was hard at work, bringing up from the cellar the bottles of cider made from last year's apples, ready to be decanted, mixed with extra ingredients, and then further fermented into the distinctive Skydark brew which Prince Alfrecht always enjoyed so much. He knew it was an ancient Boscan tradition to make Skydark cider and drink it at the autumn equinox, and he enjoyed emulating any tradition which involved getting blind drunk.

He didn't know the significance of the cider, or of the equinox. Or that the Boscans still carried on the tradition, in their own way.

He didn't even know that the Boscans still existed.

Masena came to the top of the cellar stairs, saw Lariselle holding the leaf, and stopped in the doorway.

'It's time, then,' she said.

Lariselle just nodded. They had both known this time was coming—they were already preparing for the Crown Prince's arrival—but they hadn't known exactly when. They never did. Neither the Boscans nor the unicorns used the royal calendar, imposing an artificial grid onto the days and seasons. They went by the goldenoak.

'Do you want me to go with you?' asked Masena.

'Best not,' said Lariselle. 'You know how skittish they can be.'

Now it was her mother's turn to nod silently. There wasn't much to say. Sometimes, a thing just needed to be done.

'Will you be all right here?' asked Lariselle.

'I'll be fine. Your brothers can help. We'll have dinner ready for you, when you get back.'

'Thanks. Well, see you later.'

Another nod, and that was that. Lariselle spent a few minutes getting everything she needed—a small pack with food and water, an apple tucked in her pocket, her hat and sturdy boots, the carved silver knife. This was normally kept in the Prince's dining room, hidden in plain sight as part of a display of antique weapons. Then she set off, walking down the path which led from the hunting lodge to the road. She turned off down an unmarked side track long before she reached Forest Gate, and went to the real village.

While the hunting lodge was much more populated than it first appeared, the opposite was true of Forest Gate. At first glance it seemed a flourishing village, but nobody at all actually lived there—they just watered the flowers, and kept it in a state of picturesque semi-disrepair so that it looked nice for Prince Alfrecht's journey. Everyone lived instead in the real village, which didn't have a name because nobody had ever needed to call it anything other than 'the village', hidden down a narrow path in a part of the forest that the Prince and his hunting party never visited, because Narol the huntsman never took them there.

In the real village, nobody actually grew buckets full of flowers in their gardens—they grew fruits and vegetables and kept goats for milk. They also kept pigs, which at this time of year were largely set to roam in the forest, eating apples and acorns and beech nuts. The half-wild hogs provided an occasional prize for the hunters. After the hunt, they would be rounded up, and most of them would be slaughtered to provide bacon for the winter.

There were even a few pet unicorns, although the domesticated beasts never grew coats of quite the same lustre as the wild specimens, that pearlescent sheen which made their skin so perfect for gloves to wear at the royal balls.

Lariselle walked through the village, waving hello to Narol—who was milking his own goat—and to all the others she knew. Which was everyone she saw, because it wasn't a very large village. They all gave her the same solemn nod—they recognised the knife she held, they knew she had an important job to do, and they knew nobody else wanted to do it. Or even could do it—the unicorns would only respond to someone with at least some Boscan blood, and there weren't many of them left. Lariselle was the last of her father's line.

At this time of year, after a hot summer, she could pass easily enough for a normal Skydark villager with a tan and sun-bleached hair. The Prince and his friends had never particularly commented on her appearance, or even really noticed her. They generally brought all their entertainment with them—she just brought them their food.

If they ever saw her in the depths of winter, they might think differently. However, in the cold months, the road through the forest was always rendered impassable by the snow—and so nobody ever came to the hunting lodge until the spring thaw, when the royal ladies arrived for the forest flower festival. Lariselle always tried to avoid their sharp eyes. They preferred to be served by her half-brothers anyway, who provided the right kind of roughed-edged virility to set off their delicate flower displays to perfection.

On the other side of the village, the track continued, surrounded by ever-more thickly growing trees and undergrowth. Lariselle kept going, as the sounds of humanity gradually faded behind her, replaced by the silence of the Skydark Forest. It was here, in the quiet places at the heart of the woods, that she really understood how it had earned its name; looking up, she couldn't see the sky at all, only the canopy of leaves that almost completely blocked the light.

Luckily, she had eyes that were well-adapted to seeing through the perpetual green twilight of the deep woods.

Eventually, she found the place she was looking for: the other village with no name. The village that was so hidden most people outside the Skydark Forest didn't even think its inhabitants still existed. The Boscan village.

The houses were built partly on the ground, and partly up in the trees, linked to each other with ladders and ropes. And this village wasn't made just from the houses; the trees themselves had been tamed, their branches woven in ways that created connections—and barriers. The Boscans had lived here for hundreds of years, shaping the forest to suit them. Now, there were only a handful of them left.

A handful of that handful met her at the edge of the village, each of them holding a single goldenoak leaf. They had seen the sign too, and knew what it meant.

Lariselle bowed her head in greeting, and they did the same. When she lifted her head again, they looked back at her, their eyes filled with sadness, and then they parted ranks. This wasn't supposed to be a part of their year—and yet, they had adapted to survive. As they parted, they revealed the herd of unicorns standing behind, waiting for her.

Although she had done this many times before, the sight never failed to take her breath away. The beautiful satin shimmer of their skin, standing out in the forest gloom. The long pointed horns of the females, transparent and tinged faintly green with the venom they bore. The thicker, opaque horns of the males.

The softly rounded horns of the juveniles. The gleam of their long manes and tails, the hush of everything around them.

They were holy to her people, and she was here to help kill one of them.

Crown Prince Alfrecht didn't care about what was holy. He would never see them like this, magnificent and eldritch in the soft still darkness. He only ever saw them as sources of his pleasure: the thrill of the hunt, the tang of fresh blood in his Skydark cider, another trophy mounted on the wall of his hunting lodge, more pairs of fancy gloves for himself and his mistress.

Lariselle hated what she had to do—that didn't change the fact that she had to do it. It had long ago been decided that there was only one way to keep the Boscans hidden, and to prevent the unicorns being hunted to extinction. In order for the herd to survive, one must die.

She stepped forward. With one hand, she pulled an apple from her pocket; with the other, she raised her knife. The knife made of Boscan silver, passed down to her by her father. She could wield it, as few of the human villagers could, and she could approach the unicorns. But while she had some Boscan blood, she wasn't fully of them—she didn't live in this village, she didn't drink the Skydark cider around their autumn fire, and she didn't—couldn't—share their horror of shedding unicorn blood.

The herd all raised their heads to her in greeting, lifting their horns to show that they trusted her, even though they knew why she was here and what she was going to do.

Then one of them slowly shuffled towards her. An old male, his eyes mostly clouded, his skin increasingly pale and dull. Lariselle felt tears pricking her eyes as she recognised the markings on his nose. Only last year he had seemed still in the prime of his long life; now he was half-wasted away, ravaged by disease. She suspected that, if the Boscans hadn't been taking care of him, he'd already be dead by now.

Instead, they had kept him alive, so he could be killed by the Crown Prince.

Lariselle approached him gently, and murmured his name. It was a name her father had taught her, as he had taught her the names of all the herd who lived in the Skydark Forest. Names that were not suited to be spoken in human company, names that could not be written down. He lifted his nose, sniffed the air—he could clearly still recognise her scent—and accepted the apple she had brought him.

She stroked his nose and his mane as he ate it out of her palm, and whispered to him the words she had long since memorised, and which now felt more meaningful than ever.

'Your sacrifice will not be in vain. Your blood will spill this day, and the ruler from beyond the trees will soon take your life, but your herd will live on. Your children will eat the fruits you have sown, and run free through the forest. This much I promise you.'

And then she drew the knife across his throat.

He accepted his fate in silence, although several of the younger unicorns made sounds of distress. The Boscans ran to catch the silvery blood as it flowed, humming a wordless hymn as they did so. Lariselle knew they would mix it into their brew for the Skydark cider, and leave it to ferment. The Prince's own version of the cider would be made with fresh blood, so it wouldn't be quite the same. It was a small difference, and yet Lariselle felt it was an important one—the Boscans used the cider to achieve transcendence, while the Prince just used it to get wasted.

She counted to one hundred, just as she always did, and then she let go of the old unicorn's head. The exsanguination was not complete– yet he was severely weakened. A Boscan young man—she recognised him as her second cousin, Prylm—took charge of the half-dead creature, holding a thick wad of cloth to his neck to staunch the bleeding, and leading him away to the place where they tended the sick.

Lariselle wiped the blade of her knife, and muttered a quick prayer to the gods—not the gods that Crown Prince Alfrecht professed to believe in every other day of the year, the gods of the Skydark Forest that he pretended to believe in every autumn when he drank his blood-spiked cider and played at being a forest dweller. The gods that she and the Boscans worshipped every single day of their lives.

The other Boscans turned away from her, and she felt a sudden stab of anger. Why did she have to go through this, every year? Why did she have to half-sacrifice an aged unicorn, just so the Prince and his wealthy friends could hunt it down afterwards and feel like they were the masters of nature? Just so Narol could take them on a long circuitous path through the trees, claiming to be following the scent of the unicorn herd, only to lead them—eventually—to this weakened specimen, and let him die to save the rest of his kind? Why did she have to pretend she lived a solitary life in the hunting lodge, while her family lived in the make-believe village of Forest Gate? Why did she have to hide half her heritage—the half that gave her the pale eyes and flaxen hair paired with the dark skin, the affinity with the forest, and the right to wield the blade? And yet the other half— the human half—meant that she was able to use the blade to cut the unicorn's throat and serve the future king. She was Boscan enough to serve the unicorns and understand their ways, and human enough to hurt one.

'Are you all right?'

The voice came from Prylm, who was now returning from his task, wiping the blood from his hands.

'Not really, no,' she answered him.

'You did well,' he said. 'He's in no pain. We'll treat him with every kindness we can, these final days. It's a worthy death.'

Beyond him, the herd of unicorns made a low murmuring sound of muted agreement.

'I just—I wish it didn't have to be me.'

'And I wish we were still the rulers of Skydark Forest, and rode unicorns into battle to stab our enemies to death with their venomous horns. But all things must be what they are.'

At this, Lariselle could only offer a sigh.

'I have a gift for you,' said Prylm, and held out his hand. Lariselle took what he had to offer: a very small glass bottle, filled with a faintly shimmering green liquid.

'What is it?' she asked, although she already knew.

'Unicorn venom. The queen of the herd consented to let me take some from her, to give to you.'

'I-' Lariselle turned to seek out the queen with her eyes, the largest of the females, with the longest horn and the most beautiful shimmering coat. 'Thank you,' she said. The unicorn raised her horn high in acknowledgement.

Then to Prylm she said, 'I never thought I would earn this gift.'

Unicorn venom was only ever given to those among the Boscans who had proved their valour. It was almost unheard-of for someone of mixed heritage to receive it.

'You have more than earned it,' said Prylm. 'You have taken on your father's mantle, and you do what we cannot, to help keep us hidden and the herd preserved.'

The Crown Prince thought that his grandfather had extirpated the Boscans from the forest, and that the unicorns ran wholly wild. What he would do if he found out the truth—that the Boscans survived, even in the very blood of his housekeeper, and that the unicorns he so loved to hunt lived in harmony with the people he thought were gone—

'Use it wisely,' said Prylm. 'A few drops added to the Skydark cider will produce vivid dreams. A few more drops will make you sleep for three days straight. And the whole bottle, emptied into someone's glass when they are already intoxicated...'

He didn't finish the sentence, and Lariselle didn't even dare to finish the thought. She knew exactly what unicorn venom could do. Prylm closed her fingers around the bottle.

'Use it wisely,' he said again.

Lariselle nodded, one last time, and then turned around and headed back to the hunting lodge.

The Tale of the Mother and the Hexed VCR

Nika Murphy

Nika Murphy is a Ukrainian-born speculative fiction whose stories appear or are forthcoming in Clarkesworld and Apex. She holds an MFA from Arcadia University and subsidizes her typewriter collection with a day job in the pharmaceutical industry. She resides in Florida with her family.

My daughter's newborn, Lili, sleeps soundly in her arms, pink and milk drunk. I want to remember Svitlana as she was in those quiet, blissful moments. Instead, I remember darkness. We had no words for it then, no pills nor potions, no therapists nor spells. We had only our own mothers to tell us the darkness will pass, with time. How much time, they never said.

I do not tell Lana about my time in the dark as she's been spared the worst of it. But I see my restlessness in her even as she settles down, settles in, settles.

The ocean breeze blows cool, humid air through the open windows and we reminisce of our days living near the Black Sea.

"Do you remember the VCR?" she says and puts her phone face down on the table between us. The rare gesture tilts me away from the light.

"Do I remember the worst day of my life?" I begin.

Lana knows the story of the VCR. How her father, Pavlo, and I performed magic on weekends for local mobsters and KGB officers. Pavlo cast illusion spells and I sang incantations. The other magicians in our band forged charms and drummed forth enchantments. Our dancers conjured wards of amusement while patrons dined and drank and tipped us in cash, jewels, and, once, a hexed VCR.

The following day, Pavlo had to visit his aunt in the hospital and would not be home until late in the evening.

"Don't touch the VCR. I'll remove the hex when I return," he said.

These parts of the story, Lana knows well. What she doesn't know is I had been skirting the dark since she was born and when she asked me to play her cartoons for the hundredth time that day, I had prayed for the darkness to take me.

In that moment, I did not see Lana's elfin nose inherited from Pavlo. I did not see her hazel eyes inherited from me. I saw an anchor, pulling me down into a life I did not want. But I do not say this.

"I was tired, and I didn't want to bother with the VCR," I say instead. "I went into the kitchen to call your father at the hospital to see if he could come home earlier."

The truth is, Lana started crying and I went to the kitchen to get away from her wailing. I have seen Lana do the same when Lili becomes inconsolable from hunger, or exhaustion, or some other mysterious childhood vexation. But Lana never lets the darkness reach inside her, dig its trenches between her ribs.

"You must have tried to do it yourself, put the tape in, and pushed the wrong button," I say, even as the memory tightens its grip on my throat. "Then you were gone."

"Gone?" Lana asks, as if she doesn't know what comes next.

"You disappeared. I looked for you under the beds, in cupboards, behind the fridge," I say. I yelled for her, at her. I cried to the neighbors. She has gone from this world, the darkness whispered into my heart, inside my head. How would I tell Pavlo? What would happen to our family? The darkness tugged at my neck, at my eyelids, made me twitch and spasm. Wasn't this what I wanted, it said. Wasn't it better this way?

"Then the VCR spit the tape out. I picked it up, but it gave off no energy, nothing I could sense, anyway. When I put my hand on the VCR, though, my palm came away wet and hot, covered with a slick of salt water." It was Lana's tears. The smell emanating from the VCR's vents was my daughter's. "I knew it was you," I say.

I tried some incantations, tried power cycling, tried to pry open the VCR, and shocked myself in the process, only to find it wouldn't turn on afterwards.

"Then you took it back to the market, the one in the hangar, where dad bought those haunted Puma sneakers," Lana says, and we tuck that story away for another day.

"I carried that VCR under my arm up and down the aisles looking for the seller, but he wasn't there, so I went to the yellow witch's kiosk and asked her for help." The woman, not much older than me, placed her hands on the black machine and cooed at it, hushed at it. She shook her head, her yellow hair falling over her yellow eyes.

"'You need a conduit,' she said. I responded with something like, 'no shit,' and then we yelled at each other for a bit. I offered her money, but she wasn't interested. 'I can't leave my table. Find and purchase these items for me and I will tell you where to find your conduit,' she said and handed me a shopping list. I ran around that stupid market like a beheaded rooster, buying cans of kerosene and condensed milk and catnip, but when I brought everything back, she told me to keep it all."

"Because what she really wanted was the VCR," Lana says, skipping ahead.

"The witch told me the hex would become permanent after twelve hours. After that, I would give her the VCR, with or without you in it."

"And the conduit?" Lana says. Lili sighs in her sleep.

"The conduit was an enchanted video tape full of Tom & Jerry cartoons with the power to soothe and calm any child."

"I loved that tape," Lana says as she extracts strands of her straight, sandy hair from her daughter's grip. On the day she disappeared, Lana's hair was wavy and white as sea foam.

"By the time I'd set out to find the magical tape, more than four hours had already passed." I push down the darkness rising through my core and remind myself that day is past. My daughter is safe. She is here, in front of me.

"How did you know where to look? How did you find it?" Lana's voice is elevated, excited. Her baby stirs and we go still. Lana transfers the girl to the bassinet, where she wriggles until Lana sticks a pacifier in her mouth. Lana is so natural with Lili. I am happy for my daughter, yet I envy her. I wish it had been easier for me. Envy turns to pity turns to anger in my gut. The darkness stole those moments from me, from us.

Yet, my child is here, in front of me.

"First, I called my bandmate, Grisha. Do you remember him? The one who always brought you lollipops?"

"I remember. He was fat and he brought my toys to life with his songs. I used to think he was Grandfather Frost."

"Yes! He had that white beard even though he was younger than your father."

His wife had just had a baby less than a month prior, and he was sleep deprived and exhausted, making stupid mistakes on stage, sniping at us during breaks. I had not been kind to him in those days and I was nervous to call him for a favor.

"Grisha's wife answered the phone when I called, and I could hear their baby crying in the background. I asked him if he had heard about the magical tape and he, thinking I was giving him unsolicited advice, grew irate and began to yell at me. 'What do you think those stupid cartoons are going to help us with when my wife can't even feed our baby,' he said and hung up on me."

What I don't tell Lana is how their baby's cry awakened something in me. Something the darkness had locked away. Lana's hungry cry was distinct and shrill, and I was one of the lucky ones who never lacked for milk.

"I drove to Grisha's house. He opened the door, eyes bloodshot, hair frayed. 'What are you doing here,' he said over the baby's crying. I pushed past him, went into his kitchen, and made a cup of tea. I mixed in two big tablespoons of the condensed milk I'd bought at the market and gave it to Grisha's wife.

'I tried that already,' she said.

'Drink,' I said."

"It definitely works," Lana says and points to her swollen chest and the empty cans of condensed milk on the counter.

As the woman drank, I pulled the memory of Lana at my breast, of her big black eyes searching for mine, of her dimpled hand kneading like a cat, her rhythmic suckling as much for comfort as for sustenance. I stripped away the darkness from the memory, the impatience, the numbness, the anger at the numbness, inside and out. I let myself feel the awe of having made a whole person and fed her from my body. Steeped in the memory, in the awe—

"I sang forth an incantation," I say. "The baby latched and the crying stopped." I leave out the part where I tried to apologize for how I'd been acting, but Grisha wouldn't hear it. In his eyes, we were even.

"I asked him about the tape again. He gave me the number of another magician, Serge. We'd worked with him a handful of times."

"Why didn't you tell Grisha about me and the VCR?" Lana asks.

"I was embarrassed, proud, stupid. I don't know," I say, and it is half true. The full truth is that the darkness told me no one would help me. That I didn't deserve help. That I deserved to lose Lana if I couldn't get her back on my own.

"You were so young. It must have been hard," Lana says, and I lose myself in the wisdom and understanding dripping from her words.

"Serge?" she prompts me.

"Serge was a shrewd, narcissistic, unprofessional asshole, and I worried he wouldn't give me the tape. First, he denied knowing anything about any tape. In the next breath, he said he didn't have the tape. I begged, I pleaded, I tried to offer him money, gigs, but he only laughed and said he could not help me."

"And what did you do?" Lana asks as if she doesn't know.

"I told him I would tell his wife about all his affairs if he didn't give me the tape. He laughed at me, and said, 'fine, go ahead,' but I could tell he was nervous. I had to find Kalina quickly. She worked at an apothecary as a potions mixer."

I keep some details for myself and replay them in my mind. The agonizingly slow wait in line behind the babusya with arthritis, the teacher with a sore throat, the whispering man with erectile dysfunction. The remnants of Kalina's preparations littered the counter. Salves, vials of sea grass nectar, blue beetle wing powder clinging to a pestle. Lana's counter resembles the same mess. Baby formula, vitamin pipettes, lotions. So many conveniences I never had. But never mind all that.

"When the last customer was gone, Kalina looked at me, annoyed, and told me the shop was closed. I told her I knew her husband and that seemed to get her attention in the worst way possible. She yelled at me, called me names I'd never heard in combinations I'd never imagined. The noise must have woken her little girl, about your age, maybe a year older, who came out of the back room and began to cough."

She coughed and coughed until she started crying and begged her mother for medicine. The cough sounded like grinding rocks, like growling wolves, and her tears tumbled from her face like falling stars. I felt pity at first, but it wasn't until I looked into Kalina's face that I recognized helplessness. She was a master mixer. Her reputation was well known throughout the town, and yet here she was, with a sick child even she couldn't heal.

"It reminded me of when you were a baby and we had to evacuate after the power plant exploded. You'd developed a similar cough and no matter what your father and I did, we couldn't get it to stop. We tried all the spells we knew. Sang every incantation we had memorized. Nothing worked," I say. I would have done anything to make Lana feel better. Anything.

As Kalina wiped the girl's tears, I remembered the auntie on the train who gave us an old country remedy.

"Is this the part with the kerosene?" Lana asks, and her eyes widen like they used to when I read her fairy tales at bedtime, even when she knew every word by heart.

"'Swab the back of her throat,' I'd said. The girl opened her mouth wide and said ahhh between coughing fits. Kalina swiped the girl's throat with a kerosene dipped cotton swab. The girl gagged but stopped coughing."

"Just like that. No magic," Lana says.

"No magic," I say. "I said to her, 'look, I don't know your husband intimately or in any capacity and I don't want to. But he has an enchanted VHS and I need it for my kid. Can you help me?'

"'I'm sorry,' she said, 'we don't have the tape.'

"Turned out the bastard taped over it," I say. "A soccer match or something and the tape lost its enchantment."

Lana tsks and rocks the bassinet with her foot.

"Serge burst into the apothecary, yelling at me, at her, and she yelled back, and all I could think about was the minute hand on the wall moving faster and faster. Eventually, he left and Kalina gave me the number of the magician who sold it to her."

"Did you know him, too?"

"No. I don't even remember his name." Funny how some details fade over time, while others stick like wet dough.

"I called him. I told him Kalina gave me his number and he said, 'sure, my wife knows her. They went to school together.' I told him I was looking for an enchanted VHS. He said 'sure, sure, can you come over tomorrow?' 'I can come now,' I said."

I don't want Lana to know I had expected the man to say "no." I was preparing a million different arguments, excuses, responses to get him to say yes, but in the end, he simply said, "sure, sure." In response, the darkness grew louder, trampled over my thoughts and yelled, "He must be lying. He doesn't have it. He's trying to trick you."

"How much time did you have left?" Lana asks.

"Four hours," I say, and skip this part of the story, as I always do.

As I drove, I rubbed the VCR strapped to the front seat. It exhaled dried, hot air through the side vents and filled the cabin with Lana's tiny breath. I drove faster.

My thoughts raced alongside my car, circling the drain of darkness, pulling, pulling. My fault, my guilt, dragging me down.

If I had been more patient, more responsible, maybe this would never have happened. Maybe if I had a more traditional job, or never moved away from my hometown. Maybe if I took better care of myself, ate healthier, exercised more. Maybe if I read to Lana more, or played with her more. More.

More.

Maybe the VCR wouldn't have taken her.

Maybe I should never have been a mother.

I covered the VCR with a sweater and locked the car.

My boots clapped up the stone steps to the magician's fourth floor apartment, the echoes ricocheting up and down the barren stairwell. I knocked once. No one answered. Scents of fried onions and sounds of yapping dogs filtered into the hallway between door cracks.

"The magician opened the door on the second knock.," I say. "'Come in,' he said, and I stepped over the threshold through a powerful ward. Inside, the apartment was bigger than on the outside, a magic way beyond my skill or understanding. All the odors from the hall faded. The magician's wife was in the kitchen, stirring sage into a stovetop cauldron. A little boy sat at the table, eating dinner. A one-eyed cat rubbed its face against my leg. On the TV, Tom chased Jerry through an animated American dining room," I say and Lana leans in. This is her favorite part.

Other details bloom and fade from memory. The entire household pulsed strong with magic. I was intimidated and running out of time. I tried to sound cool, nonchalant, but I couldn't hide my desperation. The magician could smell it, wafting off me in fetid clumps.

"He said he had some other items for sale in a large wooden chest: a mascara from France, imbued with an illusion spell to make you the world's most beautiful person in the eyes of the beholder; eye cream from Korea, infused with an age reversal spell to make you young; perfume from Japan extracted, from a cherry blossom tree that bloomed once a century and gave you the power to go back in time. There were auto-symmetrical eyeliners and 24-hour lipsticks in every color and lots of other things. He told me I must choose two items before the final transaction could commence."

"Like a test? Why? What items did you choose?" Lana asks.

"I suppose he was trying to vet me. Back then, selling enchanted items was illegal. Maybe he wanted to make sure I wasn't an undercover cop or something."

It was more than that, though I don't tell Lana. The chest itself was enchanted. Illusion magic rippled out of it. The items inside shimmered and swayed as if sat atop a hot horizon. I picked up a hair dye that promised to disguise me as someone else. The darkness perked up, told me to take it. To run away. Pavlo and Lana would be better off without me anyway.

The hair dye felt heavy in my hand. Tom howled on the TV and I dropped the bottle. The illusion glitched and the bottle transformed into a stuffed cat for a moment before turning back into the dye. For that brief second, I saw a chest full of toys. I saw a glimpse into a world unclouded by darkness.

"I closed my eyes and reached deep into the chest and grabbed two boxes. When I opened my eyes, the boxes contained a singing doll and a plastic tiara that allowed its wearer to turn bread into cake."

"I wore that tiara everywhere for weeks," Lana says.

"We all gained five pounds before that thing finally broke," I say and Lana laughs, nearly waking the baby.

"Then you asked him about the tape," she says.

"'It's nothing powerful, just a simple soothing enchantment,' he said. I asked, 'Will it extract a kid stuck in a hexed VCR?' and he said, 'Sure, sure.' I gave him all the cash I had. It was more than most people made in a month. He walked over to the entertainment center, pushed eject on the VCR, and handed me the tape. The wife and kid both had their mouths wide open. Then the kid started screaming. The wife came after me with that big wooden spoon in her hand, beet purple and steaming from whatever poison she was stirring. It could've been borscht for all I know, but I wasn't going to risk it. I still had that bag of catnip and I tossed it at her. The cat went wild and attacked her. I rushed out of there as fast as I could."

I can still hear the magician laughing and shouting after me to come back anytime.

"I arrived home with thirty minutes to spare. Back in the apartment, I hooked up the VCR the way your dad taught me. I put the tape in and pressed play."

I don't know what I expected to happen. Nothing changed. I looked around the room, tried to sense some change in the atmospheric pressure, but there was no discernible difference. The clock in my kitchen ticked, each second louder than the last. I began to panic.

The memory's tendrils reach for my throat. Lana notices my face darken.

"You okay?" she asks.

I'm not. My heart is on fire. My breath comes in sharp, small gasps. "Yeah," I say.

"Mama," Lana says, "what would you have done if you couldn't get me back?"

This question calms me because I know the answer. Because I turned it over and over in my mind a hundred thousand times that day and millions of times since.

There was a moment when I thought I heard Pavlo's car door slam. Heard his footsteps, his familiar and comforting gait tap, tap, tap lightly up the stairwell to our apartment. I imagined him coming back to a home without his little Lana. To a life without her in it.

The mind acts strangely when it's in shock. To protect itself. It'll invent scenarios in which the thing you fear most suddenly seems fine. That maybe, this, the most horrible thing to ever happen to you, might be alright. That one day you may live your life and survive it, even though, in your heart, you know you won't.

I do not tell Lana this. It is not what she needs to hear. Not what she needs to know. Not now. Hopefully, not ever.

"I would never give up. I would die before I gave up," I say.

Lana reaches out and squeezes my arm and I remember how she used to wrap her tiny hand around my finger just as her baby does now.

Time had run out. I took the tape out and turned it over this way and that. I smelled it. I stuck my finger in the reels, and turned them one way, then the other. I flipped up the guard panel and inspected the tape. The darkness was whipping me into a frenzy. I thought for sure the magician must have ripped me off. That the tape didn't work

"When nothing happened, I checked the wiring. Made sure I had it connected correctly. I unplugged it, plugged it back in, and put my forehead against the video slot. I closed my eyes and pushed the power button. The machine whirred and clicked to life."

I pressed play.

I watched the episode where Tom and Jerry go on vacation to Naples and a kindly Italian mouse takes them on a tour of the city.

"I thought about what your father would do if he was in my position."

"He would ask if you followed the directions," Lana says, and we both laugh.

I wish I'd let Pavlo help me more in those early days, after Lana was born. I wanted to be a good wife, a good mother, but I fell short of both. I let us all down. I had lost Lana. I had lost our only child. I thought, still think, if I could go back in time, I would do so many things differently.

"I rewound the tape to the beginning and hit play. It seized, the first few seconds lost to some defect, and then, the Jekyll and Hyde episode came on," I say.

"That was my favorite one," Lana says.

"It was my favorite too." For many reasons. "It started with a low hum. There was a vibration and, for a moment, it felt like I was on a ship, the ground beneath us swaying and undulating as if I was surfing or riding an earthquake. The feeling and the sound subsided after a few moments and a curtain of silence fell all around me, blurred the rest of the room until only the VCR and the TV were in focus.

"Time seemed to stop completely. The cartoon went on."

I want to tell Lana more. About how the colors and characters jumped out of the TV and splashed pixels across my face. How, with each frame, I felt lighter and lighter, like a balloon filling with helium and lifting off the floor.

But if I tell her, I'll also have to admit that it was the only time when I didn't feel the weight of motherhood standing on my chest, on my shoulders, my back. In those few minutes, I felt like myself. A singer, a magician, a wife.

A woman.

A woman with a child.

A mother.

Lana says, "Then as soon as it started, it was over. The room was back to normal?"

I was back to normal. My normal. With the darkness scratching at my periphery, with the dishes stacked in the sink, with spells strewn across the kitchen table waiting to be memorized.

"You were sitting on the couch watching the TV, as if you'd never left. I smothered you with hugs and kisses, and you whined until I started to tickle you and then you giggled."

"Did I ever say anything about it?" she asks.

"No, never."

Lana puts her arm around me, and I pull her close. Lili spits out the pacifier and wiggles out of her blanket. She stretches her limbs and opens her eyes. Lana asks me to swaddle her again while she runs to the bathroom. I tell Lana to take her time. That she can trust me with her baby. She laughs from the hall and says she's not sure after the VCR story.

I laugh too, but remnants of the darkness turn her comment from a playful tease to a sharp sting. Her baby whimpers, searches my face looking for Lana.

"Mommy will be right back," I say. I press Lili tightly into her swaddle and rock her in my arms. I kiss her and breathe her in and remember Lana's scent. Magic shimmers in the baby's eyes.

When Lana returns, I pass her the child and ask, "what made you think of the story?"

She shrugs and says, "I don't know if I could have done what you did."

Lili touches her mama's face. The image of them both banishes the darkness. It retreats like the fanning blades in a camera's aperture and exposes my heart to brand new light.

"You won't have to," I say as a promise. A prophecy. Still, I tell her to smell the girl's head. To commit Lili's scent to memory.

Just in case.

Lana rolls her eyes, but holds her daughter close and inhales.

The Doula

AKMay

AKMay is a writer of horror and
fantasy, a prairie witch, and secretly a
suburban mom with a day job. She lives
in Oklahoma with two dogs, one toddler,
and one mystery snail.

Ilena watched the seconds tick down on her phone's clock. The woman in front of her, forehead shiny with sweat, hands gripping the toilet seat, tensed and let out a moan.

"Don't hold your breath," Ilena said. "Breathe. Breathe."

The woman, Molly, stripped off her shirt in frustration, desperate for comfort, her belly a large brown gumdrop hanging beneath her. The contraction ended and she sighed and sagged into Ilena's arms. It had been hours but Ilena was strong. She put the cool washcloth from the sink with ice water and lavender oil on the back of Molly's neck. Molly bent over the toilet, her sweaty head on her forearms and Ilena got behind her. She gripped Molly's hips with her long arms and pressed her hands together, trying to relieve the woman's back pain and help the stubborn baby move into position. Molly's muscles rippled and spasmed. A warm gush and the musky smell of amniotic fluid flooded the tiny bathroom.

"Sorry!" Molly gasped.

"It's all natural and it's a good sign. How are you feeling?"

"I want to go to the hospital."

Molly clutched Ilena's hand while Molly's husband hailed a cab.

Ilena practically carried her body, sagging in exhaustion and disappointment.

"There's nothing wrong with going to the hospital," Ilena soothed. Her cooler pressed into her shins when she put it on the floor of the cab. She hoped the nurses wouldn't give her any trouble. She too was disappointed they were going to the hospital.

In the cramped birthing room, full of so many people and machines, Ilena watched the doctor like a hawk when the placenta slid out. "We are saving the placenta for encapsulation," she said again firmly. They often forgot such requests. The doctor looked at it closely. Ilena held her breath hoping there was no reason to send it to pathology. It was beautiful: richly dark, heavily veined, and glistening; the only organ made by an adult human. The nurse looked bemused. Molly's husband looked horrified, like he was seeing something that should be on the floor of an abattoir. Ilena put it as carefully into the heavy-duty gallon Ziploc bag as the doctor was placing the pink baby into Molly's arms.

"So big!" Ilena exclaimed proudly. Molly thought she meant the baby and gave a beatific smile.

Ilena took the subway home, picking an empty car so that no one would note her bloody clothes. Not that most people would. She sat, the rocking motion of the subway car putting her into an exhausted trance. An unpleasant smell underneath her own pungent odor made her look around. Her sneaker touched something. Under her seat was a disturbingly large pile of chicken wing bones. Disgusting. Worse than a cat leaving its kill.

Her apartment building was large and anonymous, around the corner from a Trinidadian market where women in head wraps sold fruit. Ilena paused at her mailbox for the usual thick, shiny sheaf of colorful advertisements, subscriptions to midwifery journals, New Age catalogues of paper lanterns, and chakra crystals. Only one was personal, an invitation from Marina to dinner at her new condo. She went back down the steps to put it all into the recycling bin. As the lid banged shut, she felt a prickle at the base of her neck. The wall behind the trash cans was dirty and covered in graffiti and children's scratchings. A dirty handprint was so faded no one else would have noticed it. Ilena brushed a finger along it and dried reddish mud flaked away.

In her studio apartment, a black shadow darted across the floor and threaded itself between her legs. Nushka jumped onto the window sill, butting his black head into her hand. His tail flicked as they both looked out over the fire escape. Cars rushed through the street below like blood cells through veins.

To fill the quiet room with noise she turned on the old boxy TV. *Cat People* was playing on the classic movie station. She liked the old movies and besides, she couldn't see color. The odious therapist with his unctuous mid-Atlantic accent was telling Simone Simon that she was crazy. Or was it an English accent? Language was still not easy, learned so long ago, it was hard for her to tell

"I love loneliness," Simone Simon purred on-screen.

***

The next morning Ilena woke early. She opened the curtains and let the sunlight stream in through the leaves of her hanging pothos plant. She unrolled her yoga mat and went through a vinyasa though her body ached to stay in bed, stay in the dark. After a scalding hot shower, she opened a can of foul-smelling cat food for Nushka and put it on a plate.

Ilena settled down at her kitchen table to work. She opened her laptop and checked her calendar, looking anxiously at the dates. She put a finger to her pulse and noted the faintness of the color under the delicate skin of her wrist. Shaking herself into readiness Ilena pulled up her to-do lists. She read her emails and questions forwarded from her website.

At ten she took her first video interview with a Manhattan couple expecting their first child. The woman was very put together, her anxiety somewhat allayed by a pastel-patterned calendar with meticulously labeled dates, appointments, and reminders. The man with a fashionable haircut the shape of a shark fin spoke like he was being graded on creativity.

"We just want to do things right," the woman said. Birth plans, co-sleeping, vaccines. So many decisions she wanted to agonize over. As if there was a right way. Mothers these days were so terrified. Many of her clients were without immediate family in New York which left new mothers alone and adrift. She knew a lot of them liked the idea that she was an immigrant, she said Romanian, as if it connected her to some ancient knowledge. Though Ilena preferred loose linen pants and turtlenecks to kerchiefs and dirndls and kept her hair in an unremarkable bob with bangs that covered a broad forehead, she would sometimes play her accent almost to the point of parody.

She began her soothing patter; it didn't really matter what she said. Women can give birth in caves, she said. But why not pre-natal yoga and acupuncture as well? Traditional knowledge with Brooklyn sensibilities, that's what most of them wanted and it made the birthing world an idealistic if messy stew. DNA from so many cultures, it had to be, to make up for a remarkable amnesia. Ilena marveled at the ignorance. But she also loved that about America. Everyone was still inventing themselves back to their very bones. Of course, when you made it up as you went along, sometimes nothing held you up but fear.

After the interview, Ilena put an apron over her clothes and pulled out a carton of latex gloves. She turned the radio on to Fresh Air, a low background hum to her work. She got out utensils, herbs, powders, and a gray packet from the freezer, then ground every-thing in a large granite mortar and pestle and delicately funneled the contents into gelatin-free capsules bought in bulk.

Ilena looked at the bloody thing in its Ziploc bag at the back of her fridge. She closed the door and then put the finished pills into an organic cotton bag hand stamped with *om* symbols. She put them in her bag and dressed to leave the apartment. It would take her an hour to get to Manhattan at this time of day but she listened to the chapters of "The Purpose Driven Life" on her phone during the commute.

Her client told Ilena that she was feeling anxious and depressed.

"The pills should help. Residual hormones that will help you normalize and heal. Many women experience an increase in milk production after the first few days. I'll check back in and see how you're feeling."

The tired woman looked at her with grateful eyes. Ilena handed her the bag and also gave her a recipe for almond milk latte with fennel seed to help with her milk production. She made the obligatory noises of admiration over the baby, a pink frog, skin wrinkling from dehydration.

"Don't think too much," Ilena said. She could say that to every mother. "Feed the baby, your breast or formula." The most help-less creature in nature.

***

Ilena avoided her apartment for the rest of the day. She went to see a movie and then, after using the restroom, stayed behind for another film. She took a slow walk in the park and then browsed through the DVDs at the sidewalk markets. Finally home, Ilena changed into her pajamas and paced the tiny kitchen. She did some yoga positions, stretching her spine, pressing her palms together at the heart. She couldn't get comfortable. If she took it out of the fridge now, she could put it in the sink, let it warm up while she walked to the corner store.

Ilena tried one more lotus pose. She lit another cone of incense in the ceramic turtle and made a bitter, appetite-reducing tea. Nothing helped. She had been trying to give herself three weeks. It had been two weeks and three days. But she couldn't last.

She took it from the fridge, put it in the bathroom sink, and then closed the door so that Nushka couldn't get into it while she was gone. Then Ilena changed into street clothes and went down the block in order to buy milk and more cans of food for Nushka even though the pantry was full. She bought a different kind of incense and also some Tiger Balm.

Once back in the house, Ilena felt her palms itching and her slow heartbeat rising. But she wanted to savor the moment. She took a hot shower that warmed the aching marrow in her long thigh bones. A very long one that let the steam in the bathroom atomize every delicious smell rising from the sink.

Ilena was naked, every delicate hair on her arms standing on end. Every hard tooth in her head present against the soft inside of her mouth. The bloody thing was so dark against the porcelain sink. She picked up its surprising weightiness and stepped back into the bathtub with it. She caressed its slipperiness between her fingers. She made her tongue flat and wide and she gave it one long, loving lick, getting a hint of the flavor that was about to overpower her. Then she opened her mouth wide. Pieces dropped to the bathtub as her sharp teeth tore at the tough tissue. It slid down her throat and the blood dripped down her neck. She sucked the umbilical cord into her mouth greedily and it disappeared between her lips like a giant noodle and mourned the end. She licked the blood spatter off her fingers like tomato sauce.

There were always little surprises. The vegetarian who she

could tell had been eating meat. The health nut whose placenta betrayed a fast food habit in a sour twang like a guilty fart. The ones who were sneaking cigarettes. The ones who were drinking weird teas. She could always taste it in the meat.

Ilena hummed in the purest happiness: satiation. She could hear Nushka purring in sympathetic pleasure through the door and when Ilena came out she put the bloody dish on the floor for the cat to lick clean. The sensory experience lasted for hours. She could also taste their fears, their hopes, the excitement and the dread. These women, especially first-time mothers, were vibrating on a very high frequency. Every cell pumped into overdrive. Love in the meat.

She felt kinship with them then. Loved those strange weak things. Aliens to themselves, their own bodies. They were as cut off from the world and the minds of their own tribe, let alone the planet's other creatures, as if each was an asteroid alone in black outer space. A pink brain screaming to itself in the void, a brain eating itself from worry. Living in a strange tsunami of drowning language that told so much but lied so much. It had taken Ilena so very long to understand half of what humans communicated.

Ilena was connected to her past in a way that no human would understand. Her blood contained voices of all her mothers before her. But she was alone now. It was getting harder to wait between births and not merely from hunger. If Ilena was honest with herself, something she strived to do, she knew that eating this flesh was the only time she could experience what it must be like to be human.

And she was addicted to it.

***

Later that day she took the subway to Sunset Park's Chinatown.

The streets were crowded but people naturally parted for her large bony frame. The smells collided like traffic in her nose. She looked things over carefully in a shop and bought a bright plastic fly swatter with flowers printed on it. She loved plastic things.

Ilena bought the same thing every month and the shopkeeper had it ready for her. It was a mix of herbs long used for reproductive health in China and they were given to her in a grocery sack. She took the old man's word for it. It all smelled like stale kitchen spice blends to her.

Now she needed the iron supplement. She bought it in bulk at Whole Foods, her favorite place in the world. A theme park with its manufactured scents and colors. The whole concrete building vibrating with electricity for air conditioners, freezers, lights. She walked down each aisle, watching the people just as much as she inspected the jewel-like products. Drank in the craving of the girl staring at the cakes locked in clamshell packaging with her hands in her pockets. The woman frowning over the labels of two different children's yogurts. The man surreptitiously slipping a bottle of testosterone-increasing supplements into his basket.

After all her years in America, she still marveled at places like this. The affluent shoppers had almost no real hunger but incredibly enormous appetites. That was something she understood very well. Her own appetite was growing but she put that thought out of her mind.

Reluctantly, she made it to her destination in the vitamin aisle. She could feel the electric tang, like walking through a magnetic field, of the concentrated iron. It was the closest thing she felt to sexual arousal anymore

Many of her moms were vegetarian. She had often wondered why all her vegetarian clients without fail opted for placentophagia, while others needed coaxing. A tiny ferocity, a loving cannibalism, a feast of flesh after the battle. Ilena still, perhaps unnecessarily, purchased vegetarian iron for their capsules.

***

Ilena put the supplies away when she got home and checked the messages from her website. "Let me guide you through the miracle of life in a caring, supportive, nonjudgmental environment. I take a holistic approach using plant-based medicine, vocalization, massage, and acupressure just to name a few techniques." A rose bloomed in a continuous loop.

In an hour she had a face-to-face meeting with a new client. They met at a coffee shop near her apartment. The woman put her birth plan onto the small table and they went over it together. Ilena frowned when she came to a box that had been ticked *no*.

"You do not plan to keep the placenta?"

The woman laughed, a little nervously.

"It's just a little too odd for me. My husband couldn't believe that was a thing. I finally got him on board with the idea of a doula," she said, apologetically. Ilena hid a grimace. She remembered now how argumentative the husband had been. It had convinced her that the woman really did need Ilena to advocate for her during the birth. In the old days, men stayed away.

"I understand. However, there is some very sound science behind the practice. The placenta has hormones that will help you recover more quickly. It has been shown to decrease the likelihood of postpartum depression. It can help with energy and mood. It is like nature's vitamin made just for you and your baby."

"I don't know," the woman shook her head. "It just seems too... icky." She wrinkled her nose delicately and smiled politely in a way that, for this gentle woman, was a hard no.

"It's no different than taking a multivitamin. The pills are no bigger. And in this case, since there is no FDA regulation of supplements, you really don't know what you are getting. But your custom placenta pill is made by your own body. You're as free range as it gets," Ilena made her joke. "I also add a custom blend of herbs that help you recover after the birth."

The woman had been nodding slowly but shook her head again.

"I don't know. I've read that it could contain bacteria."

"The placenta is steam cooked, it's the cleanest, safest method possible while still retaining all the necessary nutrients."

"I don't think..." the woman was clearly becoming uncomfortable.

Ilena bit her lip. She had pushed too hard. But...the woman looked so *good*. She was plump, milk fat. She wasn't from here; Ilena could tell immediately. Somewhere up north where there was lots of dairy, minimal pollution, and weak sunshine. Nebraska, Ilena thought the woman had said. Lots of blue veins ran under her white skin like rivers. A woman's blood volume vastly increased while pregnant. She was full to bursting and Ilena wanted her badly.

After the meeting, Ilena emailed her a little desperately with testimonials from past clients.

"I believe in it so much, for your baby, to get these vital nutrients. How about I take off fifty dollars the storage and encapsulation fees. Just don't tell anyone!"

The woman finally agreed.

***

Ilena's phone buzzed. Her client, Ariel, would be giving birth any day and she was calling and texting incessantly. Questions, worries, hopes. Three long texts came through rapidly, describing last night's dream, an incoherent paragraph that Ilena thumbed past.

Then another text.

Decided to eat placenta n smoothie after the birth. Thinkn wolfberry ashwagandha??

You should really encapsulate. It's the safest method. Ilena wrote back.

Read there r more nutrients raw

In Ilena's first interview, Ariel had talked at length about her diet with the fervor of a fanatic. "We try to eat 80% raw every day," she had said seriously, smiling at her husband. He gave a rather tight smile. Ilena closed her phone with a frown. This one should have been a sure thing. She was becoming ravenous at two weeks now when, strictly speaking, she didn't need to eat every month. She had lost two to meconium contamination during the births. The doctors wouldn't have let her have it and, in any case, it spoiled the meal.

Ariel went into labor two weeks later and gave birth in her Brooklyn apartment. As mother and baby rested, Ilena opened her canvas bag of groceries. Organic fruit, honey from a rooftop hive, and spirulina. Underneath the scent of *nag champa*, damp linen, and perspiration she could smell earthy blood and it made her tongue grow fat in her mouth.

"Weird, huh." The husband hovered over her. Their toddler was wild from the confusion of energy from the birth. He ran in circles, screaming with unexpended energy. Ilena pitied the child, an animal pent up in a zoo when he should have been outside, following the tracks of his tribe. Instead, he would go mad, a brilliant animal clawing at an invisible cage.

"Can you check on her?" she asked the husband.

"Just did," he said. He continued to lean on the counter with his chin in his palm. Butting in. Ilena could smell another woman on him. Not that she cared but Ariel would if she knew. When you lost your tribe you could become strangely fixated on the individual

The toddler pulled at his shirt.

"Why is the dog lady here? I hate her," the toddler whispered loudly. The husband didn't rebuke him.

"Go watch your tablet, bud," he said. Children didn't like Ilena. They were good at sniffing out differences and could always sense an interloper.

"Can you ask her again if she wants honey?" The husband looked like he was thinking. "I can't remember if she said she'd had a bad reaction to it before," Ilena lied.

He went to the bedroom and Ilena quickly took the placenta from the fridge and a small sandwich bag from her purse. Inside were two organic chicken livers she had purchased on the way over. She had barely dumped them into the blender and put the placenta in the sandwich bag back in her purse before the husband returned. She smiled peacefully at him, tossed in some herbs and they watched the bloody mixture whir together.

"No honey," he said.

The husband took the smoothie in to his wife and Ilena rushed to clean. Maybe she would only do home births now, set up another website with a different name to make up the difference. The longer she waited the more vitality was leached out. She could eat it fast while it was still hot. And she had really needed this one. She felt cold and empty.

She went into their bathroom and leaned against the countertop with its Daniel Tiger soap bottles and smears of baking soda toothpaste. Ilena's jaws ached as she unwrapped Ariel's pulpy placenta. It was a big one and she put it in her mouth as far as it would go. In the ecstatic rush of blood, she didn't notice the little boy open the door.

Ilena choked and the placenta splatted onto the floor. It, the floor, the boy, and his tablet with covered in a fine spray of crimson droplets. He began to scream.

"Mommy!"

"Be quiet," his father said sharply. "Your mom is resting."

"A monster!"

Ilena thought about pushing the boy out and locking the door. Wiping up the blood quickly and finishing her meal. But the husband was already there, unable to understand what he was seeing.

"What is going on?"

"Please control your child," Ilena said and pushed past.

"What? What did you do?"

But there was no mistaking the sobs of a scared child. Ariel called out and the husband made to block her from leaving. Ilena was strong and she left the apartment.

***

She did not go home but walked and thought about what to do. She should close her accounts, stuff money in every pocket of her jacket and her backpack. Send out mass emails to clients saying there was a family emergency. Then disable the websites. But she didn't want to leave everything she had built here.

Hours later Ilena was exhausted. She thought about the letter from Marina.

Marina owned a medical spa on the Upper East Side. A private practice where she could feed on a continuous, high-quality supply of biological products. Rich women came, among many other expensive tightening and smoothing procedures, to have their own plasma extracted and spread on their faces and drilled in with tiny needles.

There was a faint red handprint on the bricks near the handle of the double glass doors. Ilena was enveloped in the soft perfumed air and classical music of the reception area. The woman at the desk recognized her and offered her chocolate, wine and water, all of which Ilena declined, before taking a seat on a plush couch.

A large pink glass chandelier hung over the waiting room. Ilena waited, looking over the women's magazines and vaginal tightening brochures splayed on the coffee table. Marina liked to keep her waiting. Ilena's nose burned from the smell of cheap wine and sharp anesthetic. She tried to focus her mind, a will to send out love and positivity, to every creature of the Earth.

Finally, Marina came out, her high heels clicking ostentatiously on the floor like claws. She always wore high heels even though they made her nearly seven feet tall. Marina had black hair blown out in carefully symmetrical waves on either side of her striking, high-cheekboned face. It was a perfect disguise, using her unusual looks to seem purposefully unnatural.

"Ilena!" she cried. "You were supposed to come to dinner!"

"Hello, Marina." They both bristled, two predators in the same habitat, but Marina turned that uncomfortable energy into loud excited gestures. The human women in the clinic, the receptionist, two aestheticians in scrubs and a cat-faced client, did not notice anything unusual. After all, they did it themselves.

"How are you, darling?"

They didn't sit in her office but in one of the procedure rooms. Ilena sat, uncomfortably, on the table, its paper crinkling, her legs dangling like she was a little girl, while Marina leaned against an ornate lacquered cabinet. They sat and smelled each other. But they talked also, being surrounded by humans.

"Can't complain. And you?"

"Business is good. Almost too good. I'm having a hard time keeping good help. They can't keep up with the hours. I'm losing my mind, Ilena. Honestly, I'm afraid I'm losing my mind."

Marina smiled brightly. Her teeth were blindingly white. Unnaturally blue white. And so sharp. It would be impossible to describe their relationship to a human. The word alpha was a poor substitute to describe Marina. She chatted about work, about the renovation on her condo which was, of course, a nightmare and an inconvenience. It went on and on.

"And you?" she finally asked. "You do look a little pale. Have you been getting enough to eat?" Marina tried to look concerned and Ilena, despite all her nature and best efforts, felt the human desire to wish evil on her. "I don't know why you resisted working for *me*." Marina viewed her as a relic. Marina was the uber-human: the technologist. She had even begun to use the injections she gave her clients on her own strong brow to soften it. She was becoming something new with the humans. Trans-human. While Ilena became more human in the wrong ways. In her need and carelessness.

"I enjoy what I do," Ilena said defensively. Marina stood and towered over her.

"Listen. Have you been in contact with anyone from...home?"

"No," Ilena said flatly.

"Ah," Marina just stood there.

"Look, I better be going."

Damn Marina. As far as Ilena knew they were the only ones passing in the city. Maybe the whole world and that alone was what kept her in sporadic contact with Marina. But damn her for making her want to stay just to feed. Ilena didn't want to talk about home and she didn't want to beg for blood even though she was starving.

"Come to dinner tonight, I insist."

"No, I really have to go." Ilena jumped down. Her sensible Crocs sank into the plush Persian carpet.

"Wait! Listen to me rambling on and you must be thirsty." Ilena was startled by the sudden change in Marina. She realized her distaste had blinded her. There was a whiff of distress, not human, in the air. Was Marina nervous?

Ilena was left to puzzle alone. She picked up one of the pamphlets on neck skin tightening on the bureau. She tossed it back and found herself listening in on a conversation going on in the room next door.

"You're going to LOVE these results," Marina told the client next door. "The plasma facial is absolutely what I recommend. Katarina will do the dermablading before and then the facial. Perfection." Marina sent the nurse out and drew the blood herself. The woman in the chair didn't see how much.

"Dermablading is the most instant gratification process that we do. No downtime. Just lay back and relax. Seriously. You'll get addicted, we all are. Your makeup will go on so much better. You won't believe how smooth your skin will be."

"It doesn't hurt?"

"No no no."

Marina came back in. She held two blood packs close to her chest. Ilena's jaw clicked. Marina smiled. Ilena could hear the sound of the blade scraping skin in the next room. Goosebumps pricked her flesh and Ilena's teeth tingled. She could feel the woman's discomfort shading into fear.

"I knew you were hungry." But Marina made no move to open them. "But I have to ask because it is important. Are you sure you haven't seen anything...anyone? Anyone...." Marina faltered and whispered a word. It was an old word no one used anymore. Something like those in the far northern caves. Ilena's mouth went dry and her heart felt like a stone.

"No," Ilena said.

"No?" Marine stared into her eyes intently. She shook her head brightly. "That is good." She handed one of the packs to Ilena. She could feel the fading warmth of it and cursed Marina silently for letting it chill while she asked her stupid questions. Ilena used one of her eye teeth to tear into the bag and she sucked the contents down.

The warm blood filled her senses. It was a poor substitute. Within the blood came just perceptible currents of insecurity and sadness. Mortal fear. Not the fear of death as in old times, or, if it was, it was sublimated in the more immediate fear of looking old. Ilena's distaste for Marina waxed with it. Americans loved those ridiculous vampire stories. White, pure, invincible. Like these women with their violent needles chasing beauty. They would be vampires if they could, surviving aesthetically on liquid-like juice fasters. Blood was weak, insipid, nothing compared to the sweet, thick exultation in womb tissue. Dark when the other was bright. Love and life when the other was sad and stale. Addictive.

She was lost in these thoughts when once again she was distracted by the women in the next room.

"Has the anesthetic been on her chest for an hour?" someone asked.

"Yes."

"How is Jake?"

"Good, considering. I'm going to Barney's right after I finish this. I think I have time."

"I thought you had, like, twenty black dresses."

"No. Not appropriate ones. Sleeveless ones, yes. Not for a funeral though."

"Maybe throw a cardigan on one?" the voice suggested. The sound of the scalpel going over the soft skin was incredibly loud to Ilena, humming with blood as she was.

"Well.... I just feel like, it's his grandmother. You know? I mean, I think it's respectful to get something new."

Ilena had eaten her grandmother. And her mother too, when her time came, like all her people did. How long had she been here? She had been in a trance, filled with blood and the human chatter. The human world she had slipped into and didn't want to ever leave. Marina was staring at her.

"You have been making too many mistakes."

Ilena growled, unable to control herself. All noise stopped.

"What was that?" Someone said.

"You've been watching me," Ilena accused.

"Be quiet," Marina hissed. "It affects us all," This was a confession. Marina had not wanted to admit that she was touchable.

Ilena's back arched. She turned quickly to reach the door and Marina used all her strength. Her steps were so heavy the chandelier in the reception room tinkled. They didn't kill or lie. That was what humans did. *You always resisted working for me.* Maybe Marina was more cunning than she had thought. Ilena had been right to avoid seeing Marina in her home, privately. Ilena's guts wrenched at the sad blood and all the old feelings of helplessness. The feelings of betrayal. Her betrayal. Everything she had left behind.

Ilena growled again, her only shield the sad women paying Marina to open their veins and inject them with needles. Ilena opened the door and the receptionist was frowning at her desk. Something was bothering the women but they didn't know what. The technician with the scalpel in her hand trembled, looked sharply behind her as if expecting a predator.

A quick intake of breath.

The scalpel slid across the woman's cheek opening the tissue cleanly before piercing her eyeball, spearing it like a cocktail olive. The seconds seemed agonizingly long before the woman began to scream.

This is your survivor's guilt, Ilena told herself. *Do not get involved. You've come so far in America.* She cursed her nostalgia that kept her near Marina. They were safer alone, always had been. The women screamed and Marina had to turn her back to her. In the chaos, Ilena slipped out.

Leaving the cat is hard.

Don't let your past define you, Ilena said to herself like a prayer.

***

She had eight missed calls from an expectant mother, the one from Nebraska. She was going into labor early.

"Shit," Ilena said. She bit her lip. "Nevermind," she told the cabbie. She would go to the hospital first. Was she making up for misdeeds by not abandoning her? Or was she looking to satisfy her hunger?

Ilena arrived, afraid and unsure, but that all melted away when she saw the woman on the bed. For the next few hours, they would work through this together.

"It's too early," the woman said. Tears were streaming down her face. Her husband sat in the corner looking a little shell-shocked.

"It's ok. Everything's going to be fine."

It was a long, hard birth but a healthy boy finally came crying into the world. The woman's placenta was stubborn and the doctor struggled to get it loose. It finally came and an alarming flood of bright red blood followed. Ilena, hand clutching the mother's, was overcome by her closeness to the heat of the wound. She could sense exactly where it was, ragged and red, gushing with each heartbeat. In the old days, this would have killed the woman. In fact, still could kill her as these pitiful doctors couldn't or wouldn't save some women even now with all their technology.

Ilena put her finger on the belly of the woman where she knew it was. The doctor looked at her in surprise but followed it. The woman was saved.

When she asked for the placenta, the husband looked at her.

"What for?"

Ilena froze.

"For the encapsulation."

"No, we're not doing that," he said.

The doctor looked at both of them. Ilena turned to the woman but she was in no condition to have this argument.

"We'll make sure tomorrow, let her sleep now." Ilena tried to put any power she had remaining into her voice. The woman asked her husband to get her suitcase and nurses came in and out. Ilena needed to go but this was also the reason to eat now, her teeth told her. *You need it. You deserve it.*

It was sitting in the pan by the bed. Ilena jumped to her feet and took the giant exercise ball in her arms. She swooped to her other hand, rudely in front of a nurse, and caused commotion in the tiny room while the nurse and doctor gave her baleful looks.

"Oops, sorry! Let me get this out of your way!" Ilena said.

She grabbed the placenta behind her and stuffed it into her hoodie pocket while the enormous purple ball was in front of her.

"Nurse, where is it?" the doctor asked.

"What?" Confusion erupted behind her as everyone in the room looked in disbelief at the blood-smeared but empty tray. Ilena quickly moved out of the room and down the hall. She could hear questions behind her and opened a room door and slipped inside. She put the ball down and gripped the warm bloody meat in her pocket

Ilena couldn't wait. She needed to feed, too. She took out the placenta. Fresh blood oozed from the end of the umbilical cord. The surface shone dully in the dim light of the hospital machinery. It smelled so good. She tried to eat quietly, loosening and opening her jaw wide to consume the thing whole. She squeezed it all into her mouth and closed her eyes in pleasure as it slid down her throat. It was a rush to consume it so quickly. It was so good when the woman was kind.

She opened her eyes. The room had not been empty. Two wide, terrified eyes glistened in the half-dark. Her arms tightened around her baby but neither seemed to breathe; they were that still. Ilena got up slowly, quietly, like a cat. She felt the blood dripping down her chin as she wiped at her face with her jacket lining. She didn't want to kill the woman.

Ilena could picture embracing her, draining every last milky, red, delicious drop of her, eating the soft baby whole like just fallen fruit. Full of the necessary energy to do what she had to do for the next few hours. But that wasn't the life she had decided on. She wasn't a predator. Humans had made her a scavenger. She was something that humans could never understand. They shared a distant grandmother. A very old female from the same caves but they were not the same. Ilena stored all her past in the rNA, every memory of her species and she knew more about humans than they would ever remember about themselves. From before, when there had been so many different talking tribes. Cities they had built and lost and who they had killed along the way. She was very, very old. Almost the last of her kind, who remembered the world the fairy tales half-remembered.

But Ilena could feel that tiny piece, that tiny dark, inscrutable patch of her own human DNA, the product of some cave tryst millennia ago, that made her like them. Made her want to be like them. To use her brain to excavate that dark, impenetrable place in herself that she was blind to. It helped her dream, it had helped her to survive, she thought. Or it could be what was going to cause her to eat herself to death.

Ilena put her finger to her lips.

"You're dreaming," she whispered to the mother as she backed out of the room. "It's a bad dream."

Home for the Rising Sun

Devon Borkowski

Devon Borkowski is a writer, artist, and actor from the New Jersey Pine Barrens. She graduated from Rutgers New Brunswick class of 2022, with a BFA in Visual Arts. Her poetry and short stories have appeared in The Dillydoun Reveiw, The Closed Eye Open, and Room Magazine.

For the first day and a half he could pretend he hadn't noticed it starting. Like the itchy, borrowed knowledge in the back of his brain that cows lie down before a rainstorm—like Fern always said, don't want to know it'll rain? Don't look at the cows.

He kept the car radio low on those rare occasions he still had to drive, stopped wearing headphones on the subway, and started wearing them to stock shelves at work, the jack hanging loose, wire pulled through the belt loop on his jeans. And if Fern followed a little closer behind, if her put-on breathing seemed just over his shoulder? Well. Don't look at her either.

At a certain point, though, there's no stopping the weather.

"There is...a house...in New Or—"

He hooked his headphones over his ears, hiked his pants up as he walked. He kept his face turned to the road until the street player and his guitar were well out of earshot, past a Rite Aid, a Five Below, and the Tavern on Stokes. The bar was tempting, but the jukebox whir he could hear passing the door kept his feet carrying on—*"they called...the rising—"*

The corner ahead was choked off with foot traffic, and a cyclist squatting in the bike lane. The red lit walk sign held them all in place. Fern stood in the center of the little clump of bodies, between a baby carriage and two boys carrying penny boards. She was dressed for the last time he took her dancing. Red lipstick, sleek green gown and pearl lined décolletage. Her hair played to its own private, muted breeze.

He ducked around the far side, stepping down off the sidewalk and clipping his hip on the cyclist's gear shift as he brushed by. He didn't give the light time to change, facing the intersection with a flat '*don't try me*' stare. The laid-on car horns and cursing had a twang to them, almost the pickup of a guitar riff. *"...and God, I know, I'm one—"*

He thought about going home. Lying down in bed with the lights off, hitting his pen until the edges of the world dulled, and finishing off the bottle of Pink Whitney stashed beneath his mattress. But there was his mother to think of. His sister. And the little guy, too. He wouldn't bring this on them again

Two blocks down and a left turn brought him to the parking deck. This early in the afternoon it sat vacant. Just him and Fern—barefoot now, and in sleepwear. Her eyes were backlit, gleaming out of every shadow.

His mother's car was on the second level, a Honda from the '90s. She'd bought it used four years back, trying to cut down on Lyft fees, and time spent walking alone at night. He pulled up the family chat. *Taking the car for a road trip.* He waited until the screen read *Delivered*, then set cellular status to *off*. His sister would be pissed. His mother...was better not to think on. They'd both have four days to come around towards forgiveness.

The spare key was taped behind the front license plate. He dropped his useless phone into the cupholder, backed carefully out of the space. Driving never seemed to get any easier.

He figured it was just one of those things that had to be taught young. Otherwise you spend the rest of your life approaching it with the strained intentionality of a new language.

He didn't touch the radio dials. Not even when the song started up, faint and full of static.

"My father was a gamblin' man, down in New Orleans"

Ten miles down 206 the static had all but bled out. The volume, to contrast, had grown with every turn of the tires. It was loud enough now that he was catching glares at stoplights. He kept his chin high, leveled back a long look through his lashes. Still, his top lip was starting to chap where he'd been worrying it with his teeth. His palms left sweat prints on the wheel. City driving was hard, sure, but at least it wasn't personal.

There was something sheltering about a city skyline, the way the buildings came up to cradle the street. A veritable fortress. The cozy crunch of urban infrastructure had fallen away over an hour ago, replaced by rolling yellow pastures, and far too much sky.

The people, too, kept him on edge. This far into hick country he stuck out, an outlier in the land of white farmers and white housewives.

He turned on Powell, side street cramped as ever. The radio calmed just enough to hear gravel grinding as he hugged the curb too tight. He pulled into the shoulder and rocked to a stop.

It was an empty stretch of bleached gray asphalt lined on either side by wheat. Wind rippled across the swaying yellow sea. There was the telephone pole—wrapped in wilted pink ribbons, a bedraggled teddy bear still tied below its limp, weather-beaten arms. And there, toeing the cracked pavement edge, was Fern.

If she'd had her thumb out she'd have looked like any other hitchhiker. Her wind-teased, tangled copper hair, black flannel tied above her midriff, bralette peeking through undone buttons. Her jeans rode low on her hips. They were torn out at the knees, and rolled to cuffs above the pull straps of her cowboy boots.

She still wore her dorm key. It hung from a cord around her neck. He watched her through the windshield, the glint of a bronzy key blade flashing as she pretended to breathe.

He stretched over the center console and popped the passenger lock.

"I'm not your fucking valet, alright? You can get your own door."

He held his breath, she held his gaze. Eric Burdon still crooning on the radio was the only thing not in stalemate.

Then the radio crackled. The song skipped, restarted with a buzzing mechanical whine. Fern was in the passenger seat. Her back was a bowstring line, her hands sat stiff on her thighs, above the torn edge of denim. A constellation of moles marked the knee closest to him, a coin-sized bruise blooming from the ball of it.

"You're early."

He shifted the gear back to drive and pushed the gas pedal down. The radio volume raised just enough to be heard over the engine.

"It's not the anniversary," she said, more obstinate now, "you're early."

"You started on your shit earlier this year."

"Last year you were late."

He bit hard on the inside of his cheek. Over the road ahead the sky was deepening to a rich, cornflower blue. March meant a 6 p.m. sunset. He pressed the gas a little harder: he wanted as many miles behind them as he could get before then.

"I don't understand why you're still angry." Fern's voice permanently lay along a register of monotones. This one was low in her throat, somewhere around the range of *annoyed*. "You're the one who made us late."

"You came in my fucking house, Fee! Of course I'm pissed at you."

She shrugged, or at least made a stiff approximation. "I haunt you always. House, no house, what's the difference?"

"My siblings live there, man. It's different."

The radio cut. He glanced towards her, and found her staring back.

"I would never hurt them."

He believed that. Whether it was couldn't or wouldn't, she hadn't caused any real harm in the last six years. At least, not directly. Even so, hearing Fern's heralding song drift out from under his sister's bedroom door had twisted a knot in his stomach.

"Doesn't matter, I don't want you near them."

"Well. Some things never change."

A part of him really wanted to have that argument again. To give in to the pressing *what do you mean by that?* and let things devolve from there. Instead he spun the radio volume dial. Pointless as it was.

"Just play your music, Fee. Stop tryna start shit."

***

It had been his favorite song once. Of course, Fern knew that. They'd only been about three months in, still tentative and mostly undefined when it first came up. She'd been on aux, legs swung over her dorm bed's headboard while she flicked through a *"dad rock"* playlist. It was hard to picture now, the way her eyes had lit. He could remember loving that look, though. Half the things he'd confessed to her had been for the sheer enjoyment of watching her squirrel the knowledge away. The way she treasured each easy admission.

That the song now made him nauseous was undoubtedly why Fern picked it. She'd handled his heart carefully back then, but she knew how to twist a knife.

"There is... a house...in New Orleans,"

Fern swayed along. It looked less like dancing, and more like her head might be too heavy for her neck, lilting her from side to side.

"You can't possibly be enjoying this."

The swaying paused, leaving her stuck with her neck at an odd angle, "I like car rides."

"I meant the song."

"I don't know. I guess I don't really *'enjoy'* anything anymore." She tipped her head the other way. Her hair brushed the center console, "It doesn't bother me though."

The *not like it does you* was left implied.

They were on 295. Daylight had sunk from the sky, and the road was cast in blue. Traffic stayed sparse. He tried to be grateful for the easy drive.

Fern was starting to make herself comfortable, slouching in increments until she could tuck her knees against the dash. It was that way every year. The gradual loosening as they drove. In some ways he preferred the initial...wrongness. It kept him in the present.

He rolled his shoulders back, shaking out the tension. "So, can we talk?"

"Uh oh." She pursed her lips, "I don't remember liking what comes after that."

"Fee." She smiled. Sort of. For a second, at least, he could see her teeth. "We're gonna need to establish some ground rules on the music crap."

Fern sunk further into her chair. She drew her knees up towards where her arms were folded across her chest. "You tried to ignore me last year."

Sometimes the years between twenty and twenty-six felt like lifetimes. Every year the gulf between their ages grew. He wondered when Fern would start to look like a child to him. He wondered who that would hurt more.

"Yeah, I know, and I'm sorry about that." The radio popped. "Honestly, I am!"

He stopped at a yellow; other cars rolled past them as they waited for it to turn red. He put his hand on the back of Fern's seat. She was pushing her tongue into the inside of her cheek, her face tight.

"I promise. I won't do it again." He sighed, "Just...you can't be starting a week early. It throws a lot of shit off for me."

"What's your proposed solution?"

"Just go back to starting the day before. I'll get the message."

"And if you decide to ignore me again?"

A honk from behind alerted him to the changed light. He flipped the car off as it swerved past them.

"You can trust me."

The radio went static, and when the song came back on it was playing again from the beginning. *There is...a house...in New Orleans.* As far as he could tell, that was the closest Fern could get to a laugh.

"Maybe you should just focus on the road for a while."

***

It was half past one in the morning when he blinked his eyes a second and woke up in the wrong lane.

"Mother fuck—"

A semi's horn blared as he yanked the wheel to the right. He was breathing hard, his heartbeat thrumming in his fingertips.

"Maybe you should start looking for a motel," Fern said. She'd changed at some point into a band t-shirt—some DIY underground group she'd probably dragged him to basement shows for. Her key was now on a loop of yarn tied to her belt, and her Docs were on the dash.

"I'm fine."

"Sure. I guess it would be kinda funny if we both died in car accidents."

"Oh, are we calling yours an *accident* now?"

If she had a response for that he didn't catch it. He pressed his forehead to the steering wheel and let the air out through his teeth.

"You can't blame me for this forever."

"Who says this is blame?"

He tightened his hands at ten and two. "The fuck would you call it then?"

"Maybe it's love," she said, chipping black flecks of polish from her nails, "I loved you at one point, this could be what love looks like now."

Somehow that was worse than blame. Fern shrugged. "Or maybe it's just another terrible, tragic thing that happened, in a life already oversaturated with terrible tragedies."

"Your life, or mine?"

"Both. Neither."

"Fuck you."

"I wish you had."

The radio whined. He ran a hand down his face, pushing his bangs back from his eyes, "Shit. Fee—"

"—And it's been...the ruin...of many a poor boy," volume blasted up to thirty-five. Conversation over. He tried to sit up straighter, to will the blurs of yellow and green in front of him into mile markers and headlight. The music had droned to white noise by that point, even the increased volume hadn't helped. He started scanning for any signs of an upcoming motel.

***

Fern ended up being the one to find it—noting the sign while he was busy pinching his thigh to stay alert. It was instinct to thank her with a pat on the knee, and he tried to hide the recoil when his palm met cold skin.

It was the Holly Motel. Holly Hotel would've sounded better. Fern pointed that out in the parking lot, but *hotels* were for people who don't pack boxes in department store stockrooms.

The clerk came out from a back office when they got to the front desk. She had eyebags under blonde bangs, and looked less than thrilled to be talking to him (and somehow even *less* thrilled when "House of the Rising Sun" started playing over the intercom), but she took his card without fuss. Fern followed the receptionist as she retrieved their key, trailing stiff fingers down her cheek. He wanted to tell her off, but there was no point. Not like the girl could feel it anyway.

They ended up in room seven. His phone speaker nearly blew out when he put the key in the door, so at least Fern found it funny.

The carpet felt a little grainy once he'd kicked his shoes and socks off. There was a framed print of a heron hanging above the double bed. He kept his t-shirt on but dropped the jeans, then lay down on top of the covers. Fern was floating a few feet down from the ceiling, lying back in the air to let her legs flutter.

"The front desk girl was pretty."

He pushed up onto his elbows. "Okay?"

"Didn't you think she was pretty?" He couldn't see her face, just her long hair dangling.

"Fucking—come on, Fee. Cut it out."

It had been a long time since he'd looked with the intention of finding anyone pretty. With the last girl who'd loved him a permanent figment in his peripheral vision.

He took his phone out of his pocket, turned cellular back on and waited for the messages to come through. He could guess what most of them would say—Are you seeing things again? Are you drunk? Are you high? Is your head fucking cracked?

He checked the last received for each contact. From his mother it was, "Baby if you need help we can find another program." From his sister, slightly less gentle, "I fucking can't with you. If you're dead I'll hate you forever." He shut it off again without responding to either.

He rolled over, buried his face into a scratchy pillow case and closed his eyes.

***

Another hour saw him lying on his back, hands crossed over his stomach. It was hard to see Fern beyond a dark shape drifting near the corner.

"Your note blamed me."

His phone was on the nightstand. The song still played from it, but hardly any louder than the radiator. His eyes were starting to itch. Shutting them brought him no closer to sleep, though.

"What?"

"In the car you said you didn't blame me. Your note said otherwise."

"I didn't see it that way."

Whether she meant the conversation or the note she didn't specify.

"You know what I don't get?"

"Taxes."

"What? No—"

"Therapy."

"Stop it, no." He brought his arms up over his face, "Why would you write a note at all if you were going to do it as a car crash?"

Fern landed at the foot of his bed. The mattress didn't shift to accommodate her weight. He could see her a little better though, in the crack of streetlight coming through the blinds, just a sliver of silver tracing the outline of her head.

"I'm not sure I understand the question."

"I mean it would have looked like an accident, right? Without the note?" He pinched his lips together, "Why not just...let it be that."

She sat in perfect stillness for a while, considering. He found himself making his own breathing shallow to match the statue set of her shoulder.

"For closure, I think."

He sat up, "How was a letter supposed to give us closure?"

The speaker on his phone flared, popped like a gunshot. The song vibrated.

"Fuck—What?" He caught himself on the nightstand just short of tumbling out of bed.

Fern shrugged, "It's funny. That's all."

"What's funny?"

"How my whole life became, in an instant, just another bad thing that's happened to you."

His hand drifted towards her, but he snatched it away before it reached.

"I didn't mean—"

"It was closure for me, not anyone else," she said, "I had things left to air out."

"Is that why you're still...around, then? Still got something on your mind?"

Fern tipped back, disappearing over the lip of the bed, then buoyed up again toward the ceiling.

"Not right now. Maybe ask me again in the morning."

***

He woke to a full face of afternoon sun, and the sinking feeling they were going to be late for checkout.

He showered, which only made pulling on yesterday's jeans feel worse, and cursed his lack of foresight in not picking up a toothbrush. His whole mouth was fuzzy, and rubbing his teeth with a wet paper towel only went so far.

The woman at reception this time was older, mid-sixties, with a broad face and soft hands. He stuck his tongue out at Fern while she had her back to them. Fern made a show of pretending not to see.

There was only one other car still parked when they stepped outside, and it looked like they were also packing to go. A man struggling to fold down a double-seated stroller, and a boy with a bowl cut running laps around the car, mindful to step around the occupied baby carrier at his father's feet.

Icy fingers closed around the cuff of his jacket. Fern was watching the children with distant, pained eyes. The father was nearly mangling the stroller now, biting off curses under his breath. He looked back to Fern, then to the family again. He sighed.

"Need any help with that?"

The man looked wary, watching him approach, but he was used to that this far south. The man looked between his two kids and the awkwardly balanced stroller, and seemed to decide it was worth the risk.

"S'pose I could use the extra hands."

He knelt down to look for the release button on the bottom seat.

"So what brings ya out to Knoxville?"

He popped the bottom seat loose and set it off to the side, then started on the adaptors. Fern was sitting cross legged in front of the baby carriage. She ran her pointer finger along the knuckles of his curled little fist. The baby's blueberry eyes were locked on her face. She sometimes had that effect on infants, like maybe they could see her too.

"A road trip. It's an annual thing."

"My boys and I are on a road trip ourselves."

Fern was making noises for the child now, a sort of melodic cooing. It took him a second to realize she was trying to hum, vaguely in the tune of "You Are My Sunshine."

He stood and lifted the stroller's folding joint, then flipped the locks around the frame. He pushed it over for inspection. Fern, seeing the job was done, leaned down to press her face to the baby's forehead. She held there for a moment before standing to go.

"I really appreciate the help."

"No problem, man. Have a good one."

Fern followed him back to the car without complaint. He opened the passenger door for her and pretended to be checking his glove compartment as she climbed in.

"Got your baby fix for the rest of the drive?" he said, trying not to look at her. Fern had always been so good with kids. She would've made a good mom. They'd talked a lot about it at the time, how different they'd be from their own parents, how ready they'd always been for the tantrums and the bad days.

He turned the key in the ignition and left the motel parking lot behind.

***

As soon as her mood improved Fern started whining about breakfast. He wanted to refuse on principle—*you don't actually eat, Fee*, but the rumbling of his own stomach forced capitulation. He went through the drive through at a Culver's. He ordered chicken fingers, and fries, which he put in the passenger cup holder for Fern to sniff at.

She was fully lounging in her seat—elbow propped on the center console, one foot on the upholstery. He rolled down the window so she could hang out her other leg. With anyone else he'd have worried about it catching on something, but that wasn't really an issue for Fern.

"I'm pretty sure you're not supposed to sit like that in a dress."

"No one can see me but you, what does it matter?"

"Maybe I don't want to see your panties either. Ever think of that?"

"Prude."

She was in a red cotton scrap that could generously be called a sundress, and a decidedly familiar lightweight bomber.

"That's not your jacket."

Fern shrugged, "You threw it out when I died. It might as well be now."

She sniffed at her fries again, touched one to the tip of her tongue. By the face she pulled it wasn't as satisfying as she'd hoped.

"Do you remember the chicken fingers we got when we drove to PA?"

"Oh my god," he laughed, "that was somehow the best chicken I've had in my life."

The radio crackled, Fern tipped her head back with a smile. "Fucking PA chicken."

"And I wasn't even high!"

"I would've killed you if you were."

He merged into the left lane, cool air from the open window fluttering through his hair. "I wasn't about to smoke before meeting your sister. Give me some credit."

"My friends always said I gave you far too much."

There was the echo of a sting there, dulled by a lack of surprise. He remembered their old dorm parties, sitting at Fern's desk chair with her in his lap, trailing his fingers over her sides and catching her around the middle when she doubled over laughing. The way her friends would politely avoid eye contact, then tactfully cap his drinks at two. He didn't go to the funeral. He figured the only person there who might've ever actually wanted him around was already ash in an urn.

***

He parked on North Rampart Street and walked to the cemetery. The trees they passed along the way were hung with thousands of strung plastic beads. It was just past four when they reached the wrought iron gates, the cemetery closed for the night. The filigree was easy for his sneakers to find purchase on as he boosted himself up and over. He nearly rolled an ankle, though, dropping off the other side.

Fern watched with a smile, arms crossed over her chest. While he was dusting grave dirt from the knees of his jeans she stepped up to the gate and put her hand to the metal. With a squeal they swung open. She stepped inside.

"The fuck, Fee!"

She turned her palms up, "It's like I've got a house key, I guess. It wouldn't have worked for you."

They walked, winding through the raised tombs. Bodies were

buried above ground here, Fern told him once, to keep the coffins from floating. She, of course, didn't have a real grave. Dust to dust and all that.

"If your ashes sorta blew away, why is this your...resting place?"

She pursed her lips and hummed. "Maybe they didn't get very far."

Their jackets brushed, hers still rustled like real fabric moving against his.

"Did you want it to be this graveyard?"

"I just asked to be brought to New Orleans in the note," she said, "I don't know who had to actually pick the place."

"If you *had* picked?"

"Scattered over the Mardi Gras parade, for sure."

He snickered, "For sure."

She led them over to one of the tombs. Marie Laveau, according to the plaque, which sat in stone above a planting urn of blue flowers. The stone was scratched in x marks, clustered in threes. He sat with his back to the grave and Fern sat down in front of him, the curve of her spine between his shins. She was warm, her ribs expanding with each breath. He spread his legs and let her slot herself between them. Her back to his chest, head tucked under his chin.

"She was called the Voodoo Queen."

"Hmm?"

Fern gestured absently behind them, grazing his cheek in the process, "The woman buried here. They say she can still grant wishes. It was on my list of things to see when we came together."

He wrapped his arms around her and squeezed. Her hands settled over his. There were so many places he'd promised to take her. New Orleans was the big one, of course, but then there'd been the beach (his promise on the worst of her bad days. *Don't be like that—I'll take you to the beach! Who could be sad at the beach?*), and the Met, and one nearly blackout drunk vow to take her little sister to Disney World. He ducked his chin, buried his face in the crown of her hair.

"I never wanted to hurt you, Fee."

"Oh. But you were so good at it."

His eyes felt tight. He squeezed them shut, breathed through his nose. One hand slotted just under Fern's jaw. The other, around her waist, she intertwined her fingers with, and ran her thumb over the back in soft circles. She leaned into the hand around her neck.

"Why did you leave me?"

He kissed the side of her head, let his mouth linger, "Could ask you the same question."

"You left first."

"I had a lot going on...it was complicated." A laugh heaved out of him, and the dam behind his eyes cracked, "I thought you'd be better off."

She reached up to run her knuckles below his lashes.

"I wasn't."

"Yeah, I get that *now!*"

He bowed over her, absorbing her body into his as he shook. He was too tired to be embarrassed to cry. She molded into his hold, locked her arms over his, shushing and soothing and letting him pull her close. His mouth was over her forehead now, dark hair tickling her face, but she made no move to push him away.

"It's not my fault. It's not my fucking fault."

"I know," she said, "I never meant it to be."

"I didn't fucking kill you, Fee."

"I know."

She turned into the hand on her jaw and kissed the palm. Her warm, dry mouth against his calluses. Then she took the one from her stomach, where their fingers were linked, and kissed the back. She pet at the nape of his neck, and trailed fingers over his arms until he felt like he could breathe again.

When all but the trembling had subsided, she pointed to the horizon, just visible through backlit monoliths. Pink clouds were drifting over the setting sun.

"My mom used to call that the sun's pink blanket," she said. "When I was really little, she'd pretend the sun was tucking itself in for bed."

"You must miss her." His throat was raw.

Fern rubbed her thumb across the ball of his wrist.

"Yes. It seems I do."

"I'm sorry."

"That's not your fault either."

Her head lolled onto his shoulder. She turned in, kissed his clavicle.

"I think it's almost time."

The phone speaker hummed, nearly mournful, *oh mothers...tell your children...not to do what I have done*. He kissed her forehead, then her crown. He held her as close as he could. When the sun slipped below the sea of graves she whispered his name against the back of his hand, and was gone.

"See you soon." He would. It was never very long before she started to pop up again. A head of copper hair in a crowd, the flash of a green dress, the figment drifting closer and closer across the year.

His knees popped as he stood, stretching his back experimentally. He gave a pat to Ms. Laveau's tomb. It crossed his mind to leave behind an x or three of his own, to ask for a wish, but he couldn't think of anything worth wishing for. Not anything a dead woman could do for him, anyway. He started the walk back towards his car. It would be a long drive. Longer still without the radio, his ears ringing in the silence.

The Soundtrack of Your Life

Lesley Morrison

Lesley Morrison lives and works in New York City, dreaming of an eventual escape to somewhere with palm trees. She dabbles in speculative fiction and has a tendency to be a bit obsessive about certain authors, series, shows or games. Her short stories have appeared in Canadian magazines TransVersions and On Spec, The New School's DIAL Magazine in NYC, PIF magazine and a horror anthology "From the Yonder II."

"So when someone's wife had a baby, why was he hearing 'We Are the Champions' instead of 'Morning Has Broken,' or 'Hallelujah,' or some soaring instrumental bullshit?"

"'We are the Champions' is top of list for favorite song for 'winning,'" Kiran says, his doe eyes reproachful. "We are fine-tuning the algorithm, but micro-expressions are harder to quantify for happiness. Human response to–"

Felix cuts him off. "Yes, yes, we know, the mod response covers fifteen levels all the way from ennui to heartbreak, but we need to keep tweaking on the other end, even if most of these music lovers are bored depressives."

About a dozen of us, the tech team plus my two-person marketing team, are sitting around a long table in one of the many conference rooms on our floor in the Winchester building near the Chelsea piers. The rooms are along the east side of the building with floor-to-ceiling glass and a view of lower midtown, the Empire State building rising behind the sun-warmed orange and yellow brick backs and sides of the warehouses that block the first line of sight. From this height, the city is calm; the only movement is the occasional familiar tiny sparkle, sunlight on a passing drone moving between buildings. It's a respite from our windowless work area.

Felix, the project lead, is beating up on Kiran, the tech lead. I've been trying to figure out Felix's pattern, some days he is cajoling and some days he's much more of an asshole. He tends to wear his hair one of two ways; it's jet black and shaved on the sides with a mop that either flips forward in a relaxed wave, or gets gelled back in a solid crest. Today it's the former. My idea is that it's an indicator of his mood, but so far it's been an elusive theory.

He glares around the room. "Are you getting your feedback from everybody?"

Mine is in, but Lalla next to me shifts guiltily. Overall, our mod is working well. We've all been beta-testing and tagging responses for the tech team. There's just a final remaining problem with inconsistent responses to positive reactions: the mod gets mixed up between joy and triumph, for example, the subtler contentment of snuggling with a pet versus the self-righteous satisfaction of proving someone wrong.

After delivering the usual lecture and extracting multiple assurances from Kiran that the next series of updates will fix the issue, Felix morphs into a pleading pep talk. "Let's make this the next climate control," he finishes, referring to the mod that's held up as the aspirational goal throughout the industry. I assume everyone else is as sick of hearing this as I am.

Climate control was the first third-party leech mod to hit the market right as the Sphere's main competitor, the Protector, came out, pushing demand for both models beyond supply for months. I was doing marketing for a startup that was integrating micro-expression recognition into a mod for pharmaceutical research when we were bought out by one of the big three, and the underlying technology was split into several development paths. Someone had the bright idea that people wanted more drama in their lives and a mod that curated a personal musical soundtrack would be just the thing to do that. I'm fine with the project in general, but I miss the startup atmosphere. We all know the rug can be pulled out from under us at any moment; Felix, for all his tattoos, is from corporate.

***

Once work is over for the day, I abandon Manhattan for Brooklyn. Emerging from the subterranean depths of the subway, I squint in the late afternoon sunlight that turns the pavement into a glittering expanse of tar line crisscrossed patchwork, the haze of heat thickening the air in the narrow space between buildings and street. I enable climate control in my Sphere with a curt nod at the console that floats leeward, and bat away an ad drone that swoops too close. The opening instrumental burst of "Here Comes the Sun" that heralds my return to daylight stutters and is replaced by Tech N9ne's "Get the Fuck Out of Here." Making a mental note of the mod's abrupt mood swing, I ease into the fray on the sidewalk, threading my way between the other pedestrians, as walking becomes an intricate dance– if the approaching pedestrians are wearing a Sphere, a wider berth, if not, just enough for mine. You can tell by the slight fuzziness around the edges of the perimeter, and I slither around and between, feeling my gait adjust to the track's synth bassline and staggered rhythm. The homeless proselytizer on the corner of Metropolitan pauses his ranting to give me an appreciative leer. I give him a thumbs-up and a few extra credits in his digital cup. I'm brimming with what passes as goodwill at the moment; I am remote the rest of the week to run interviews. I stop at the bodega across the street for a six pack, setting my Sphere to pass-through with a quick twitch of my head so I can traverse the narrow aisle and get the beer from the cooler.

About the Sphere. It's everything. It's better than sliced bread. It's a personal field that surrounds you like an almost transparent egg, ranging in protective ability from basic air filtration (a necessity with the mutating corona variants, along with the requisite pollutants) to a protective weather mode that sheers off wind and rain, to hardcrack mode, which can deflect a knife or even a low velocity bullet. One of the viral early ads showed it shooting out from under a dropped grand piano, with a dummy in it, of course. It takes some getting used to when you first start wearing it; there's a certain amount of contained area that has to adjust if you change your point of gravity.

Keri, the day clerk, gives me a bored nod from within his cage, eyes briefly swiveling away from his media screen as I aim my six-pack and then my iris at the receptor. Outside again, I turn on to Union Street, towards my apartment building. The Tech N9ne song that faded into the background as I entered the bodega has now turned into some silky down-tempo electronica, music to get home by, apparently. I feel as if I'm starting to wind down, so that's okay.

Now don't get me wrong, New York City is still shit. This is no bright utopian future, clean-swept and shining; just the same old haves and have-nots, the new technology mixed in with the old, electric vehicles not polluting while the older models carry on with it. Getting all the buildings up to code will take years. And there is still a homelessness problem, an affordable housing problem, rising prices, frozen wages, rats, cockroaches, piles of garbage, bad subway service, same as it ever was. But personal comfort and safety have taken a huge step forward; that must be acknowledged. And like all technology, prices for the Sphere and its competitors have dropped until the same population that generally has the latest high-tech items has one; you can hardly walk around Williamsburg on the weekend and see anybody without one.

I let myself into my apartment building's small lobby and glance inside the mailroom. The usual clutter of packages on the floor; I kick them out of the way to check the mail. Then I stop to stab futilely at the elevator button, but it's stuck on the third floor again; I hear it chiming up there, doors opening and closing. I take the stairs, panting hard by the time I reach the seventh floor.

Inside the cool dimness of my apartment, I tell the Sphere to shut down. I shiver my way out of the backpack that carries my laptop and Sphere's battery pack, letting it slide onto a chair behind me. I am not quite ready to turn on the lights and confront whatever state I've left things in, so I open a beer and put the rest in the fridge. I take a long slow swallow, feeling the promise behind the cool prickly bitterness. My silhouette in the dresser mirror regards me in turn, face shadowed, a sturdy, compact frame, shorter than I'd like, but good hair, straight, shiny, hanging in a dark curtain to my shoulders, and good ass, so I've been told. Soon, some packet of dinner to microwave, general decision-making on cleaning myself and/or the kitchen, and then the nightly preparation begins.

To sleep. That's my dream, just to lie down and sleep. But the night has other plans. I know I do sleep; because sometimes I come to sprawled like a dead crab washed up on the beach before returning to my monotonous routine, the semaphoring limbs, the heaving groans, my eyelids autonomous flaps of muscle over my reddened eyes, reopening inexorably of their own accord so that I can fixate on the slow march of the arms of the glowing clock face on the bedside table. And now I have a new nemesis who isn't me, or my brain, or even sleep, but someone who has moved in upstairs.

***

Today is the first of a series of interviews I have to run, signing up volunteer beta-testers for our mod. The man on my screen is named Gerardo, a stolid fellow, probably mid-20s, square head with closely shaved dark hair. He lacks affect, but seems amiable enough. I introduce myself as Moira. My name is Janice but I like to mix it up. I check the input form. "You signed up through our online ad, it says here—what made you want to try our mod?"

"Well, I'm on furlough and I liked the sound of it. Timing is right." The background behind him must be his parent's house; the white wall with a line of cross-stitched flowers in round frames doesn't seem like his style.

"So the mod installs on your Sphere, and we start with some basics; some of it you give us, some of it we get from your stats, where you lived, who your influences were; you can link to any of your playlists or personal channels and that gets worked in too."

He nods. I can tell he isn't going to be one of those types with a lot of questions about privacy, AI, tracking, storage of personal data. I've got answers for all that anyway.

"I see you were brought up in Raleigh, North Carolina, joined the military and moved to Fort Bragg for basic training, and that you had an uncle who played blues guitar and took you to clubs."

I pull down the rest of his profile and send a request code to his Sphere for installation. He accepts it. "The mod is going to play you some tracks, or parts of tracks...just to get some data points, see how we're doing. Relax, you can close your eyes if you want."

Once installation is complete, I start the test script remotely. The mod has chosen "Tell Mama," an old Muddy Waters song. Gerardo's face remains impassive but at the first break point he says, "I like that." Apparently his micro-expressions have been sufficient for the mod to interpret his reaction; the readout agrees. I open my mouth to tell him about the next phase, but there's a sudden barrage of thumps from upstairs, and I automatically mute my mic, much as any New Yorker does for a passing siren.

When my upstairs neighbor first arrived, I put the tumult down to the movers: the stamping of hard-soled feet over my head in a sporadic back and forth, too unpredictable to become familiar, a suppressed violence in the force of each step, intermittently spiraling into a violent culmination of bumps that shook the walls, only to return to the pacing. At first I was perplexed by the anger in those steps. When a week had gone by, I could no longer pretend that he was still unpacking or moving furniture.

If we are both home during the day, it's infuriating, but at night, it becomes an assault. He goes to bed later and rises earlier than I do. He goes out in the evening, and I forget about him, only to be startled by the brutality of his homecoming.

I unmute; the noise has paused temporarily. "That would be fairly neutral music, maybe for when you're occupied with something familiar, like driving—music you'd enjoy while doing that."

Gerardo nods, and the script continues, pulling partial tracks from his reactions, keeping it low key, just getting his baseline profile. Once that's established we work up to some unexpected outliers based on his responses—he has a self-pitying streak—his strongest emotional response is to "Whipping Post" by the Allman Brothers Band. We arrange a callback the following week to debrief, and I explain to him that his reactions and responses to his soundtrack go into a testing database for our tech team, and how he can tag anything he finds good, bad or interesting for us to discuss in our follow-up.

***

After the beer run to the bodega and some dinner, the real work begins. I prepare carefully, my methodical ritual. The beer will be imbibed, the mindless media offerings watched until I'm in a state of relaxed stupor. Yes, yes, I know, drinking to sleep is a terrible idea, but I have already been through the rest, the breathing exercises, the meditation, the white noise, the rain noise, the ocean noise, the relaxation music, the relaxation mantras, the hypnosis, the sleep studies, the biofeedback, and finally the drugs and the resultant sleep walking, sleep eating, hangover effect, anxiety, depression, and eventual resignation.

I can bear, I have borne, the lack of sleep if I can lie there in my familiar pattern, but I can't lie there while being assailed from above; it's tough to maintain a mindset of bleak acceptance with a warm rage kindling in my core. I tried going to bed with the Sphere and using the noise cancelling feature, but the external noise is merely a distraction, not a cause, and the complete silence is claustrophobic. It makes me feel as if I'm in an isolation tank, and still sleepless. So that's where I'm at now. And it's been three months.

***

The week progresses. Another day of interviews. Everyone thinks they love music more than other people. It's a good thing for our marketing, that, and the fact that a large segment of the population is apparently bored out of their minds and searching for meaning in their daily existence.

"I have tons of my own playlists," says Annie with a stubby

unicorn horn modification on her upper brow and a halo of purple curls. "How is this better?"

She seems curious rather than argumentative. Her profile says she loves Broadway musicals and Disney movie soundtracks.

"You ever watch a movie?" I say. "You know how the soundtrack fits in with what's going on? It doesn't just play song after song. It drops out for dialogue or tense moments, it enhances the mood, or it sets the mood; it follows dramatic moments; some of it's instrumental, or orchestral, or audio effects, sometimes songs play that tie into the plot, or portray mood, or character, new songs, old songs, obscure songs, well known songs—without the soundtrack, movies would be really dull, right?"

She nods, there's nothing to disagree with there.

"And you can still have playlists, or play any song from your subscription tier of the extended catalog anytime you want. That's all included. But—" Here I like to pause for effect. "—what if you had your own soundtrack, personalized for you, based off of the best data we have, not only on you and your tastes, your background and your exposure, but from what the entire data cloud says about everyone—everyone else who responds in a similar way to a song, and how they respond to other songs—we can predict not only that you'll like a certain type of music, or song, but *when* you'll like it—what sort of mood you'd be in when you'll respond to it."

"That sounds pretty cool," she says, warming to the idea.

"And it learns with you, it's AI—it improves over time, if it ever plays anything you don't like you just let it know and it adapts."

The ability of our mod to recognize micro-expressions comes from a well-researched and peer-certified branch of research used for psychological therapy. Even if you're not depressed, our mod still has the ability to figure out how to help you feel happier and more productive. If you feel sluggish, it can play music that inspires you to get going, and so on.

"It's going to help you understand your own story," I tell her. I like to say this rather than, "It's going to make you feel as if your life has meaning."

I wish I had that answer for myself. When do things go from feeling like anything is possible into a routine that seems impossible to escape from? You don't know what you want to do, only that it isn't what you're doing. I can't even put my finger on when it changed.

Both my pitch and my reverie are interrupted by a track of purposeful stamps overhead, the creak and slam of a door, then a high-pitched keening that I realize sounds like a dog crying.

A few more days, interviews, six-packs and broken sleep patterns later, I have established there is a dog, probably a puppy, upstairs, and it is here to stay. It cries when he leaves and barks when he comes home, and now the pacing is complemented by a four-legged padding. It's a relief to go back to the office.

***

"So who is our audience?" asks Maddie, the intern. She's the newest member of our marketing team, very fresh-out-of-school and businesslike, with a crew cut and a cowlick like a rosette above her left temple. She poises expectantly, fingers on her touchpad. She's the third to join our small group; so far it's been just me and Lalla, steely gaze, long brown hair and vestiges of a Staten Island accent she tries to suppress.

We are back in one of the identical conference rooms; the view today is grey gloom, mist blocking the view and obscuring the top of the Empire State building.

I explain. "Single people, independent types, but at least people who spend a lot of time alone. We don't see a family with younger children at home as our demographic."

"Makes sense," Maddie says, fingers tapping crisply. We are onboarding Maddie this week, getting her up to speed on the project and ready to work with Lalla on poking through the testing data for marketing ideas.

We settled on a name for the mod the week before last. I am still pleased with what I came up with, the Soundtrack of Your Life, or SOYL, and the logo idea, rounding out the Y to a U shape and dropping the descender down to a line under the rest of the acronym. There was some initial argument for Soundtrack of *My* Life from Felix, but it died quickly once I pointed out that with my suggestion we could call it the SOUL Mod. The idea had gone straight to Design, and would be ready in time for the pre-rollout marketing.

After our marketing meeting, the tech meeting. We move into an identical conference room two doors down. Although I feel for them, tech is not my problem. Happy to give the feedback, then it's their problem. The onsite tech team is seated around the table, and Felix is beating up on Kiran again over the updates. Today his hair is gelled back and he's still being an asshole, but I'm not ready to give up on my theory.

"Themes." Felix turns and fixes on me, catching me off guard. "We need a marketing plan."

My eyebrows rise before I can stop them. I'm still neck deep in pre-rollout, plus I have to follow up with all my beta-testers.

"Doesn't matter," he says, as I open my mouth. "We stay one step ahead. Next rollout after deployment is personalized themes. I need the first draft by Monday."

I drag myself back to the work area. That means working this weekend. My mod pensively introduces "Dear Mr. Fantasy," echoing my despondency. It fades out on the second verse as Lalla starts in on a beta tester story.

"So my user says he doesn't want to hear creepy music when he goes down to the basement, and I'm trying to explain that when that happens in a movie it's for the audience, but now the soundtrack is just for him. I mean, if he's on a rollercoaster ride it could enhance it, but if he's really scared it's not going to scare him more. We go back and forth, he keeps adding more scenarios, like what if he's all alone in an alley at night and someone is following him, what if his brakes fail when he's driving down a winding road, but he finally gets it."

I smile along with her, but Mr. Fantasy creeps back when the conversation is done. Nonetheless, I nudge my laptop to life, create a new ad package, wait for all the templates to load, title it THEMES, and open the notes panel.

My mod introduces a tight little percussion track—it's subtle, but I have to be impressed with the no-nonsense, let's-get-to-work vibe.

I type randomly, brainstorming. *Imagine. Your own theme. Personalized for you. Built from your SOUL profile.* Maybe better to emphasize that *they* build it.

Themes you create. Themes that grow with you. Themes that change with you. Themes for what and who is important to you.

Scratch that. *Themes for what's important to you. Themes for who's important to you.*

I sneak a glance into the lab on the way to the bathroom. Joel is in today. I've had my eye on him for a while. One of these days I'll see if he wants to get a drink after work.

I actually do have some sort of dating life, or I did. I tend to be a serial crusher, getting infatuated with one man at a time, and then taking it upon myself to initiate something. It's more than how someone looks, and I don't have a type. Usually something they say piques my interest, and then I find myself making up personalities for them that turn out to be more compelling than the real thing. Or so the trend goes. If I don't lose interest first, they seem to find my expectations peculiar and inflexible, and after some negotiations they bow out, and I move on to the next one.

What was it Joel said? He had been on the phone, arguing patiently with one of the offshore developers when I was in the lab talking to Kiran until the rise in his voice caught my attention.

"It would work if we fixed it?" he was saying incredulously. Amused, I'd looked over and decided I liked the looks of him, lanky body and Mediterranean complexion. He wore his hair a bit long, in loose dark curls. He had seen my glance and grimaced back his frustration, which animated his normally serious face with all sorts of interesting lines.

Wary of prior misjudgments, I've been letting this one sit for a while, but my take is that he's shy and a bit lonely, work is the most important thing to him, and that he needs to be drawn out.

But right now I need a marketing plan, and as usual, I'm exhausted. I focus my waning energy. I just need a foundation to work from. By Monday I need short blurbs, slogans, and longer descriptions. Also an executive summary, a project sub-plan, a timeline, proposed media channels and release dates. But the latter are templates I need to fill in; that's just time, it's the ideas that don't come out of thin air. They need time to percolate.

After a couple of hours, I have enough to consider it a start. My mod settles into a relaxed beat, some instrumental Ska which morphs into Bad Manners' "Walking in the Sunshine" as I prepare to leave the office. That one I have to check the credits for. I haven't heard it before, but it seems to mirror my sense of relief. I tag it to report back to Kiran. The lab is empty, they've already left, so no drinks tonight, which is probably just as well.

Oh, I figured out who is living upstairs. I saw a heavy-jowled, stubble-faced brute complete with sports jacket and baseball cap in the mail room with a small dog, some sort of Shepherd mix, brown with black points, trailing him on a leash. And all too soon, what began as the soft padding became a louder romping, and as the beast gained size and strength, those legs beat a rapid tattoo over my head from one side of the room to the other.

It makes sense. If the owner can put that much angry force into his steps, that energy will rub off on the dog. When he leaves, the dog howls and cries. When he comes home, it barks unceasingly and gallops around like a demented pony.

I complain to the management company. They say they'll speak to him. It doesn't help. I thump on the ceiling when it starts up in the middle of the night, but I finally give up, as it just makes me angrier and it takes longer to relax afterwards. I bear it with icy resolve during the day, but at night, my anger turns to fantasies of homicidal ideation—you know, like suicidal ideation. You don't want to do it yourself, but if someone else was to do it, that would be fine. Or maybe an accident? An accident would be good, too. Maybe some scaffolding could fall on both of them. Could one weaken it? Too many cameras, and timing would be critical. How about carbon monoxide? That would be quiet, at least, but would involve tubing, and the drilling of holes, not to mention a source for the gas. Murder is hard these days; especially murder that looks like an accident. Between all the security cams and drones, handhelds, digital tracking and personal field protection, it's almost impossible. But you can't stop a girl from dreaming, can you?

I know his name now, too. Bradley Wosinski. I get his mail sometimes, and take gratification in tossing it out.

* * *

Work is meetings and more meetings, with plenty of time wasted fluffing the executives, most recently with a series of demos of the proposed ad series, just our logo and the launch date, meant to mysteriously titillate, along with the endless rejiggering of my executive whitepaper for the Themes rollout, which Felix just can't leave alone, having me change it one way and then another until it's back where it started.

I follow up with my beta-testers, making sure they're happy with the results they're getting. Gerardo missed his last check-in, but when I bring up his profile it's deactivated. Kiran is walking by in the hallway, so I call out to him.

"Do you know what happened to Gerardo, that guy from Raleigh?" My mod, which has been gamely playing Skillrex in an attempt to keep me focused, fades the volume back.

"He's off the project," he says, then stops and comes over to my desk. He adds in a low voice, "I was going to tell you. Actually he's been accused of murder." At his words, my mod surges to a brutal dubstep drop in tandem with my stomach, and goes silent.

"I guess he thought his girlfriend was cheating on him. When the police got his Sphere disabled before picking him up, I got an alert that the mod's access had been blocked, so I did a quick search and saw some local news reports."

"That's horrible." I picture his lack of affect during our interactions. Should I have sensed something?

***

Gerardo is on my mind a lot this week. Felix brings the event up briefly at a meeting and says that although it's very tragic, it's something that's bound to happen now and then within our customer base, as they're made up of the general population. "Maybe if he'd had a mod for monitoring his mental state it could have helped, but we'll never know for sure."

After that it feels kind of like bad taste to talk about it, although I want to talk about it. I want to be absolved for not seeing that he was fucked up, though I don't know what I could have done. I need comforting, but tonight Lalla is going home to babysit her niece, and Maddie is staying late to finish something. It may be time to check in with Joel about that drink. The bar scene in this area is not to my taste but there's a legitimate dive nearby that is generally quiet enough to at least have a conversation, with a pairing of intimate stools between the wait station and the grimy window at the end of the bar. I picture confessing my guilt about Gerardo and getting the necessary reassurances: Joel gazing into my eyes with sympathy and understanding, and after a couple of beers, our knees brushing, casually at first, then with a firm pressure.

And a mere five minutes later, I'm heading home, trying not to feel humiliated. Joel has plans. He said it nicely, but he didn't take a raincheck, either.

"Guess I got...what I deserved..." The mod has selected Badfinger's "Baby Blue," which is melancholy enough, but I find the first line offensive. "Fuck you," I snarl, and the mod breaks off, silent for a few long moments before easing into a series of gloomy drawn out chords from a string quartet, a quavering digital digeridoo bass holding the root.

The tech team's latest upgrade to tweak the mod's upper-end emotional response is deploying over the weekend. We're all to report back about any results, but it's hard to intend to have a strong feeling of satisfaction. In fact, I plan on *not* having one anytime soon.

***

The dog upstairs gains size and strength daily. It's holding its own as far as the amount of racket it produces. The lonely howling has ruined the time in the evening when I'm accustomed to winding down. Being awake is not quite like being awake anymore, it's like a dream, or a drugged haze. I go through the necessary motions automatically: showering, dressing, getting on the train, saving my last bits of brain power for work. I haven't called my parents in weeks or gone to one of my neighborhood bars for even longer. I can't put on any sort of social facade beyond what's necessary for work, and that's taking everything I have.

Also, I think my mod is fucking with me. It's playing sadder songs all the time. I mean, I found tears on my cheeks yesterday during Debussy's "Rêverie." I'm just so tired. And I keep thinking about Gerardo.

One night as I'm leaving late, I see Kiran's light still on in the lab. I almost don't bother, but somehow my body propels me in, and I roll a chair over next to him. I ask him to bring up Gerardo's last week of data. It takes a while. The testing data records all the personal tags on beta-testers, in production the data will be anonymized. Kiran correlates time and date with the soundtrack and overlays the emotional response data. He scrolls through the week. The music gets angrier, switching to a steady stream of old punk in the last few days: Black Flag, Sex Pistols, Dead Kennedys, culminating with GG Allin and the Murder Junkies' "I'll Slice Yer Fucking Throat."

"I guess this is when he did it," Kiran says, pointing at the graph, which spikes to an extreme level of response, then falls to almost nothing. After the named tracks stop, the data dissolves into something called Koka's Soundtrack Box No. 1. We download it and listen. It seems to be a series of strange and random atmospheric audio effects, played by the AI behind the mod. There's a sense of release in it, but otherwise it's devoid of any emotion.

We look at each other. The lab is silent, only the sporadic twangs of something like a door stopper spring being plucked. Kiran's dark eyes are troubled.

Hesitantly I say, "So...what happens when someone is going to do something wrong? If they have a SOUL mod, is that going to feed off their reactions...help legitimize what they're thinking? Maybe it gives them that last little push?"

He shakes his head. "I don't know. They can do what they want with or without the mod. They could still play any music they want, right?"

***

Final deployment is here, then the official launch of our mod the day after. We have to be in the office by noon and stay until it's done. I have no hope of getting much sleep as it's already late. I'm just getting off the train, and I still need to wind down. My nemesis will be coming in late and getting up early. The dog will be intermittently howling and pacing. And I am mortally tired.

My evening is laid out before me, my night as well. And all the nights after that. The imagined relief of a successful rollout is already overshadowed by the knowledge that after this rollout comes the Themes rollout, and then the one after that, and the one after that. All I know is that something has to give, something has to matter. Portentously, my mod plays "Tristan and Isolde," the insistent strains demanding some sort of resolution that feels beyond my grasp.

I get my beer and head home. The streets are quiet now; the darkness sucks the color from the parked cars and awnings, turning the building bricks and painted storefronts to shades of grey. A few spots of warmth and light from windows of occasional bars and restaurants don't beckon me in. I am outside of all that.

Now my mod eases into "Dead Souls" by Joy Division, and I walk in step as it builds into the full strength of the refrain, perfectly embodying my overwhelming sense of futility. I feel like some great beast of the plains, plodding on in the face of a driving blizzard, snow up to my hocks.

The chance comes so easily, so naturally, it's barely an intention. There is the dog, running around the lobby, barking hysterically, leash streaming behind it, and the partial view of a grey sweatshirted figure in the mailroom, burrowing through the packages. Easy to put my Sphere on pass-through, open the door, fumble my way in, keeping it from the automatic close with my backpack, my eyes up as the dog dashes out through the sudden opening, still barking, while my nemesis turns, his mouth a round o of alarm. Easy to slowly rotate as he shoves by me, flinging the door wide, my pose one of surprised dismay, to catch a last glimpse of the dog as it tears into the street between two parked cars, to see him throw himself after it, his body twisting gracelessly as he maneuvers the narrow passage between the cars. Easy to put my hand to my mouth as I hear the screech of brakes, a heavy, satisfying thud, and a bystander's shriek. Time freezes for a heartbeat; I feel my senses struggling to connect. Then I hear the barking, which I realize has never stopped, recede into the distance, and I am flooded with a sensation I barely recognize, a lightness that feels almost like floating. Inside my Sphere, the triumphant chorus of "We are the Champions" starts up. Reflexively, I tag it for Kiran.

Last Letter First

Kristina Ten

Kristina Ten's stories have appeared in Lightspeed, Nightmare, Fantasy, Split Lip, Passages North, Weird Horror, and elsewhere. She is a graduate of Clarion West Writers Workshop and the University of Colorado Boulder's MFA program in Creative Writing. Born in Moscow, she has lived most of her life in the U.S., in the company of mischievous dogs, melodramatic plants, and bookshelves full of fairy tales.

Duri begins. "Category is..."

On their way to the Nova satellite colony, three hundred miles from home in Earth's low orbit, Duri and Margosha play a game to pass the time. It's an old game, one their society has largely forgotten—more sophisticated amusements are invented every day. This one is simple, boring even. It's a relic of another age, before flashy graphics cards and total-immersion headsets, before massively multiplayer networks, before the proliferation of wires and screens.

Of course, these old things have a way of coming back to us when we need them.

Margosha waits for the boredom the game promised to set in. Before launch, the pilot announced that their projected travel time was just over four days—they got a suboptimal slot, screwed up the matching trajectories, and now there's a debris field to circumnavigate—but she's certain she and Duri have been playing for months, years, decades, centuries. She longs to be bored, for that one feeling to drape a heavy blanket over her other feelings. Namely anticipation. Namely terror. Namely dread.

Drape a heavy blanket over them and kiss them goodnight. Tell them to hush, go to sleep now.

"Animals," Margosha offers, and there's that stupid shake in her voice. She thinks about blaming it on the airbus's rocky suspension, a way to save face in front of her new seatmate. But the truth is Margosha didn't know a thing about suspension systems back on Earth—or alternators, transmissions, carburetors, spark plugs. She was always setting off her auto shop's dumbass-city-girl detector, too, always getting taken for a ride. The techs could tell just by looking at her. Another dumbass city girl, barely passed her driving test, got a used clunker just to go with her cousins, twice a year, to the wineries upstate.

So up here in the cramped passenger airbus, everything more alien than it's ever been, feels like a bad time to start playing mechanic.

Besides, it's actually been pretty smooth since they broke through the stratosphere.

"Good one," Duri says. "Animals, animals..." She chews the ends of her straight black hair, considering her next move, and when she pulls her mouth away, the strands are a bright, lemony yellow. Duri must have one of those color-changing mods, Margosha realizes, the new moisture-activated one from J&J. The ads light up the buildings on her way to work each morning. Mousy-haired girls transformed while running through sprinklers. Graying women whose hair goes all psychedelic Roy G. Biv jamboree when they're dancing in the rain.

From her seat in the middle-back of the bus, Margosha can peer up and down the aisle and see plenty of mods. A few seats up, a blue tail with fat spikes flops over the armrest, before its owner, a kid who can't be out of her teens yet, reaches over and tucks it back under her seatbelt. There's an older woman sitting catty-corner with a hyper-realistic tattoo of a wolf on her shoulder, curled in a tight ball with its tail warming its snout. Suddenly, the wolf stands and stretches, seesaw-style—creaking forwards, backwards, forwards again—then begins stalking the pair of tattooed swallows flitting on the back of the woman's neck.

Margosha expects Duri to take the hint and say wolf, but instead, for her first word, Duri picks:

"Aardvark."

"*Aardvark?* They have many of those on the farm?"

"Oh, shut up." Duri laughs. "Just play."

Even though they've been breathing the same dry, circulated air since they boarded the airbus and wound up, by chance of fate, sitting side by side—and even though Margosha has told Duri a safe, small amount about her life in the city and Duri has told Margosha a safe, small amount about her own life in the rural reaches of the opposite coast—Margosha didn't think the two of them were close enough to say a thing like "shut up" to each other. But then, time loses meaning when you're hurtling through black sky, without sunrises and sunsets to hold onto. And Duri has a rough-edged familiarity about her that Margosha isn't used to. A matter-of-factness that she imagines Duri perfected during a lifetime on her farm, surrounded by Earth's more gentle creatures. Creatures who want only what they need—food, water, sleep, sun—and who have no talent for doublespeak, no interest in controlling others.

"Aardvark. Ends in 'K'…" Slowly, Margosha traces the long seam of the seat in front of her, then brightens. "Easy. Kangaroo."

"Kangaroo, huh?" Duri smirks. "They have many of those in the city?"

Margosha thinks to stick her tongue out but at the last second pulls back. She wanted the mod that lets you program your taste buds to perceive certain flavors no matter what it is you're actually eating: hazelnut liqueur truffles instead of fried bologna, beluga caviar instead of a bowl of Lucky Charms. But it's not cheap, and even with the funding the airbus organizers managed to raise, she had to pour all her savings into this trip.

And surely she and Duri aren't stick-your-tongue-out friends quite yet.

So they play. It's kangaroo-ends-in-"O," then octopus; salamander-ends-in-"R," then rabbit. Tarantula, "A." Antelope, "E." Earthworm, "M," then macaw, walrus, snake. At one point, Margosha gets stumped by her seventh "O" of the game until Duri cough-hints "ocelot." At another, Duri begs Margosha to go with the full word, "rhinoceros," instead of the shortened "rhino," because those are the rules, or if they're not, they should be—and besides, Duri already gave Margosha "ocelot" and she's pretty sure there aren't any other animals that start with "O" on their entire godforsaken planet—and Margosha, ever the good sport, relents. Late in the game, stalling on a tricky "G," Duri suggests they should get extra points for animals that are extinct, and Margosha agrees that's not a bad idea.

Except maybe the last thing they need right now is to introduce further complications. Or to start obsessing over all the things they'll never see again.

Come to think of it, nobody's keeping track of points in the first place. Because this game is about the grace of distraction. And if winning means the end of the game, they don't want it.

To win, to really win, would be to get to Nova in one piece. To get back to Earth with what they came for—*that'd* be a miracle.

***

"Category is..."

It's Duri's turn to choose. "We've done all the usual ones. How about...body parts? And before you ask, yes, *human* body parts."

Margosha grins. "Mods or no mods?"

Duri scans what she can of Margosha above the tray table her seatmate dropped over her lap hours ago, and on which she's since accumulated half a dozen empty bags of airbus-brand trail mix. Margosha has strawberry-blonde hair, buzzed short on one side. Lips so chapped they're cracked at the corners, close to bleeding—it's that dry in here—and two eyes the color of honey. No mods that Duri can make out. Not so much as a sharpened canine or a heart-shaped freckle, not even a harmless little piercing, grandma stuff. Strange, Duri thinks. There must be gills hiding beneath the hood of that baggy sweatshirt. She figured someone from one of the cities would have had just about everything done.

"Let's go old-school," Duri says. "No mods. The natural stuff."

"All right," Margosha starts. "Nose."

"Hm. Ends in 'E,' so...ears."

"Skin."

"Nail."

"Liver."

Normally, on one of her long drives into town, or to drop meat or eggs off at a neighbor's, Duri would look out of the window of her rumbling pickup and think. She did some of her best thinking gazing out at that dusty, low-shrub country, blinking up at the wisps of clouds as they crawled lazily by. Now she's sitting in the window seat of a patched-together airbus without windows, chewing her nails down to the quick. She turns instinctively to her left, but finds only a thick plate of sheet metal there.

"Rib," she manages.

She should be focusing on body parts, on calling to mind the anatomy worksheets she had to fill out back in high school, but instead she's still thinking about the last round. About animals. Duri's always been more of an animal person than a person person, and when she stares at the rivets bordering the metal plate, they remind her of the blank, wet eyes of cows.

Which makes her think of an old tradition her grandfather told her about, back when he owned the farm, when the fields were still productive and Duri was shorter than the stalks. It was once customary, he told her, for newlyweds to spend their wedding night in the barn, clutching at each other in the stalls, the hay giving their skin new texture. It was said their lust would improve the animals' fertility. Like making babies was something contagious.

And she said, "Grandpa, *ew*," and her grandfather chuckled in his quiet way, scrambled her not-yet-modded hair.

Which makes her think of something her mother once told her: that after the last of the animals go, it won't be long till the barns fall. One depends on the other. It's the barns that give the animals shelter, and it's the heat of the animals—spreading out to the walls, the ceilings and foundations—that keeps the barns standing upright. Without that heat, the materials will grow cold and brittle and start to cave in on themselves. Soon, her mother warned her, hundreds of thousands of acres on Earth will be nothing but fields of crumpled brown carcasses, and the barns keeled over with them.

And in the fields, among the dead: all the children playing.

The airbus's temperature control is out, and the little hairs on Duri's arms are bright, lemony yellow with sweat. She tries to do superpower mind games on the rivets, bore through them to open windows to whatever lies beyond. She has this nagging feeling that this will all be over soon, and this is her one real shot to see the stars up close. Even though she gets that's not how space works.

Whatever body part Margosha says next, Duri doesn't register it. Instead, she tells Margosha about the barns in her part of the world, how they freeze to death when they're no longer useful, done being vessels for something warm inside.

Margosha is lost in thought, making a crinkly tower of the bags on her tray. Finally she says, "It's funny. In the city, when the buildings are empty—it doesn't happen often. There's always somebody up late, or up early. Always a few of those yellow squares still on. But when it does happen, when you do manage to find a building that's totally barren, it's the opposite of what you're saying. It's almost better for being empty. It feels somehow..." She grasps at the air in front of her, as if trying to pluck the right words from it. "Somehow..."

"More alive," Duri says, and her heart trills, imagining.

***

They take a break to play hangman, then tic-tac-toe. One of the airbus organizers seated at the front walks down the aisle to distribute another round of water bottles and trail mix. She hands Margosha and Duri a pair of small, thin blankets folded in squares, and Margosha is momentarily overwhelmed by the kindness, the enormous risk the organizers must be taking in championing such a controversial project. Duri rolls the blanket up, shoves it in the space between her cheek and the airbus's metal wall, and falls asleep.

Margosha eavesdrops on a conversation between the spiky-tailed girl and her seatmate about how stars are born when great clouds of dust and gas called nebulae collapse. The spiky-tailed girl's neighbor says something like, isn't it kind of beautiful how the nebula sacrifices itself to bring the star into existence? And the spiky-tailed girl, young and bitter, retorts that isn't it pathetic how the nebula has no choice. Margosha pictures her own body disintegrating, swirling pain on a colossal scale, until nothing but the hot core at its center remains. She knows someone somewhere would call that beautiful, take pictures of it, print them in textbooks.

The wolf tattoo on the catty-corner woman's shoulder, having caught one of the swallows, pins it proudly between its paws and howls.

Its owner, surprising Margosha, promptly howls back, and it's clear that they do this all the time, their duet ringing, comfortable, and pure of tone. Duri wakes, and gradually the rest of the passengers on the airbus join in the howl. Margosha thinks she sees one of the organizers smile.

The howling reminds Margosha of the youth sleepaway camp her parents sent her to every summer upstate, and the songs the campers sang while marching to their assigned cabins or to the flagpole at sunup, obedient little soldiers in training. Call-and-responses and songs in the round.

And the green grass grew all around.

It reminds Duri of the stories passed down to her, of real soldiers with their own versions of the chorus howl. Energetic voices in unison as the Humvee rolled into battle. Crystalline hymns as the dead were lowered into the ground, their babies being born the very same minute, bathed in light for the first time on the other side of the world. One in and one out, the census numbers perfectly level, indifferent.

Ghosts shout-singing, *I'll be a ranger the rest of my life.*

When the racket dies down, Duri begins. "Category is..."

Margosha wishes the howl wasn't over. She liked the way she and Duri sounded shifting in and out of harmony. She wonders if, maybe, wanting the same thing, being willing to travel three hundred miles through Earth's atmosphere to get it, means they do understand each other well enough after all. They understand each other better than anybody, don't they? Gone chasing the things they're not allowed to have.

"Regrets?" Margosha ventures cautiously.

The women have grown accustomed to speaking in code. The game is just another way of doing that. Even though the airbus organizers promised them that they can speak freely now, that they're safe here—from the moment the hatch went down to the moment they touch down on Earth again, they're *safe here*—it's an awfully hard habit to break.

Margosha is on a performing athlete visa, Duri is on a temporary agricultural worker visa, and one is every bit as bogus as the other. The organizers who secured the project's funding also arranged travel documents for every passenger aboard, and by all appearances they knew what they were doing. The airbus flies steady despite being a bit in disrepair, and the documents look pretty convincing. When the uniformed men at the departure dock reviewed them, they gave clipped, perfunctory nods before waving the travelers on to the next stages: vitals check, extensive cavity search, then baggage scan.

Five years ago, both Margosha and Duri could have traveled under legitimate medical treatment visas, but since the recent mods policies went into effect, everyone has had to get a little creative. Select treatments were moved out of the medcare column, where they had previously sat for more than a hundred years, and were lumped together under the new body modification column, then under the *voluntary* body modification column soon after that. Which has turned out to be convenient for some, less convenient for others, since at the same time vol-mods were declared entirely subject to government approval. Meaning they're evaluated on a case-by-case basis, permitted or denied.

There were protests, for a time—cries that they were all regressing dangerously into another, darker century. But lawmakers insisted that the past was worth returning to: these old things, they said, have a way of coming back to us when we need them.

Duri's color-changing hair is a piece-of-cake level-one vol-mod—J&J rigged it so most of their cosmetic mods are—and the prowling, animated wolf tattoo is a level one-point-five. The latest out of Prada is a fatty tissue transplant to the heels and balls of the feet that allows the brand's loyalists to endure the shoes for more consecutive hours. It debuted at level two, but was upgraded to level three when one unintended side effect became apparent: the springy transplants improved the wearer's ability to sprint short distances. The mod's opponents dubbed it "the escape advantage."

Levels four through six get into the experimental mods, and those heavier-duty ones that call for some prerequisite training. J&J's

injectable tans and sunscreens got cleared as entry levels, but their offshoot, an injectable camouflage, is never going to drop below level six, ensuring the military holds a monopoly on it.

The procedures Margosha and Duri were seeking when the organizers found them and offered to help, plucking them from their lives thousands of miles apart, are categorized as level sevens: the highest level currently assigned. By design, level-seven vol-mods are harshly stigmatized, and they remain virtually impossible to get licenses for on Earth.

Nova is another story, one everybody's heard. The colony broke away two decades ago, when Earth started becoming a truly intolerable place to live and the wealthiest of its citizens realized that they did not, in fact, have to tolerate it. Only the most well-off can afford to stay on Nova permanently, expats in their peaceful, progressive society orbiting Earth. But people like Margosha and Duri, and the rest of the passengers on the airbus, can pay the satellite a brief visit. For a price.

What Margosha wants to modify is there's a baby inside her she doesn't want to be there.

What Duri wants to modify is the fact of her body being able to carry babies at all.

The four days in the hot, crowded airbus will be worth it, the organizers remind them again and again, to arrive at the plush Nova clinic, with its simulated gravity, its sympathetic doctors, its pillows stuffed with the last of Earth's real goose down. There'll be some discomfort. Not pain, never pain—only *discomfort*. Nova doesn't recognize mod levels or license requirements, but rumor has it the colony does share Earth's penchant for calling things something other than what they really are. All the level-seven mods get sanitized, labyrinthine names to match Nova's sanitized, labyrinthine environment: fetal tissue evacuation, absolute uterine transfer, breast tissue alleviation. Pudendum reconstructive therapy, from the Latin *pudere*: to be ashamed.

Still, in comparison, a sanctuary.

"Regrets?" Margosha repeats softly.

Duri is silent for some time, staring out of her not-window at the not-arid not-land not-outside. At long last, she replies plainly, "None."

Margosha agrees quickly: "None." Even though it means losing the game. Because if she were playing by the rules, she'd have started with "E." It would have been so easy. If the game were more important, she could have said any number of things: "Eavesdropping," or "Ending it," or "Everything."

But instead she says it again, with more force this time, "*None*," and the twin cracks at the parched corners of her mouth split open.

***

"Category is..."

Exhausted from the hunt, the catty-corner wolf is snoring loudly, a pile of tattooed bones and broken wings forming a jumbled graveyard at its feet. The crackly-voiced pilot announces that they're very close now, everyone should make sure their seatbelts are fastened—he'll let them know when it's time to brace themselves for final descent.

"Wishes," Duri finishes.

Earlier, while playing tic-tac-toe, the O's made Margosha think of empty cavities: subway tunnels after the trains stop running, holes in tree trunks, vacant bellies, cracks in sidewalks. Hollow spaces responsible for holding nothing, free to simply *exist* as they are. The X's made Duri think of the way people get buried sometimes, with their arms crossed neatly over their chests. Because the person preparing the body wanted the dead to appear penitent when meeting God. Or just because it made it easier to fit the corpse inside the box.

When they played hangman, Duri drew a single straight line for the middle part of the hanged man's body. Margosha was grateful, even though the truth—a circle middle with a stick baby inside—would have given Margosha an extra guess. It meant that Duri couldn't tell what Margosha really had under that baggy sweatshirt, or that even if she could, she wasn't the kind to commit another person's secrets to paper. In the end, Duri drew a couple of little shoes at the ends of the hanged man's little legs, so Margosha got the extra guesses anyway.

"Wishes, wishes..." Margosha murmurs. "Well, I've heard Nova has a great view of Earth."

"The best in the galaxy!" Duri knows the tagline well. She's seen the ads, too—they're inescapable. She might not get them full-res on the side of a skyscraper, but they come through just fine on the tiny smart screen she keeps in her kitchen and turns on once a day to check the weather and the progression of dust storms across her county each morning.

Margosha smiles sadly. "Then my wish is for Earth to be better to us from a distance."

Duri nods. She knows exactly what Margosha means. She reaches over to the tray table, where Margosha is nervously drumming her fingers over the gulch cut half an inch into the plastic where the cup is supposed to go, and she takes Margosha's hands into her own. Again, Margosha marvels at Duri's shamelessness, her willingness to feel something and act on it right away. The way Duri's eyelashes are turning a bright, lemony yellow and she's leaving her hands right where they are, isn't even bothering to wipe the tears away.

Margosha sticks her tongue out at her new friend. They're nearly there; they'll get there together. She licks the split corners of her lips, tastes blood.

***

It happens faster than anything. Fast as these things happen sometimes.

It happens before Duri can take her turn in the game. Before she can put together that she's been thinking about death, about nooses and hanged bodies and burials, for a reason.

Before she can realize that the way she's been holding Margosha's hands, it's with the same combination of firmness and gentleness she used to cradle the cows on the farm as they died. How do you make steel latticework of your fingers? How do you keep a body from coming apart and at the same time give the soul the space it needs to float up off the ground?

When the airbus organizers come down the aisle this time, they're not holding packets of trail mix or water bottles. They're not squeezing the passengers' shoulders. They're not wearing their calm, reassuring expressions anymore.

They're wearing the kind of vests Margosha sees every day without exception and the kind Duri sees on the special days she goes into town. The vests the armed guards wear while patrolling in front of the government buildings, in front of schools and grocery stores, post offices and corner markets, medical clinics and law offices and drugstores.

The organizers of Project Storm Port, of the airbus meant to ferry Duri, Margosha, and the others to safe-haven clinics on Nova, are carrying stun guns and zip ties, and rolls and rolls of military-issue restraint tape. They cover mouths and eyes, bind arms, legs, talons, and tails, methodically working their way down the narrow aisle. The passengers in the first rows are too taken aback to do anything but go compliantly, but the others, witnessing the sudden change in the organizers' demeanor, are screaming, flailing, shooting up from their seats. With nowhere else to go, they stampede in place, in this windowless metal tube gaining speed toward a destination they now understand is very different from the one they had set out for.

The organizers are close now, and Margosha and Duri can just make out the blocky white letters across their vests:

OFFICER.

And:

NOVA INTERPLANETARY CORRECTIONS.

The wolf on the woman's shoulder awoke at the first commotion and now, sensing danger, snaps wildly and snarls. It bucks and bites, defiant to the end, while the officers struggle to contain it to the surface of the woman's skin, one long, sticky strip of black tape after another.

Duri is frozen, astonished. She can't believe she's been so naive. People from the cities, like Margosha, sure. But *her*? No. Her county was one of the first to incite citizen militias to enforce the level-seven mod bans in their own communities. Self-appointed bounty hunters lurk in the shadows back home, snatching shoppers as they come out of drugstores and rifling through their bags. Hackers tap into personal networks, monitor order histories. Groups of men follow groups of women down the street, waiting for them to separate when they reach their cars.

It should've always been a possibility in her mind for Nova to be not paradise but prison.

Duri looks at Margosha, in her two eyes the color of honey, and reads in them, in an instant, a million urgent things. Namely rage. Namely wrath.

And something else—something strange.

Something like satisfaction.

As Margosha begins her transformation, both women think, not for the first time, that here and on Earth, they really are regulating the wrong things.

Margosha got the Deere vol-mod last year. Rated level five for commercial machinery. She and her cousins, fellow city girls, were taking their biannual tour of the wineries upstate when she saw the ad in a gift shop. The auto cashier spit it out to her along with her change and a coupon for a local reds tasting class. It was Deere's first foray into cosmetic mods, designed to mimic the manufacturer's line of combine grape harvesters, only on a much smaller scale: the scale of the human body. It was meant for family vineyards that didn't have much ground to cover and whose owners couldn't afford the bigger external equipment. And it was recalled almost immediately—while the ads were still running—because the mod had a tendency to clog and overheat, and because it came with a non-negligible risk of permanent disfiguration.

Margosha got it for a steal. The shop couldn't wait to be rid of it. Practically gift-wrapped it with a bow.

She never expected to use the mod for its intended purpose. What's she know about tractors and combines? Half the time she can't get her own little sedan to start.

But it sure has helped her feel safer walking home alone late in the city, when the men at last turn out their sickly yellow squares and the buildings, fed up, spit them out. Every night she thought, if the men *had* to look at her, why couldn't they do it the way they looked at the stars? The harmless admiration of some remote, unreachable thing, more dream than anything. But no. She was, to them, all too attainable.

The Deere mod has helped her feel safer then.

Here, too, it'll do just fine.

Margosha's mouth stretches wide, wide, then wider, ripping apart the scabs at the corners that never heal quite right. Gears snap into place and sprockets turn somewhere at her center. Her lips stretch out to her jawline—ends in "E"—then to her ears, and steel blades, painted company green and yellow, erupt from her gums and begin to rattle and whir. Before the combine's face can overtake the rest of her, reconfiguring her eyes into plate-glass windows, Margosha throws Duri a don't-you-worry wink.

The blades start their sputtering and churning, and the liquid trickling down Margosha's grill balances out to equal parts fuel and blood. The Nova officer nearest the hungry machine clutches her useless roll of tape and tries frantically to backtrack up the congested aisle. But the airbus is packed with the hopefuls Project Storm Port baited, and they do all they can to get in the way.

Margosha bears forward and begins to harvest.

By the time they dock at Nova Interplanetary Corrections Facility, Duri's moisture-activated hair is more yellow than black, and more deep, syrupy red than yellow at that. Chunks of flesh and bone decorate the airbus's walls. The passengers have yanked off one another's bindings and stand ready at the hatch, mods out and confiscated stun guns in hand. The pilot is pinned against the cabin door, blubbering about how he has *daughters*, and don't his daughters need their *father*, the sharp spikes of a scaly blue tail pressing triangles into his throat.

The wolf, freed, howls, and the others howl back.

Duri thinks, as the hatch clicks open and the passengers pour out onto a world woefully unprepared for them, that Margosha is merely continuing the game they started. The simple, boring game they've been playing on and off for the past four eternal days of their doomed road trip: last letter first.

They are, technically, still on wishes. Last Duri can remember, she said something about wanting a good, solid meal—all the trail mix getting tiresome, not even being the kind with chocolate.

Which makes it Margosha's turn.

The cheering and baying, the sounds of Margosha's inner mechanisms patiently digesting the officers, overwhelm the echoing shuttle bay. And while Duri can't quite make out what her seatmate says, she figures she can guess well enough.

Friendshop

Zoe Marzo

Zoe Marzo lives in Los Angeles where she is studying for a PhD in Depth Psychology. Her fiction has appeared in Popshot Quarterly, Tahoma Literary Review, and elsewhere. Find her on Instagram @zoe.marzo

It was full dark now. The sun had set. Streets were lit by alternating red and green and yellow traffic lights. Neon signs with kiwi green and fuchsia lettering. In a bubble of yellow light that poured out of a storefront, I stopped, feeling the breeze of bodies pushing past me. I held perfectly still, staring into a cube-shaped shop faced with transparent glass. There were two signs on the window, words in lilac neon—so soothing and vivid I could almost smell the color. Delicate. Floral. Wafting on seemingly clean air.

FRIENDSHOP

it said.

Blinking on and off next to it:

24 HOURS ONLY

24 HOURS ONLY

24 HOURS ONLY

The real eye-catcher was beyond the glass of the storefront. Floor-to-ceiling rainbow on all three walls. I opened the glass door and it buzzed at my entrance. The rainbow was made of bracelets woven of embroidery thread. Friendship bracelets, the kind that kids made at summer camp—or so I was led to believe from movies I watched growing up. I had an impression of kids sitting at picnic tables amidst sun and pine trees.

Each bracelet was unique in color and design. Chevrons and stripes. Diamonds and hearts. Twists and braids. Multi-colored and monochrome. Beads woven into the thread.

"Welcome!"

I noticed, for the first time, the shopgirl boxing up bracelets in one corner of the shop. The girl's eyes crinkled with her smile. There were tiny stickers—heart, smiley face, star—decorating the corners of her eyes. She wore a green and pink floral kimono on denim short-alls, and a nametag that said "Taffy Jones, manager." I thought Taffy could have been either twenty-two or forty-two years old.

"You made it just in time!" Taffy sang. "We pop up for one day only every spring, and *you* look like someone in need of a friend."

Taffy gestured at the rainbow walls so the sleeves of her kimono dipped and Leah saw that her arms were adorned wrist-to-elbow with bracelets.

She made me nervous, and I laughed uneasily, looking to the walls of bracelets. I stepped toward the wall for a closer look and one that caught my eye. It was simple—a pattern of repeating daisies, like a chain. I reached out and touched it.

"Looks like you found a friend," and with that, Taffy reached around me, taking the bracelet off the wall and wrapping it around my wrist, tying it in a tight knot. I stared at the knot, stunned, uncertain of how Taffy even came to be standing next to me.

"How much is it?" It was the wrong thing to say. I should have said, *No, thank you.* But I asked how much, knowing there was only thirteen dollars in my wallet in ones and fives, all the cash I had left in the world, aside from a checking account so depleted I couldn't bear to check my balance, and a credit card for emergencies. This whole month had been an emergency. I had no intention of buying anything. I just wanted to get out of the car, stretch my legs, maybe window shop a little bit. *Right?* I asked myself. *Right?*

Taffy smiled. She looked at me like she was looking *into* me...

"It only costs thirteen dollars, no tax. Small price to pay for the perfect friend."

...or into my wallet, counting everything I had left, and noticing a desperate, friend-shaped gap in my life. My hand reached for my wallet of its own accord. My head nodded as if it brainlessly believed we'd stumbled onto *the most amazing deal.*

Can't pass this up, my mind rattled, senselessly.

It's not my fault, I argued with myself. It's not my fault this woman tied the bracelet in a knot. I shouldn't have to pay for this. I didn't need—of all things—a *friendship bracelet*. It would just have to be un-knotted. No, no, no.

I held the money out to Taffy, resignation washing over me.

Who was I kidding? The tension of having nothing had to split at some point. Maybe the bracelet could be a talisman, a good luck charm. Maybe it would help manifest an actual friend. Maybe I didn't need to eat dinner tonight. Maybe I didn't need to eat tomorrow.

Since arriving in Los Angeles and finding myself with no job,

I was usually nauseous, a lump in my throat every time I spent money. I didn't feel it now, handing the bills to Taffy.

I must be disassociating. No one is occupying this body. Taffy didn't even count the money, she took it out of my hand, smiling, crumpling the bills around the middle—the way a cartoon character might grab money. Then, she put her arm around my shoulders and led me toward the door of the shop.

"I hope to see you again next spring. Good luck in LA and *have fun!*"

She opened the door and Melrose engulfed me. I faced a now trafficless street. There was a *click!* as the door was locked behind me. The square of yellow light disappeared along with the soothing violet neon, and I turned to find the windows blackened, the interior invisible, and just my own reflection looking back at me.

My phone said: 12:01 a.m.

I started walking back to my car and saw something round and shining on the sidewalk and made a reflexive jerk toward it. The reflex was jarring to me, all in the hopes of finding a quarter or change, and it was only a scrap of plastic reflecting light. I looked at the bracelet, daisies dancing around my wrist. I looked back at the black cube of a shop wedged between a trading card store and an arcade. Then, I looked up at the sky. How did it seem so oppressively close without any stars in it? The full moon was low and huge, blending in with the streetlamps as if it was just another light fixture.

Nothing in this city is real, I thought.

***

The coffee shop had a patio in the sun. A couple of men in suits talked about their screenplays, air pods hanging out of their ears. A group of women in yoga clothes shared a table, ate French toast dusted with powdered sugar and breakfast burritos with silver ramekins of salsa. Students stared into textbooks and scribbled in spiral notebooks.

Lured in by the birds and the shade, by the brightness of it all, I was tempted to sit down at a table without buying anything, but my body was in charge again, and I found myself approaching the counter and ordering. I found herself handing over my probably maxed-out debit card. The cashier swiped it, and miraculously, the screen went from *Processing...*to *Approved* and a receipt printed. A moment later, two alerts pinged on my phone—my bank account was less than the fifty dollar amount, and my account was overdrawn. Available balance: $-4.25.

Don't panic. The money would come back to me. Something would come up, because it had to. It had to. I found an empty table near a woman with platinum blonde hair and sunglasses sitting cross-legged in high tops, and sipping a pink smoothie, reading a book. *She's so aesthetic,* I thought, sitting down at the empty table, watching the woman's lips curl as she laughed at something in the paperback in her lap.

The mesh seat was too low for the height of the metal table, making me feel like a child with an oversized, bowl-sized cup of matcha. Liquid motivation, steeling my courage. If life wasn't working for me, I'd play at it. I'd browse jobs in case—

But I didn't want to think about the other job not coming through. *It had to.* It's what I came here for. I focused instead on my latte. There it was, cradled in glossy ceramic. I had yet to take the first sip, always hesitating to wreck latte art—a feathery white leaf floating in a frosted willow green sky. I opened my laptop.

A pigeon flew low, and I felt the breeze of its wings near my cheek. A couple tiny sparrows hopped onto my table, one tilting its head to regard me. I could hear the twittering of its family and friends in the branches overhead and felt encouraged by their presence and proximity.

The bird took wing between me and the platinum blonde at the other table. As it passed between us, we made eye contact through the blue lenses of the woman's sunglasses and smiled at each other.

There's at least one friendly person in LA, I thought.

The birds tweeted and hopped around on the branches above. There was a *Crack!* followed by a *Plop!*

A small branch dropped out of the tree landing *smack!* in my matcha latte, breaking the art and spraying green onto my jacket and cheeks, splashing the screen and keyboard of my laptop. I sat there stunned. Next to me, the platinum-haired woman giggled, making me laugh too.

"Here," said the woman, and flipped up her sunglasses. "I have some napkins."

"Just when I was starting to feel hopeful," I said, taking napkins, dabbing at the drops.

"The universe is such a jokester, am I right? Is your computer okay?"

I tried to wipe at drops on the screen, smeared and smudgy.

"You, uh, have a few more spots on your hair and forehead."

I cringed, embarrassed, feeling for the sticky spots on my face

"I hope this isn't how the rest of my day is going to go. Or my week." *Or my life.*

"I have a feeling it'll turn around," she said and reached out her hand. "My name is Daisy, by the way."

When I gripped her hand, I felt a static shock.

"Oops," she said. "Sorry about that, I'm always creating static electricity. What did you say your name is?"

"Leah."

Daisy slipped the book she had been reading into a striped tote bag.

"Leaving?" I asked—my voice operating without me, and sounding strained. I realized how desperate I was for any human interaction at all.

"I'm actually on my way to the beach," Daisy said.

"Oh, I haven't been to the beach yet." *My mouth is being chatty,* I thought.

"You're kidding."

"No, I just moved here."

"Do you—want to join me? I'd love the company."

"Really?"

"Yeah, really," Daisy laughed.

What gripped me? Impulsiveness? Desperation? A feeling of connection? The job search was important, but the possibility of a friend was too tempting, too necessary, too more-important-than-anything else.

"Yes," I said. "Yes, I'd love to join you. Please."

Daisy smiled. "Do you need to finish that first?"

We looked at the latte, a partially submerged branch sticking out of it, and burst out laughing.

***

I exhaled through the rolled-down windows as Daisy's car carried us forward and away. Soon, I could taste the salt on the air and then I could see it—the road before us leading directly into the ocean. We parked on a small, crowded street. Daisy grabbed beach towels from her trunk. She even had extra flip-flops, and the two of us half-ran, unsteady through the sand toward the water. "You have to jump in, even if you don't have a swimsuit with you," Daisy insisted.

That's what I wanted to hear. I wanted to be swallowed up by the ocean and cleansed of all the ill experiences thus far. Even fully dressed, the cold ocean gave me goosebumps. The waves knocked me down, but pulling myself up, I imagined the weight of the water on my clothes was Los Angeles, holding onto me, wanting to keep me. Dripping, Daisy and I spread out them, colorful floral prints only slightly faded by sunshine. As we unfurled the towels, old beach sand flew off the threads and sparkled in the sun before settling back where they belonged. Pixie dust.

Daisy disappeared for a few minutes and reappeared with a paper basket of fries, sticky with fresh minced garlic. We shared them, stretching out in the hot sun.

"Love a spontaneous new friend," Daisy said, turning to lie on her back, shading her eyes with her forearm. I turned my head, squinted at Daisy through the sting of saltwater and bright sunshine.

I couldn't respond. *Spontaneous.* Not reckless. Not impulsive. Not throwing every penny I had away on a hope and a whim. *Spontaneous.* Daisy's feet dug into the warm sand, and I gasped— seeing something around Daisy's ankle—an anklet embroidered with the very same colors as my new bracelet. I sat up, looked closer—daisies. Just like mine. They matched.

"I'm so happy you decided to come along," Daisy said, her voice sounding sleepy and distant, almost syrupy, as she lay in the sun. "I felt like I needed a friend."

***

Daisy dropped me off back at the café where we met. A yellow butterfly flew by as I stepped onto the pavement. The light through its wings made it look like a moving fragment of stained glass.

"Call me anytime," Daisy said before she drove away.

I walked back to my car on sidewalks dotted with some kind of smashed brown fruit that must have fallen from the palm trees. I took a deep breath, feeling more myself than I had since moving to L.A., energized by half an order of garlic fries and the after-glow of a day at the beach. Then I saw my car—the only one remaining on the street.

Closer, I noticed the envelope tucked under the wiper blade. Inside, a strip of paper, as thin and slender as a receipt. It was a parking ticket. Breath left me. I leaned against the side of my car, unable to support this new weight. My eyes were still focused on the seventy-five dollar fine when my phone pinged. I looked: Charges to account exceeded available balance. An overdraft fee for a matcha latte I never got to drink. *Charged money for not having enough money.* I looked up from the phone's blue light into the rusty light as sunset turned palm trees black along Beverly Boulevard.

***

The next day, I stood outside the office building where I was supposed to work. It was empty. Totally empty. There was a sign in the window.

FOR LEASE

It said.

I could see inside, an expanse of concrete foundation. Only a few weeks earlier, they'd offered me a job which I'd accepted with enthusiasm over the phone. I drove west for this. When I tried to call, the phone rang without switching to voicemail. I checked their website.

404 NOT FOUND

Anxiety mingled with exhaustion. What do I do? Do I even have enough gas to get out of the city? Probably not. Heavy trucks lumbered by, the clanking of their gruff metal and thud of bulk moving over potholes unsettled me. The sound itself felt harsh like a vibration shaking me from the inside. I got in my car. My body operating without me. Turning onto the freeway, ready to leave, counting the ticks of my turn signal when—*Slam! Crash!*

At first I didn't know what happened. I wasn't sure what I was looking at. There'd been an almost-benign sound of crumpling metal. My car, scraped across the asphalt and the world turned over. The KITCHEN box slammed against me, sliding from the passenger's seat. It took a moment to get my bearings, to realize I was hanging upside down from my seatbelt. The car was facing a totally different direction than I'd been traveling, having spun then flipped. The cream plastic of deflated airbags crumpled at the window, the felt lining of the car's interior burst open. Paramedics pried the door open and I crawled out, already a little bruised and scratched, unsteady on my feet. My things spilled into the road, broken glass lit by the sun. A sauce pan was dented. I wished I'd never brought any of it with me. Cars drove around the wreckage without stopping. A box had split and let loose a blanket. Cars rolled over it, pinning it down, leaving tire treads across its surface, one corner trying hopelessly to lift in the wake of speeding cars.

I found out the other car ran a red light, ramming into the side of my car. They were fine. Their car hadn't flipped over. They never spoke to me. Never got out of their car. Maybe they were more traumatized than me. Maybe if I wasn't exhausted and disappointed I could have reacted sooner. It wasn't my fault. Everyone said. But the feeling of failure was ripe and in full blossom inside my chest.

***

At the hospital, I gaped at my skin as I tried to change into a hospital gown. Already there were purple bruises where the seatbelt strapped me in. After a few X-rays, they released me from the Emergency Room. I had no car and nowhere to Uber to. I looked down at the medical bracelet printed with my name and patient number and insurance I'd signed up for when the ambulance dropped me off. Side-by-side with the medical bracelet was the embroidered friendship bracelet with the daisies, looking bright and optimistic and new.

Daisy had typed her number into my phone the day they went to the beach, and now, I didn't know what else to do. I hadn't met anyone else in LA. Daisy answered after one ring.

"Hey-a Leah! What took you so long to call?...Hello? Lay?"

"I'm sorry." I wanted to apologize for my existence and what I was about to ask for. "I was just in a car accident—"

She never gave me a chance to explain myself.

"Where are you?"

***

I was stretched out on the hospital bed staring at the wall when Daisy got there. They'd let me wait. I heard her voice coming around the curtain.

"Welcome to Hell-A, am I right? You're not wasting any time—jumping into the Pacific, flipping your car. I'd say you got your initiation to the city out of the way," Daisy's voice was light, and she was gentle as she helped me up. "I have a sofa with your name on it."

***

Daisy lived in Koreatown, a ground-floor corner apartment with hardwood floors and a plush, well-loved sofa that opened into a bed. She had ivory curtains that let in the sun but blocked out views from the street. Her bedroom was small and the bathroom was tiny, but after sleeping in my car, the space felt luxurious.

"It's not much, but it's home," Daisy said after a quick tour that involved mainly pointing at things.

Daisy ordered Chinese food then went to pick it up. "When

you're well enough," she said, "I'll take you to this place. It's just around the corner and I love it." The food revived me. There were doughy noodles in thick black sauce and spicy red soup. There was so much of it that I couldn't finish, hungry as I was. I felt better.

"I'm so sorry for putting you out—" Daisy was already waving my words out of the air, swatting them away like she was trying to stop the sound from landing on her ears—"I'll leave as soon as I'm feeling better I promise—" Daisy shook her head as if an obnoxious fly was circling. "And I'll pay you back for the food and—"

"Listen, money is just energy and energy needs to be fluid and in motion. We have it, we let it go, it comes back, or it goes somewhere else. Sometimes it's stagnant. If I have some that I'm not using, you may as well be using it. Money is a made-up system, and nothing really belongs to any of us."

Who says *things like that?* I wondered. *Who says things like that and means it?*

***

The light through the curtains the next morning and many mornings after that taunted me as bruises surfaced like mottled florals on my body. When we finally went out, I seemed to bring clouds with me, but I gradually started to feel revived in spite of myself. Rain clamped down the smog. The city was grey but shiny, and my soreness subsided enough to get out of bed at Daisy's urging. "LA is magic. One day you'll see." We strolled down Hollywood Boulevard across a slippery Walk of Fame.

At Grauman's, measuring sneakers against high-heeled impressions and hovered our hands over puddle-filled prints to discover we were both exactly the same size as Debbie Reynolds—so we danced in the rain to celebrate.

Daisy shined bright on the grimmest days. She wore clothes that looked like they were made from recycled inflatable furniture from the early 2000s. Pink transparent plastic dresses with balloon sleeves or shiny skirts over tights. Somehow everything looked right on her and nothing looked out of place. She seemed to be deriving nutrients directly from the cosmos, soul-fed. She was a mystery, an enigma, and I felt at once enchanted and confused by her.

Daisy possessed the spirit of the city, or so it seemed to me, a playfulness and edginess, that was an embodiment of the best of it. "How can that be?" I wondered out loud, and Daisy just shrugged and said, "It's easy if you've always been here and never known anything else."

***

One day, driving home in a new-to-me car, I started singing along to an Ace of Base on the radio and caught a glimpse in my rearview mirror of the girl in the car behind me doing the same—raising her arms in the air and moving to a beat as we were stopped at a light. The man in the car next to me was doing the same—all of us in our totally separate, enclosed spaces, listening to different songs, moving and singing along. I didn't realize until then that something had shifted in me, that I was different. It wasn't so long ago I'd been sobbing in my car, feeling alone and isolated, trying to change lanes and feeling totally shut out, rejected by the city, wondering what I was even doing.

I still felt the trauma of the accident, still tensed at intersections, had to steady my breathing turning onto freeways, felt my body respond when I approached the site of the accident, even if I wasn't consciously thinking about what had happened there. But it was manageable. Maybe I wasn't totally better, but I felt okay, I was functioning better.

I started to believe that LA was magical. The kind of place where you a bracelet you buy with the last of your money has the power to manifest a friend who doesn't make you feel bad for the things that have happened to you or judge you or ridicule you or give you a hard time about sleeping on their couch. Now and then, I caught a glimpse of Daisy's anklet peeking out from under the hem of her jeans. Always a reassuring sight with its repeating pattern, like mine. By the end of the year, my bracelet had faded and it was barely hanging on, frayed, and falling apart. It was knotted too tightly to take it off for showers or swimming. Daisy's, on the other hand, stayed pristine. Exactly as it had been when I first noticed it. Exactly as mine had been when I first bought it. My bracelet now was getting ragged and frayed, but I felt so attached to it. A good luck charm.

But one day, it caught on my jacket and I pulled to get it free. There was a fell whisper against my skin as the last delicate thread separated and it drifted to the sidewalk, dropping into a puddle. I felt a twinge in my chest. At first, it sat on the surface of the water and in slow motion, sunk, as water took hold of it, and drew it under. I watched it disappear as if in slow motion.

What did it feel like then? Like a smartphone slipping out of my fingers, the corner hitting pavement, splintering into spiderweb cracks that would leave fiberglass in my fingertips—that's how it felt, in my heart, a sickening loss that couldn't be real.

The puddle—a gross, downtown, LA puddle, brown and yellow and mysterious in a way I didn't want to know. The bracelet was unsalvageable. I said a silent goodbye. Farewell, friend, and rubbed my naked wrist as I walked on.

***

Daisy was late to meet me at the Moonlight Rollerway. It was Retro Night with music from the 70s, 80s, and 90s—our favorite. I sat on a bench with my skates on, and Daisy's skates that I'd already rented sitting next to me. We were the same size. We were celebrating the new apartment I'd moved into, and I wanted to treat her. I put her skates in a locker and went into the rink for a few laps to "Grease" and "Hit Me Baby, One More Time," with my phone on vibrate, all the while scanning the crowd. But Daisy never showed. She didn't answer her texts. She tried calling, but the phone just kept ringing.

I drove to Daisy's apartment, but Daisy didn't buzz me in. Discomfort settled in my chest. I looked around the neighborhood before climbing over the low wall and up to Daisy's corner windows to peer inside. No curtains. The apartment was empty. Bare walls and empty hardwood. I couldn't even see dust marks to show where furniture had been. Daisy was gone, and she hadn't said goodbye. My heart pounded. Someone was leaving the building, a flash of pink velour, I rushed over to see the upstairs neighbor with her dog—the dog was tinier than I imagined. They both wore pink tracksuits.

"Excuse me, I'm looking for my friend. In apartment 2B." Leah pointed to the corner windows. "Do you know when she moved out?"

The woman looked me up and down. "I never met a tenant living there."

"Her name was Daisy. She has platinum blonde hair—" *Never met? I'd heard them talking by the mailboxes.*

"Listen, I never met anyone in that apartment and I never peered through their front windows either, as far as I know, it's vacant, and has been for a while. I think you should stop snooping around the property before someone calls security."

* * *

I walked the neighborhood as if I might bump into Daisy.

Smashed dates littered the sidewalk. I went to the ice cream shop with the cute, fish-shaped cones, and walked through H Mart, lingering in front of the kimchi. I even walked by the empty building where our favorite Chinese restaurant had been—the one with the huge bowls of noodles in black bean sauce and the spicy beef stew. The building was empty now. I kept trying Daisy's phone as the days went on, and it kept ringing. It didn't even switch to an answering machine. I drove through Daisy's neighborhood again and again. I walked the courtyard in Little Tokyo with the Japanese lanterns where we'd sung karaoke on an open stage. Someone had put a $5 in a jar for us. I passed the studio where we'd stood in line for an open audition even though neither of us could act. It was just "*so* LA" and Daisy said, "You *have to,* at least once!"

I got into my car and started home. I zoned out, lost in thoughts of our friendship. It got dark as I drove. On Melrose, I caught sight of a cube of light and a lilac neon sign. Then I realized—it was spring again. It had been one year since I moved to Los Angeles. The pop-up had reappeared. It was almost midnight. I pulled into a parking spot so abruptly the car behind me honked before zooming past and laying on its horn. The noise didn't mean anything to me now. I'd changed. I'd survived a crash. This city couldn't hurt me any more than it already had. I parked quickly and ran down the sidewalk. Many of the shops had changed in the past year but the crowd on Melrose remained the same. Denim and leather. Bright hairstyles. I opened the glass door to

FRIENDSHOP

and heard the welcoming buzz. Taffy, in her floral kimono, turned around to greet me.

"Welcome back," she said. "You look like you could use a friend."

THANK YOU TO OUR SUPPORTERS

Many thanks to our patrons and supporters, especially:

Johanna Levene • Kate Boyes • Wichael Tellez
carol shoemake • Cathrin Hagey
Natalie Weizenbaum

S Klotz • Amy Meng • Alex grehy • Alina Kanaski
Myz Lilith • Erik DeBill • Frederick Stark
Bonnie Warford • Felicia OSullivan • Salomao Becker
Anna O'Brien • Martin Cohen • J'nae Spano
Tory Hoke • Matthew Bennardo

EM Gaucher • Thomas Moulia • Elana Gomel
Maria Brekke • Ana Wang • Lorna D Keach • smokestack
Lisa Short • Sian Jones • Kristina Saccone • BethOfAus
J. Askew • Dirck de Lint • Wanda • Karen Anderson
Charlotte Nash-Stewart • Liz Warner • Suzanne Thackston
Jen G • Emily Anderson • Maria Haskins • GriffinFire

Want to see your name here? Become a patron!
patreon.com/lunastation

About the Cover Artist

Indicreates is a freelance artist from Germany.

She graduated in game art studies and works full time as an Illustrator. She focuses on character illustrations for books, games and more.

indicreates.com

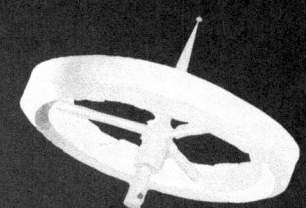

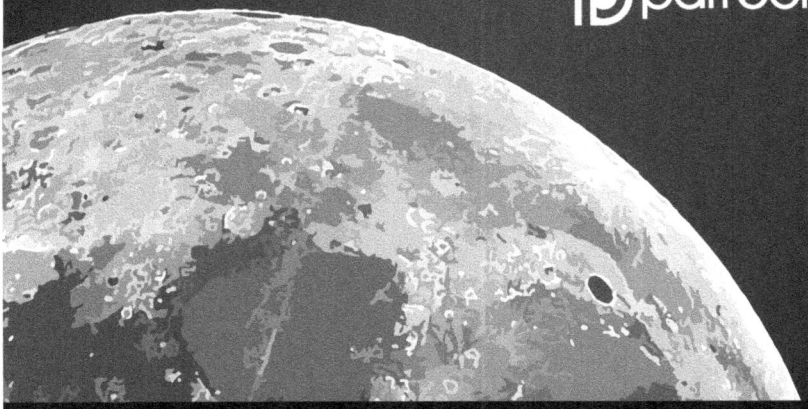